# THE
# RAGING
# SEA

# THE RAGING SEA

*a novel*

## Sonia O'Brien

Covenant Communications, Inc.

Cover image © PhotoDisc/GettyImages

Cover design copyrighted 2004 by Covenant Communications, Inc.

Published by Covenant Communications, Inc.
American Fork, Utah

Printed in Canada
First Printing: April 2004

10 09 08 07 06 05 04    10 9 8 7 6 5 4 3 2 1

ISBN 1-59156-452-2

Dedicated to my children

# Acknowledgments

I express my sincere gratitude to Angela Colvin, the entire Covenant publishing family, my readers' group (who now have this book memorized), and my family for their constant support in helping to make my childhood dream a reality. To my Heavenly Father—when the words would not come, You whispered.

# CHAPTER 1

The rain fell in torrents on the roof as lightning flashed across the night sky. The wind howled and thrashed like a wounded animal, tossing everything in its path. Kaitlyn yanked the soft feather pillow from under her head, plopped it over her ears, and snuggled deep into her covers. She could feel the house rumble and echo with each thunderous strike. One exceptionally fierce crack of thunder caused her to sit straight up in bed. It was not that she was frightened. She usually enjoyed listening to a good storm; there was something exciting about the sheer power of nature. Tonight was different though. In the morning she was leaving for spring break with her two best friends, Gracie and Amber. The three of them were scheduled to fly from Minnesota to Miami, where they would then take a cruise to the Caribbean Islands. Sitting under an umbrella on a tropical beach—to stay out of the rain—was not what she had in mind.

Another strike of lightning lit the room, but the thunder that followed it was not as intense as the last. Kaitlyn peered at the fluorescent digits on her alarm clock. It was one thirty in the morning. For the next twenty minutes, she watched as the wind twisted the branches of the willow tree outside her window. With each flash of lightning, the branches threw distorted shadows across her walls.

Mesmerized by the show of light and shadow, Kaitlyn listened as the rumbling of the thunder drifted into the night until it was nothing more than a gentle murmur in the distance. Then she shut her blinds, shifted the pillow under her head, and drifted back to sleep.

The next sound Kaitlyn heard was a steady stream of loud pounding from the other side of her bedroom door.

"Get up!" came an all-too-familiar voice.

"Go away," Kaitlyn said as she launched her pillow at the door.

"Okay with me. I'll bet Gracie and Amber would much rather go to the Caribbean with a good-looking muscle man, anyway."

"You wish, little brother," Kaitlyn teased.

"Just for that, I'm not saving you any breakfast," Kenny retorted.

Kaitlyn rubbed at her eyes and then climbed out of bed. She could see the first hints of morning streaming in through the slits between her wooden blinds. When she pulled them up, she smiled at the scene before her. The sun was just beginning its climb into the morning sky, and the only signs of rain to be seen were the droplets that slowly fell from the overhang on the roof. Kaitlyn opened the window and breathed in the cool morning air, where the fresh smell of rain still lingered. The effect was crisp and inviting. Kaitlyn's smile broadened. This storm would not ruin her vacation after all. With that thought, she cheerfully headed to the bathroom to get ready for the day.

Kaitlyn peered at herself in the mirror as she brushed her teeth. She could not help but notice how much she was beginning to look like her older sister Leslie. The extra hours of sun working as a life-guard at the community center had bleached Kaitlyn's hair the previous summer. With the highlights she'd gotten over the winter, the look was strikingly like her sister's. Plus it had grown about four inches through the winter, putting it just above her waist. Of course, Leslie had those big brown puppy-dog eyes, and Kaitlyn's were light aqua blue, a recessive gift from Mom; but the likeness was definitely there. Kaitlyn had been more keenly aware of it in the last four months since Leslie's death. Kaitlyn's throat suddenly tightened.

She bent down and splashed water on her face to stop the inevitable, but just as they had so many times before, the memories of that day flooded her mind.

Kaitlyn could still remember the frigid bite in the air that morning. It had snowed heavily the night before, which had brought down many power lines, leaving the majority of the residents of St. Paul, Minnesota, without power, including her family. Kaitlyn's dad had quickly built a roaring fire while her mom gathered thick, hand-made quilts to wrap up in. Kenny, Kaitlyn's twelve-year-old brother, had fumbled through the pantry in search of marshmallows and graham crackers. He had already snagged two chocolate bars from his bedroom, which he intended to use to make several gooey s'mores. He saw the whole situation as an adventure.

Kaitlyn sat on the couch with her feet propped up on the coffee table, relishing an unexpected day off from school. Leslie was sitting on the hearth, leaning close to the fire with her chemistry book tilted toward the flame. She was in her junior year of college and, like with everything else she did, was excelling. Kaitlyn sighed heavily as she watched her sister study.

"Come on, Leslie," Kaitlyn pleaded. "Classes have been canceled today. Forget about the books. Let's have some fun."

Leslie slowly looked up. At first she appeared a little annoyed at being interrupted, but when she saw her sister, her expression quickly softened. She brushed back the long, sandy strands of hair that fell over her shoulder, then snapped her book shut.

"I think I'm ready for this test, anyway. What did you have in mind, Jelly Bean?"

Jelly Bean was a nickname given to Kaitlyn by her father. One Easter, when she was three, she had tried to shove a jelly bean up her nose. It didn't stick, but, as Dad always liked to put it when he was telling the story, the name did.

"Let's visit the Keaths," Kaitlyn began, "and see if they need some extra blankets or something."

Leslie smiled mischievously over at Kaitlyn. "Or something, huh?"

The Keaths were family friends of theirs, and had been for years, but it wasn't the Keaths that prompted Kaitlyn as much as it was their twenty-one-year-old son, Greg. Greg had recently transferred from an out-of-state college to one back in Minnesota. Growing up, there had always been a little casual flirtation between the two, but now there was a definite attraction. Leslie winked over at her little sister, fully aware of what sparked Kaitlyn's sudden concern for the Keaths.

After a little bit of coaxing, Leslie managed to get the car keys from their dad. He was a pushover when it came to Leslie. Kaitlyn thought it was because of their dad's mother, whom she so strongly resembled. She had the same pair of warm, thoughtful eyes, which always seemed to be half hidden in the pages of a good book—just the image their father most cherished when he thought on the girls' grandmother. The two girls gave their father a quick kiss, then slipped out the back door.

The Keaths lived only about a mile away. In the spring it was a nice walk, but with six inches of snow on the ground, the girls decided on the car as the only option. The temperature had plummeted over the past few hours, causing the top layer of snow to crystallize. Kaitlyn could hear the crunch of the snow under her feet as she made her way to the passenger side of the car. Leslie wiped at the snow-covered windshield with her arm and then quickly climbed into the car. The powder still clung to her coat sleeve. When she started the car, it sputtered with the chill of the morning, shooting long puffs of smoke out the tailpipe.

"Are you sure that you don't want to just hang out at the house?" Leslie asked as she breathed into her hands and then rubbed them together for warmth.

"A little cold isn't going to kill you," Kaitlyn said, shoving her own hands deep into her pockets.

Leslie shook her head, then backed out onto the street. There wasn't a lot of traffic out, so most of the roads still had fresh powder. On some of the back roads there were no tracks at all, only a deadly undercoat of ice hidden beneath a beautiful, white blanket of snow. As they neared a less-traveled intersection not two blocks from their house, a man in a white pickup approached the same intersection from the opposite side. He seemed to be totally oblivious to the stop sign just feet in front of him. Finally, at the last possible moment, he slammed on his breaks. At first the truck fishtailed, but then spun violently out of control. Kaitlyn and Leslie both stared in horror and tensed in anticipation as the truck headed for them. Kaitlyn could feel adrenaline surging through her entire body as she'd watched a spray of snow shoot up from the back tires of the truck, showering flecks of white powder all over the intersection. She wanted to reach over and buckle her seat belt, but there was no time to do anything. It was over in seconds, the shrill sound of metal smashing into metal. The last thing Kaitlyn heard was Leslie calling out her name.

Kaitlyn had woken up a few hours later in a hospital bed with a concussion, a broken arm, and several cuts and bruises. Leslie never woke up. On impact, her head had hit the steering wheel; she was pronounced dead at the scene. In a split second, Leslie's life was over, and Kaitlyn's would never be the same again.

Kaitlyn shook her head with the memory and then splashed more water on her face. As she did, her eyes went to the scar on her hand. Though the wound was completely healed now, its purple hue was a constant reminder of that day. Why had she suggested going to the Keaths? The question plagued her like a recurring nightmare, except that bad dreams dissipated with the dawn—this dull ache never left.

"Kaitlyn? Are you in there?" Marjorie Winters called out as she tapped softly on the bathroom door.

Kaitlyn spun around to stare at the closed door. Then she turned back and looked at herself in the mirror. Her face was red and blotchy from crying. She wiped at her cheeks with the back of her hand and then swallowed hard in an attempt to dislodge the lump in her throat.

"Just a minute, Mom," she called back, trying to control the emotion in her voice.

"Don't take too long, sweetheart. I'm going down to start breakfast."

"Okay, Mom," Kaitlyn responded, wiping the last of the tears from her face.

\* \* \*

Thirty minutes later, Marjorie lifted her head from her cooking as Kaitlyn entered the kitchen.

"Hey, save some for me," Kaitlyn said in mock fear as she took a seat next to her brother. He was downing what was probably his third or fourth piece of bacon.

"You snooze, you lose," he mumbled, his mouth crammed with food.

Marjorie shook her head with a smile. Kenny was thirteen and going through a major growth spurt. He could easily inhale two sandwiches, a bag of chips, and an apple, and thirty minutes later be asking what was for dinner. Now, where he was storing all that food was a mystery. It had to be in the three extra inches he had grown that year.

"Would you like some scrambled eggs, sweetheart?" Marjorie offered her daughter.

With that Kenny sprang to his feet. "Scrambled eggs! I must have missed them."

Marjorie watched as half the contents of her frying pan disappeared.

"Your dad is going to have to get a part-time job just to feed you, and we see him little enough as it is."

Kenny opened the refrigerator with his free hand and grabbed a jug of milk.

"I can't help it, Mom. I'm starving."

Marjorie watched her son with affection. After having two daughters, it had been fun to have a son and see the dynamic that created. In physical appearance, Kenny had taken after her side of the family. He had the sandy hair, the broad shoulders, and the squared chin, but other than that, he was a carbon copy of his father. He loved sports and was extremely competitive, almost to a fault, especially savoring the rare opportunity to whoop his dad.

Marjorie's eyes then fell on her middle child. Though Kaitlyn was twenty, she still seemed to be finding herself. In Kaitlyn's eyes, she wasn't the stellar student that her sister had been, nor did she seem to have the headstrong determination that Kenny possessed. Marjorie hoped that this trip would give her some time to work things out and develop some confidence in her potentially bright future. The past few months had been so difficult on her. It had been for all of them. Marjorie had even noticed a few changes in her own appearance with the stress of Leslie's death. Her hair was starting to gray, she had put on ten extra pounds, and she was on the losing side in the fight against wrinkles. Under different circumstances this might have been hard to accept, but now it all seemed trivial. Other things were so much more important.

Brent Winters poked his head around the kitchen entryway. His dark but graying hair was in disarray.

"Let me guess," Brent began after seeing Kenny at the table. "The bacon's gone."

"Do you want some, Dad?" Kenny offered, holding up the last half-eaten piece.

Brent tousled his son's sandy mop and then bent down and kissed Kaitlyn's forehead.

"The bacon's all yours," he said with a grin. "I'll just grab some granola after my jog."

Brent was forty-five, but he easily could have passed for much younger. His hair was not the shocking black crop that it had been when they were first married, but the gray around the edges made him look surprisingly distinguished. He still jogged three times a week and played racquetball every Sunday with some guys from his work. In the past, he had almost always asked Marjorie to come and watch him play, but lately she had noticed that he was slipping out more frequently by himself. It hurt her feelings, though she would never admit it. She figured that it was just his way of dealing with the accident.

"Good morning, sweetheart," Marjorie chimed in.

Brent flashed her a quick wave as he headed for the back door.

"I won't be long. Then we can take this world traveler to the airport."

Marjorie watched as the screen door creaked open and then slammed shut with a big thud. She sighed wearily, then turned off the stove and took her own plate over to the table.

\* \* \*

Kaitlyn had just finished her breakfast when the phone rang. Kenny sprang to his feet, knocking the table with his legs. Marjorie had to grab her glass of orange juice to keep it from spilling.

"Would you please sit down, young man? Or better yet," she began with a look of inspiration, "why don't you kiss your sister good-bye and go do your chores."

Kenny twisted his face in disgust. Apparently neither the chores nor the thought of kissing his sister appealed to him. Kenny plopped his baseball cap on his head and darted out the door. Marjorie shook her head as she watched him go.

Kaitlyn jumped up and answered the phone, knowing full well who it would be. For the last few months she and Greg had been inseparable.

"Hello?" she said cheerfully into the taupe-colored phone on the kitchen counter.

"Hi, Kaitlyn." Greg said eagerly.

Kaitlyn held the receiver with her shoulder and hoisted herself up onto the countertop to sit. "I wasn't expecting to hear from you today. I thought you had that big *important* meeting with your uncle this morning."

"He'll just have to wait," Greg announced boldly.

Kaitlyn smiled and then began twisting the phone cord with her fingers.

"Let me guess. He had to cancel."

Greg started to laugh. "Am I that obvious?"

"No, just that ambitious. I know you wouldn't cancel anything because of how important eventually joining the firm is to you."

"So, is it too late to stop by and see you before you go?"

Kaitlyn looked up as her mom pointed at the clock and then left the room.

"I'm supposed to meet Gracie and Amber at the airport in forty-five minutes. How fast do you think you can make it over here?"

Kaitlyn smiled as the other end of the phone went dead.

* * *

Greg pulled up in front of the Winterses' home just as Kaitlyn's father reached the driveway.

"Good morning," Greg offered as he crossed the driveway to shake hands with Kaitlyn's father.

"I thought we might be seeing you here this morning," Brent admitted, a little out of breath from his jog.

"I hope you don't mind," Greg began to explain.

Brent held up his hand. "Not another word. You're welcome here anytime. You know that."

Brent had never hidden the fact that he liked his daughter and Greg going out. The Winters and the Keaths were practically family already. Greg's having a full scholarship, with plans for law school afterward, was just icing on the cake. Placing his hand firmly on Greg's shoulder, Brent escorted him into the entryway.

"Kaitlyn," Brent called up the stairs, "there's a young man down here that would like to see you."

Brent slapped Greg on the shoulder and then wiped at the beads of perspiration on his brow.

"I better head for the shower."

Greg watched as Mr. Winters climbed the stairs and then disappeared around the corner. With no one else around, Greg quickly stole a look in the brass-trimmed, oval mirror that hung in the entryway. He brushed at a few stubborn strands of hair that kept falling toward his eyes. He scowled, acknowledging that he needed a haircut. His hair was a bit too trendy. He needed a more clean-cut, professional look.

"Admiring yourself in the mirror?"

Greg jerked around to face the stairs. His face, though slightly red from being caught, lit up when he saw Kaitlyn. She had her arms folded as if scolding a small child, but her eyes were sparkling with amusement.

Kaitlyn arched her eyebrows. "And they say women are vain."

Greg smiled up at her. She was very much enjoying having the upper hand. He watched her as she descended the stairs. It was obvious that she was a swimmer. Her build was athletic and her limbs tanned. A few wispy pieces of hair highlighted her face, while the rest of her hair fell long over her shoulders. Her T-shirt, baggy cargo pants, and flip-flops attested to a casual and unassuming personality. Her nose was just a bit pink from too much sun, and freckles dotted her cheeks. Greg mused on how much her appearance matched her personality. She was unpretentious and sunny. She was also very attractive, but not at all obsessed with looks—which made her all the more appealing.

"Actually, I was just thinking that I can't believe I came over here looking like this."

Kaitlyn reached out and touched one of the soft curls around the nape of his neck.

"Well, you look good to me, shaggy hair and all," she teased.

Greg reached out, pulled her to him, and kissed her firmly on the lips. When he pulled back, Kaitlyn shot a quick glance around to make sure that they were still alone. Greg smiled and then took her hand.

"Come on, let's go sit outside for a minute."

Greg sat down on the porch and then patted a spot next to him for Kaitlyn to sit.

"I know it's selfish," Greg began, "but I wish you weren't going to be gone a whole week."

"I'll be back before you know it. Then we can spend the rest of the summer together."

"Actually," Greg began with just a hint of apprehension in his voice, "I've been thinking about spending a lot more time with you than that."

"What do you mean?"

Kaitlyn searched the handsome features of Greg's face, lingering on the dark green eyes fixed on her. Something in their depths seemed to pull her in and whisper exactly what he meant. Kaitlyn instantly felt breathless, as though an enormous siphon were sucking all the oxygen from her lungs.

Greg traced her face softly with his finger and then bent and kissed her.

"I love you, Kaitlyn."

Kaitlyn's brain was apparently beyond all function. "I—"

Greg lifted his finger to her lips. "We'll talk more when you get back."

Kaitlyn stood on the porch to watch Greg leave. She was so deep in thought that she didn't hear her father come up behind her.

"Did Greg leave?" he asked, disappointed.

"He just did," Kaitlyn said, still staring down the road as his car disappeared.

Brent put his arm around his daughter's shoulder.

"You've got a good young man there. Greg's got a lot going for him. He's polite, he has ambition, and he's smart—he's dating you, after all."

Kaitlyn turned to face her father. It was no wonder she adored him. "Thanks, Dad."

Brent squeezed her shoulder. "Well, it's the truth. Now let's get a move on before your mother leaves us both."

# CHAPTER 2

Kaitlyn's eyes took in the whole of the busy airport. Business people with cell phones in one hand and briefcases in the other were rushing toward crowded terminals. Families were huddled together talking excitedly, totally oblivious to anything else going on around them. Then, as if the scene were not chaotic enough, little utility vehicles pulling luggage threaded in and out of the crowd.

Kaitlyn had never flown before, so she felt a little uncertainty mixed in with the excitement. She quickly checked her baggage and then walked with her parents toward the long line of passengers waiting to make their way past the security checkpoint.

"Do you think Gracie and Amber have made it here yet?" Kaitlyn asked as she scanned the crowd.

Before Kaitlyn could say another word, a girl in a bright orange shirt that was printed all over with giant pineapples and palm trees came running in their direction. She wore a wide-brimmed hat and had her camera dangling from a strap around her neck. Her arms were stretched out and she was running as if she were in slow motion, like a farewell scene from a movie.

"Kaitlyn! Kaitlyn! It's been so long," she shouted, doing her best airport reunion imitation.

All eyes were on them. Kaitlyn just shook her head. "Gracie, you're crazy," she muttered.

Brent Winters's face was a deep shade of crimson. "I could have told you that a long time ago."

Amber came trailing up behind Gracie. She was dressed considerably more mainstream than her counterpart. She wore a soft pastel pullover and tailored cotton shorts. Her auburn hair was pulled back in a neat ponytail, which drew immediate attention to her lovely heart-shaped face.

"Gracie did the same thing to me," Amber began, "only she used a French accent. When my parents saw her coming, they handed me my luggage and went the other way."

Kaitlyn's father burst out laughing.

Marjorie just smiled and then turned to Amber. "I was hoping to see your parents."

"I think they're trying to keep at a safe distance," Amber said with a flippant grin.

Gracie put her hands on her hips in mock offense. "What are you insinuating?"

Amber put her arm around her friend's shoulder. "You know we love ya, Gracie."

\* \* \*

Kaitlyn stopped, allowing her eyes to take in the interior of the 747 that would be taking them to Miami. From back inside the airport, looking out at the metal machine that could soar through the air almost as proficiently as a bird, the plane had looked enormous. Now, though, that same marvel of technology looked surprisingly small. Kaitlyn could almost feel the butterflies in her stomach taking flight.

"Hey, what are you doing?"

Kaitlyn turned to face Gracie, who was standing in line behind her. She had her carry-on bag slung over her shoulder, and, from the expression on her face, it was heavy.

"Sorry, Gracie, I was just taking a look."

"Well, do you have to be such an obvious tourist?"

Amber poked her head from behind Gracie.

"This advice from a person with life-size fruit on her shirt."

Gracie completely ignored Amber's teasing.

"There's no assigned seating on this plane, and I'd like to get the seats in front of the wing. The last couple of times I've flown, I've had to sit in the middle. Then I couldn't see anything out the window but the wing. Everybody else got to see the Grand Canyon from a thousand-plus feet up, and all I saw was a gray slab of metal."

Kaitlyn turned to the side and watched as her overanxious friend shot past her. She cringed as the bag slung over Gracie's shoulder came dangerously close to smacking a few seated passengers. Gracie, of course, seemed completely oblivious to the trail of dirty looks and muffled comments that followed her down the aisle. When she reached the seats just in front of the wing—the seats that she wanted—she came to a dead stop. Every seat was taken. Apparently several other people had had experiences similar to Gracie's. The only seats still available were the ones in the middle, directly next to the wing, and the seats clear in the back by the rest rooms. Kaitlyn and Amber scooted past Gracie, who stood gaping wide-mouthed at the occupied seats.

Kaitlyn found three open seats together and quickly sat down. Amber sat down next to her, while Gracie struggled to get her bag into the overhead compartment. A guy in a football jersey sitting in the row in front of them stood to help her. He lifted the bulky luggage with one giant swoosh of bicep and then motioned toward the empty seat next to him. Without a moment's hesitation, Gracie slid right in. After a couple of seconds, she popped her head over the back of the seat to face Kaitlyn and Amber. She had a look of triumph on her face.

"I hope you guys don't mind me sitting here next to . . ." Gracie turned to look at the guy next to her.

"Jim," he offered with a smile.

"Next to Jim," she said. Then she turned back around before they could say a word.

"How does she do it?" Amber said in awe.

"It must be the wide-brimmed hat."

\* \* \*

After all the passengers had boarded, Gracie stood up and turned around to face Kaitlyn and Amber. She bent over toward them as if to whisper, but her voice was intentionally loud enough to reach the people in the seats in front of the wing.

"Did you hear about that plane last week that crashed into the side of a mountain?"

Kaitlyn could see a couple of heads quickly turn in Gracie's direction.

"From the reports on the six o'clock news, it was a real disaster."

Kaitlyn had not heard of any plane crashes lately. She eyed Gracie suspiciously, unsure of where she was going with this.

"Yeah, it was a bad one! The plane split right in two. Miraculously, the only people that were injured were the ones that sat in front of the wing."

Kaitlyn began to shake her head as she watched Gracie's apparent Broadway debut.

"In fact," Gracie continued, raising her voice slightly, "they had an aerodynamics expert on, and he said that the least safe place to sit on any airplane is directly in front of the wings."

Kaitlyn turned to Amber. "Aerodynamics expert, huh?"

"That's why I try to stay just as far away from those seats as possible," Gracie concluded, gesturing toward the very seats she wanted.

Gracie's words hit the mark. Within seconds, two younger girls gathered their things and scrambled to the seats back by the rest rooms. Gracie did not even wait to be discreet about her next move. She jumped to her feet, dragging Mr. Biceps with her, and darted toward the now-vacant seats. Once she had claimed the seats as her own, she shamelessly raised her hands above her head as if she had just won some huge victory.

\* \* \*

Kaitlyn watched out the window as the plane cut through the featherlike cirrus clouds that seemed to float aimlessly in an otherwise tranquil sky.

"I can't believe Gracie actually agreed to come on this cruise. I don't think I've ever met anyone so afraid of the water," Amber commented.

Kaitlyn turned to look at Amber.

"I know. I thought for sure she'd say no. She did say that she's sleeping with her life jacket on." Amber started to laugh, but Kaitlyn raised an eyebrow. "She wasn't kidding," she added almost seriously. Then they both started to laugh.

"Have you decided on a major now that your basics are out of the way?" Kaitlyn asked.

Amber sighed. "I guess."

Kaitlyn tilted her head. "That doesn't sound like excitement to me."

"I'm just not sure of what direction to go with my life right now. I mean, I'm enjoying college and everything but . . . I don't know." Amber shrugged. "So, how are things going with your mom and dad?"

Kaitlyn let out a sigh. "Still the same. They're not saying anything, but you can feel the tension between them."

"It will work out, Kaitlyn. They're probably just dealing with a lot. It hasn't been that long since the accident."

Almost instantly Kaitlyn could feel the muscles in her throat begin to constrict.

"What about you? I know it must be tough."

Kaitlyn had confided in both Amber and Gracie about almost everything in her life. They had all gone through the ups and downs of braces and acne, hormones and dating, sibling squabbles, and even Gracie's parents' divorce. Each time the three of them had made it through together, but this was different. Somehow Kaitlyn could not open up. It was too painful.

"I'm fine," Kaitlyn offered weakly, trying to hide the strain in her voice.

Amber opened her mouth as if to continue, but then reluctantly changed her mind.

"Well, I'm here if you ever want to talk about it."

Kaitlyn reached over and squeezed her hand. "I know. Thanks."

"So, how are things going with Greg?" Amber asked, trying to lighten the mood. "I half expected him to try and hitch a ride in your suitcase."

Kaitlyn laughed and then pointed to the compartment above them.

"I think Gracie's carry-on luggage is big enough to fit him."

"That's because she's hoping to stow away a gorgeous native on the return trip."

Kaitlyn nodded, though her mind was already elsewhere. "Greg wants to talk when I get back."

"Oh?" Amber began, raising her voice slightly. "Talk about what?"

"I'm not positive, but it sounded serious."

"Are you saying 'serious' as in *commitment?*" Amber began incredulously. "As in exclusivity?"

"I don't know."

"Wow! That's a big step."

Kaitlyn nodded her head, still not completely certain how she felt about it herself.

"Do you love him?"

"I've always loved him."

"I know, but are you *in love* with him?"

"Amber, Greg has always been there for me, especially since Leslie died."

"That's not what I asked you."

Kaitlyn turned toward the window. "I don't know," she admitted weakly.

Kaitlyn leaned her head back and closed her eyes. She tried to block out everything but the hum and constant vibration of the engine. After what seemed like an eternity, her breathing began to slow and deepen and her body finally succumbed to the lulling hum of the plane. Any thoughts about Greg or Leslie would soon be lost in dreams.

# CHAPTER 3

Kaitlyn stood in the lobby of the *Lady of the Islands,* the cruise ship that would be taking them to the Caribbean. Her eyes greedily scanned the entire expanse of the room before her. It was elegant, but still had an old-sailing-ship feel to it. There was an enormous steel anchor on the wall directly in front of them. Below it, a huge salt-water aquarium ran the entire length of the wall. Brightly colored tropical fish darted in and out of an elaborate, underwater city. Off to the right of the lobby was a sitting area with several plush, high-back chairs. A mural of a captain staring across a stormy sea was hung above an exquisitely crafted, antique coffee table. A vase of freshly cut flowers had been placed on the center of the table.

Straight in front of them was a man in a crisp, white uniform. He was greeting and giving directions to the passengers as they boarded, as well as handing out life jackets with instructions to keep them in their cabins in case of an emergency. Amber approached the steward, while Kaitlyn and Gracie lingered in the entryway to soak in the nautical atmosphere.

"Welcome aboard the *Lady of the Islands,*" the steward offered with a friendly smile. "May I direct you to your cabin?"

When Amber told him their cabin number, the steward turned and pointed in the direction of the elevators.

"Your cabin is on the third level," he began. "Just turn to your left as you exit the elevators."

When he turned back around, Kaitlyn and Gracie had joined Amber. His eyes quickly fell on Kaitlyn.

"Uhh, welcome aboard," he stammered.

"We're all together," Amber offered, gesturing to her two friends.

The steward nodded his head in response to Amber, though his eyes still lingered on Kaitlyn. "There will be a mandatory muster drill thirty minutes before we depart. All the safety procedures will be explained there." Then he turned and hastily grabbed three life jackets. "I guess you'll be needing your life jackets." As soon as he spoke, his eyes suddenly grew round. "I don't mean that you *will* need them. They're for emergency purposes only. Not that we're expecting an emergency," he quickly added. "This ship has been around for *a lot* of years and she's still going strong."

Amber wrinkled her forehead as she watched this seemingly professional young man try to regain possession of his mouth.

"I don't mean 'a lot of years' as in old and falling apart," he added as soon as he realized how that sounded. "Trust me, this ship is built like a tank. She's rock solid. It's a wonder she can float at all."

The three girls were now gawking wide-eyed at the steward.

"But she does float," he quickly added, almost as an afterthought.

Kaitlyn and Amber were trying not to smile, but Gracie made no such attempt.

"Where are we supposed to meet for that drill?" Gracie asked, obviously dragging out the steward's discomfort.

He looked down at his clipboard. "The section of the ship that you're in meets at the promenade deck."

"Our cabin is up the elevators and to the left?" Amber finally offered, trying to rescue the poor guy from further embarrassment.

The steward only nodded, his face bright red.

"Now, he was cute!" Gracie concluded as they neared the elevator.

"He was okay, I guess," Kaitlyn said, keeping her voice as matter-of-fact as possible.

"Are you crazy?" Gracie piped in. "He was *definitely* more than okay."

"Did you see the way he looked at you?" Amber questioned as she pushed the button on the elevator for the third floor. "He was so tongue-tied he could hardly speak."

"He wasn't looking at me any certain way," Kaitlyn argued.

"If you didn't notice the way he was looking at you, then how did you know I was talking to you and not Gracie?"

Both girls turned to Kaitlyn.

"Well . . . I . . ." she stammered.

Gracie folded her arms and smirked as she waited for an answer.

"Look," Kaitlyn finally began, "I came on this cruise to spend time with my two best friends, not to meet men. I'm not interested in that steward or any other guy. I'm completely content with the relationship I'm already in."

The elevator doors opened up to the third floor and Kaitlyn immediately hopped out, anxious to end the conversation. She turned right, and quickly walked down the hall. Amber and Gracie stood at the elevator doors and watched her go.

"Who's she trying to convince," Gracie began, "us or herself?"

Amber shrugged her shoulders.

"I don't know, but I do know one thing. If she's heading to our cabin, she's going in the wrong direction."

\* \* \*

Kaitlyn stood in the doorway of their cabin. There was a bunk bed on one side of the room as well as another bed that folded up or down that was connected high on the wall. A metal ladder was propped up on the wall next to it. A tiny but clean bathroom with a narrow closet was on the other side of the room. At the far end of the cabin was a small table with two chairs positioned in front of a porthole.

Gracie rushed over and set her suitcase down on the lower bunk bed and began rummaging through it for her swimming suit, while Amber unpacked her neatly folded clothes. Kaitlyn walked over to the table and sat down in one of the straight-backed chairs. She leaned toward the small window to lookout at the people lining the dock. Some of them were heading toward the ship to board while others waved up to loved ones on deck. A long blast from the ship's horn signaled that they would soon be departing.

"I don't know about you guys," Gracie began, "but I'm going to be out on deck sipping a little fruit drink with an umbrella in it when this ship leaves port." With that, she slipped into the bathroom.

"Sounds good to me," Amber admitted.

Amber turned to Kaitlyn who was now flipping through a pamphlet that had been placed on the table.

"What are you looking at?"

"It's a schedule of events for while we're on board," Kaitlyn answered, holding up the brochure. "Who needs the Caribbean? There's enough to do here on ship to keep us busy for weeks."

"Like what?" Amber asked, her curiosity piqued.

"To start with, it says that there's a movie theater, a gym, and tours of the navigation bridge and radio rooms. They have several different entertainers, and a dance in the Caribbean Room every night. Tonight just happens to be a luau," Kaitlyn said with a huge grin.

"Did you say luau?" Gracie called out from the bathroom.

"Yeah, why?" Kaitlyn called back.

"Go open my suitcase. I bought us all something to use in the Caribbean. I was going to wait to surprise you, but this will work out great."

Kaitlyn and Amber hurried over to the bed and flipped open Gracie's suitcase. Right on top were three grass skirts.

"Did you find them?" Gracie asked anxiously from behind the door.

"We found them, all right," Kaitlyn said, shaking her head.

"I have a few more surprises for later," Gracie called back proudly.

"Is it too late to jump ship?" Amber whispered.

Kaitlyn laughed and then sat down on the bed to continue looking at the schedule of events. Amber peered over her shoulder.

"Great!" Amber exclaimed as she pointed down at one of the activities listed. "They even have a class on scuba diving. I've always wanted to try it."

"Sounds fun," Kaitlyn agreed.

Gracie emerged from the bathroom with a big bottle of suntan lotion.

"There's only one activity that I'm interested in right now," Gracie said as she reached for her beach towel. "Introducing this ghost of a body to some sun."

Kaitlyn and Amber glanced over at Gracie. She was wearing a hot pink bathing suit and a pair of dark sunglasses. Her jet-black, curly hair was pulled up on the top of her head in a ponytail, the curls bouncing everywhere unrestrained. Her skin really was white—maybe not ghostly white, but not too many shades off. Kaitlyn had never paid much attention to Gracie's appearance before. Everybody was always attracted to Gracie because of her sense of humor and personality, but she really was pretty. Her dark hair and fair skin made a striking contrast.

"If I were you, I'd stock up on the sunscreen or you're going to end up nice and crispy," Amber teased.

"I know. The last thing I want to do is show up in the Caribbean looking like I've been deep-fried," Gracie agreed.

She squeezed some coconut-scented lotion into her hand and began plastering it across her shoulders while Kaitlyn and Amber took turns in the bathroom changing into their swimsuits. After they were finished, the three of them joined their group for the muster drill, then headed for the crowd of passengers lined up on deck to take in their last glimpse of land before they departed for paradise.

Kaitlyn could feel the fresh ocean breeze rush across her face. She closed her eyes, savoring the moment. The smell of salt water and the squawking of birds flying aimlessly along the docks perfected the experience. The ship did one more long blast on the horn and then began to move. They waved down at the strangers below them, thrilled to be heading out into the ocean. Suddenly Kaitlyn wished that her family was down there amid the crowd. Her brother Kenny would have loved this. Once, when they had taken a family vacation to San Diego, Kenny was so fascinated with all the ships that he had proudly announced he wanted to be a sea captain when he grew up. Of course, he also wanted to be a fireman, an astronaut, and a linebacker for the Miami Dolphins, his all-time favorite team. Kaitlyn smiled at the memory, then breathed in deeply. In just a short time they would be docking at an exotic port and having the experience of a lifetime.

# CHAPTER 4

The wispy white clouds above them danced in the warm ocean breeze. Kaitlyn stared back in the direction of the dock, but it could no longer be seen. The city had grown smaller and smaller as they'd gone farther out into the ocean. The beach, with its rows of fancy hotels, began to blend into a solid mass and then eventually disappeared completely. Now all that could be seen was a seemingly endless expanse of water. Kaitlyn watched as the waves rolled and peaked and then rolled again.

"Did you have any problems finding your cabin?"

Kaitlyn jumped and then swung around, startled by a voice she didn't recognize. The sun was directly in her eyes as she turned around, making the figure before her impossible to see. Kaitlyn raised her hand to shade her eyes. It took a minute for her eyes to focus and the black silhouette before her to fully materialize. Then, there he was, the ship steward who had given them directions to their cabin.

"Oh, I'm sorry," he said, realizing that the sun was right behind him. He took a couple of steps to the side and then came easily into view. His hair was a rich brown that shone as the sun hit it, but it was his smile that instantly drew Kaitlyn's attention. It was warm and genuine. He was of average build, maybe six feet, but broad through the shoulders. His shirt was clean and pressed and his overall appearance tidy. His somewhat bushy eyebrows appeared to be his only nonconforming feature, though they drew one's attention to a stunning pair of blue eyes. Kaitlyn thought she had caught him glancing at her during the muster drill, but each look had been so quick she hadn't been completely sure. Because of his possible attentions, she had missed much of the safety instructions.

"I just wanted to make sure you didn't have any problem with my directions."

Kaitlyn thought back to the elevator and going the wrong direction.

"No, not at all," she lied. "We found our way just fine."

Kaitlyn shot a glance in the direction of the pool where Gracie and Amber were lounging in the sun. It took only a second to locate them; they were both sitting straight up in their chairs staring directly at her. Kaitlyn focused back on the man before her.

"Thanks again," she said in a rather short tone, then turned back toward the ocean.

Both of them were uncomfortably aware that he had just been tactfully dismissed. The steward nodded his head politely.

"Sorry to have bothered you."

Then, as quickly as he had come, he was gone. Kaitlyn wanted to call him back. She wanted to apologize for being rude and thank him for his help, but as she turned around, Amber and Gracie were already racing across the deck toward her.

"What did he want?" Gracie asked as she looked over her shoulder at the young steward, who was now mingling with the other passengers.

"He was just making sure we didn't have any problem finding our cabin."

"Uh huh!" Gracie and Amber both sang in unison.

"Yeah, right!" Gracie smirked. "And I'm the queen of England. Wake up, girl! He's interested."

"But I'm not," Kaitlyn said adamantly.

"Well, if you're not, *I am!*" Gracie declared. Then, without another word, she made a beeline through the crowd toward the steward.

"Hey, Your Highness, it's not ladylike to hurdle lounge chairs," Kaitlyn called out, but Gracie was already halfway across the deck.

Ten minutes later Kaitlyn and Amber were sitting in front of a feast fit for a king.

"Gracie doesn't know what she's missing," Kaitlyn declared as she spread a generous scoop of honey butter on a warm scone.

"I know it," Amber agreed as she popped a juicy strawberry in her mouth.

"Hey! I've been looking all over for you two." Kaitlyn and Amber looked up to see Gracie making her way across the promenade deck toward them.

"I didn't expect to see you back so soon," Amber admitted.

Gracie sat down and then reached over and snagged one of the plump red berries off Amber's plate.

"I didn't either," Gracie admitted with a shrug.

"So how did it go?" Amber asked.

"It didn't. Apparently he only dates girls from his church."

Amber looked at Gracie in disbelief. "Did he say that?"

"No, but after talking to him for a few minutes, I kind of caught on. It's a shame, too, because he's cute."

"What is he, some kind of religious freak?" Kaitlyn blurted out.

Amber laughed but Gracie shrugged her shoulders. "It wasn't like that at all. Matthew said something about a date with him consisting of a dollar movie, a bowl of green Jell-O, and a handshake at the front door. I don't quite get what green Jell-O has to do with anything, but I am totally not for the handshake at the front door."

"Matthew?" Amber questioned.

"I saw his nametag," Gracie offered.

"What church does he belong to, anyway?" Kaitlyn mumbled.

"The Church of the Latter Days or something. I can't remember," Gracie admitted. "Really, it's no big deal. I've been turned down before. This was the first time that religion was used as an excuse, though."

"Gracie, if I know you," Amber began with a knowing smile, "before this trip is over, you'll have fallen in love at least five times and left behind a trail of broken hearts stretching from the coast of Miami to the middle of the Caribbean."

\* \* \*

After their late lunch, the three of them decided to spend the rest of the afternoon on deck. Kaitlyn and Amber slid into a figure-eight-shaped pool while Gracie put on her sunglasses, pulled out a magazine, and found a comfortable lounge chair. Kaitlyn did several laps across the pool, giving her muscles a stretch, then claimed her own lounge chair. It was close to five before the three of them returned to their cabin. After changing their clothes, they headed to the ship's kitchen, where hourly tours of the ship began. Their tour guide, a petite woman in her early twenties, made little effort to conceal the fact that she was thoroughly bored. She yawned broadly several times as she pointed to various points of interest around the ship.

After a tour of the kitchen, the group took an elevator to the fourth floor, where the navigation bridge and the radio room were located. A middle-aged man in a clean, white uniform welcomed them onto the navigation bridge with a pleasant smile. Kaitlyn was sure that he had to be the captain, but when addressed as such, he introduced himself as Lieutenant Roger Lewis, the first mate. He pointed over to a table where a man was studying several unrolled charts.

"Captain Bridges has been a captain for twenty years," the first mate began, motioning over to the captain. "The first ten years he served as a captain for the U.S. Navy. He received the Medal of Valor for rescuing three members of his crew."

Captain Bridges straightened as he turned to face the group. He had a striking head of silver hair. Kaitlyn watched him closely as he crossed the room.

"Thank you, Lieutenant, but actually I've been a captain for twenty-*two* years. I was one of the youngest captains in the Navy. After I served my country, I was asked to captain this baby." Then he gave a dismissing nod to the first mate, who saluted and then went immediately back to work.

Captain Bridges stood upright with his hands behind his back, his eyes scanning the cabin. He breathed in deeply, satisfied with what he saw. He then walked over to the helm where another member of the crew was standing. The captain put his hand on the man's shoulder to dismiss him, then took his place to steer the ship. He first looked out the large windows in front of him at the vast ocean, then glanced over his shoulder at the tour group.

"Would anyone like to give her a try?"

Gracie's hand shot up instantly, along with almost everyone else's in the group, but the captain pointed to Kaitlyn.

"Where are you from?"

"Minnesota."

"You're a long way from home," he acknowledged as he motioned for her to come over next to him.

Kaitlyn hesitated for only a second, then quickly moved next to the captain. She placed her hands firmly on the large wheel as the captain stepped aside.

"Keep her straight," he ordered, his voice intentionally gruff. Then he gave her a quick wink and led the rest of the tour group over to a wall full of colored charts and technical graphs.

Kaitlyn stared out the window before her as the ship sliced through the water. The ocean before her was a deep blue with an occasional touch of white as the waves peaked and sprayed. She could see a hint of a storm on the horizon, but the water was so mesmerizing that her focus lingered there. Her heart raced with the idea that she was steering this massive ship. The immense power of the whole thing was thrilling.

The captain paused from the tour to look over at Kaitlyn.

"Everything all right, Minnesota?"

"Yes, sir," she said enthusiastically.

He nodded and then began showing the group the different instruments that ran the length of one of the walls, explaining their functions. When he was finished, he sauntered back over to Kaitlyn.

"Does anyone have any questions?" he asked, glancing across the group.

Before anyone could speak, the door to the bridge opened and a young man in uniform entered. He promptly crossed the floor to the captain and whispered something in his ear. The captain's relaxed disposition was instantly gone.

"Ladies and gentleman," he said in a professional tone, "I thank you for your attentiveness, but I'm afraid that I have some business to attend to." He motioned for the first mate to relieve Kaitlyn at the helm. The captain then turned, and without another word led the young crew member out of the room.

Kaitlyn looked over at Gracie and Amber. "I wonder what that was all about."

"I don't know," Amber said with a shrug.

"Forget about that," Gracie rushed on. "What was it like steering the ship?"

Kaitlyn smiled broadly. "It was incredible."

The girls continued talking and giggling quietly as their tour guide led them to the radio room. After a quick knock on the door, a large man in uniform appeared in the doorway. In a brisk, no-nonsense way, he informed them that all tours of the navigational areas, including the radio room, had been canceled today. Kaitlyn stole a look past the man into the room. Several people were huddled around the captain, talking excitedly. The captain looked agitated and abruptly lifted his arms to silence the group. Kaitlyn edged in closer, but before the captain could speak, the door was briskly shut. Kaitlyn stood staring at the closed door. An uneasy feeling made her shiver. She tried to shrug it off, but when she glanced over at the tour guide, she too was looking at the closed door with a frown. When she saw Kaitlyn watching her, she quickly attempted a cordial smile.

"So what's next?" Gracie asked her friends as the rest of the group made their way over to the elevators.

"I think I'm going back to the cabin to lie down for a while," Amber said.

"What's wrong?" Kaitlyn asked.

"My stomach is a little upset. I think the movement of the ship is getting to me."

"I'm sure they sell something in the gift shop for seasickness," Gracie suggested. "If not, we could always see about getting something from the ship's doctor."

"No. I'll be fine. I just need to lie down."

"And miss the chance to meet the ship's doctor?" Gracie concluded, half joking and half serious. "I don't think so. I heard he's young."

# CHAPTER 5

Kaitlyn decided to check the ship's gift shop for something for seasickness while Gracie went with Amber back to the cabin. Apparently, Amber was not the only passenger bothered by the movement of the ship, because the little gift shop was jam-packed. Kaitlyn grabbed one of the last bottles of motion-sickness pills, paid for it, and left the crowded store. Kaitlyn could feel the movement of the ship beneath her as she made her way over to the elevator. She wasn't bothered by it, but the movement did seem to be stronger than when they had first started just over eight hours ago.

As she entered the empty elevator, a man in uniform stepped in with her. When Kaitlyn turned to ask him which floor he wanted, the crew member, who had been concentrating on something on his clipboard, looked up. Kaitlyn could feel the blood rush to her cheeks as her mind flashed to the incident on deck where, for no apparent reason, she had been rude to a complete stranger, *this* stranger. There was a moment of awkward silence as the two of them stared at each other. Finally the steward broke into a smile.

"You must think I'm stalking you or something."

Kaitlyn tried to laugh, but it sounded forced.

"I don't think I've properly introduced myself," he said as he extended his hand to Kaitlyn. "I'm Matthew Wright."

"Mr. *Right,* huh? I wonder how many girls you've used that opening line on."

This time Matthew's laughter filled the elevator.

"I only wish I could deny your accusation. The sting of certain experiences is still with me." He grimaced as he grabbed at his heart.

Kaitlyn couldn't help but laugh.

"I'm Kaitlyn Winters," she offered as she studied him carefully.

"Nice to officially meet you. Is the movement of the ship getting to you?" Matthew asked, gesturing toward the bottle in her hand.

"No, I'm fine. They're for my friend."

"The one that I talked to up on deck?"

"No, that was Gracie."

"She's quite the character," Matthew chuckled.

"What do you mean by that?" Kaitlyn shot back, suddenly irritated.

"I didn't mean anything by it. I only meant that she . . . well . . ." He appeared to be struggling to find just the right way to phrase it. "Well, she speaks her mind, that's for sure. Not that that's a bad thing," he quickly added.

Kaitlyn turned as the elevator doors began to open at the third floor. She started forward, but as she did, the movement of the ship caused her to lose her balance. With a loud bang, Kaitlyn tripped right into the half-opened metal doors. Matthew leaped forward, dropping his clipboard. He grabbed Kaitlyn around the waist to keep her from falling.

"Are you all right?"

Kaitlyn's forehead was throbbing and she was just a little dazed, but the real sting came from embarrassment.

"I'm fine," she lied.

Matthew reached up and gently brushed the hair off her forehead to expose a quickly forming goose egg.

"It doesn't look fine to me," Matthew concluded, his voice now taking on a more professional tone. "You better have the ship's doctor take a look."

"Don't be silly. It's only a bump."

"Oh, sure, you're fine *now*. Then when you go back to your room and pass out, I lose my job. Would you like to be the reason an innocent guy like me loses his only means of support?"

Kaitlyn rolled her eyes.

"Seriously," Matthew continued, "I would really feel better if you got it checked out."

Kaitlyn could tell that he was not going to let up.

"All right, but I'm telling you, it's nothing."

As Matthew escorted Kaitlyn toward the ship's doctor, she was keenly aware of him next to her, though his behavior was nothing more than casual and polite. He was handsome, that was obvious, but there was something more, something different. He had a quick smile that made him seem not only handsome, but charming and sincere. Kaitlyn was finding it difficult to dislike him.

As they walked down the corridor, they passed a set of double doors that led out onto the third-floor deck. Kaitlyn slowed her step. The dark clouds that had been distant when she'd looked out the large windows on the navigation bridge now cast their shadows across a quarter of the sky. A grayish haze of rainfall ran the length of the horizon.

Matthew retraced his steps back to Kaitlyn and then gazed out on the approaching storm.

"This ship has seen her fair share of years, but, believe me, she's solid," Matthew said, trying to sound reassuring.

"You're not going to try that whole 'she's solid as a rock' thing on me again, are you?"

Matthew winced. "I guess I better stop while I'm still ahead." Then he reached over and took her gently by the elbow. "Come on."

Just as the two of them turned to leave, Matthew's pager went off. He reached down and turned it off, then read the message.

"Do you need to go?" Kaitlyn asked, surprised that she was not as anxious to get rid of him as she had been earlier.

Matthew nodded. "Let me walk you to the infirmary first."

"No, you go ahead," Kaitlyn protested. "I'm fine, really."

Kaitlyn put her hand up to her head. The bump was still sore, but the swelling seemed to have lessened.

"Are you sure?" he asked, not yet convinced.

"Yes. Besides, I need to get these pills back to Amber."

"I will need to file an accident report, but I can get with you later on that." Matthew smiled. "It was nice talking to you."

With that, he turned, walked down the corridor, and disappeared around a corner. Kaitlyn stared after him. The feelings inside her were twisting and churning every bit as much as the distant storm. Kaitlyn puffed her cheeks out and then released a long sigh. Why was she feeling like this? She shook her head and started back in the direction of the elevators. She turned her head away from the deck doors as she passed; she was flustered enough without worrying about a storm.

* * *

"What took you so long?" Gracie asked, her tone raised just enough that Kaitlyn knew she was miffed.

"It's a long story. How's Amber?"

Before Gracie could reply, the sounds coming from the bathroom let her know exactly how Amber was doing.

"I guess not very well." Kaitlyn winced.

Gracie shook her head. "If you think this is bad, you should have seen the nice trail she left down the hall. I would hate to have been the maintenance worker that came across that little cleanup."

Kaitlyn cringed. "Gracie, you're awful."

"No, what's awful is seeing the *Lady of the Islands'* all-you-can-eat buffet the second time around. Not a pretty sight!"

Kaitlyn shook her head and then looked up as the bathroom door opened. Amber emerged, swaying with the movement of the ship. Her face was green and she was struggling just to hold onto the door frame, obviously not trusting her legs. Kaitlyn walked over and put her arm around her friend to help her to the bed.

"Are you all right?" Kaitlyn asked gently.

"I just need to lie down for a while."

"You look terrible!" Gracie offered, not at all ashamed by her bluntness.

Kaitlyn flashed Gracie a look, which Gracie either did not see or chose not to acknowledge.

"I couldn't possibly look as bad as I feel."

Kaitlyn quickly turned to Gracie. This time her look was impossible to miss. Gracie arched her eyebrows but kept her comment to herself. Instead, she took a bottle of perfume, plugged her nose, and walked toward the bathroom.

"If she's complaining now," Amber moaned, "wait until she sees what I did to that pineapple shirt she left lying on the bathroom floor."

A high-pitched scream from the bathroom let them both know that the discovery had been made. Kaitlyn burst out laughing. Even Amber couldn't help but smile a little.

* * *

Kaitlyn put on her white, one-piece swimming suit. Then she wrapped the grass skirt around her waist and slipped on a brightly colored lei she had purchased earlier in the gift shop. With that done, she stood back to inspect herself in the mirror. She had to admit she really did look like she was ready for a luau. Just then Gracie poked her head into the bathroom.

"Aren't you ready yet?"

"Almost," Kaitlyn said as she reached for the concealer in her makeup bag. She shook it vigorously and then began to apply it to the two-inch scar on her hand. Gracie watched her for several seconds before she spoke.

"Kaitlyn, Leslie knew that you loved her."

Kaitlyn flinched.

"She would want you to be happy and go on with your life."

Kaitlyn could feel her chin begin to quiver.

"I just miss her so much," she whispered.

Gracie wrapped her arms around Kaitlyn.

"I know. I miss her too."

When they pulled back, Kaitlyn wiped at the warm streaks on her cheeks with the back of her hand.

"Thanks, Gracie. I guess I needed that."

Gracie pointed to the full tube of liquid makeup.

"What you don't need is that."

Kaitlyn glanced down at the concealer in her hand. Then, slowly, she looked at the scars on her arm and hand. They had served the last few months as a constant reminder of the guilt and pain of that day. She had tried everything to erase the images from her mind, images that makeup couldn't take away. Kaitlyn stood motionless for several seconds, then slowly screwed the lid back on the tube, walked over to the waste can, and dropped it in.

# CHAPTER 6

The Caribbean Room was decorated with the exotic flair of the tropics. Enormous potted trees reached halfway to the ceiling, which was about thirty feet high. On the far side of the room was a waterfall. Water splashed over rocks jutting out from the falls, then fell into a pool below. Kaitlyn and Gracie's table was actually close enough for them to feel the cool mist as the falling water hit the pond. Lily pads in full bloom floated along the edge of the clear water while large goldfish swam beneath them. The effect was enchanting.

Kaitlyn glanced over at a woman who was mingling amongst the guests. She guessed from the nametag that she was probably the cruise director. She was in her twenties and very attractive. Her silky, ebony hair was split down the middle by a widow's peak. She had beautiful olive skin and dimples that appeared when she smiled—which was often. Kaitlyn found herself wondering if the woman knew Matthew, then immediately tried to shrug the thought off.

"Can you believe this place?" Gracie said, still taking in the whole room.

"It looks like we're already on the island. I feel terrible that Amber's missing this," Kaitlyn admitted. "Maybe tomorrow, if she's feeling better, we could come back. She'd love this."

"Uh-huh," Gracie agreed absently as she picked up her menu. "I don't know about you, but I'm starving." Then she looked down at her watch and scowled. "It's almost eight o'clock. If we eat too much we won't want to come back for the midnight buffet. It's supposed to be huge."

"We could also check into that scuba class she was interested in," Kaitlyn added quickly.

"Nice try," Gracie said, peering over her menu.

"Oh, come on, Gracie. It'll be fun."

Kaitlyn knew why Gracie did not want to take scuba lessons. A few years before, Kaitlyn and Gracie and a few close friends had gone to the lake for the day. They had played volleyball in the sand and water polo near the shore. Then, about a half hour before sunset, she and Gracie had gone for a swim. They found a man in his early twenties floating facedown in the water. Despite Gracie's panic, she helped Kaitlyn drag the man's lifeless body to shore and began CPR until help finally arrived. Since then, Gracie had refused to go in the water. Kaitlyn was grateful that the ship hadn't seemed to bother Gracie. It was probably because it felt more like a floating hotel than a ship.

"You're both welcome to go to all the scuba classes you want," Gracie said flatly. "I'll just try a little skeet shooting."

"Gracie, I know how hard it is. Trust me."

Gracie looked Kaitlyn straight in the eyes, then looked down to the scar on Kaitlyn's hand. For several seconds she just sat there silently. Kaitlyn bit her lip nervously as she watched her friend.

Gracie shook her head, then blew air out of her cheeks. "It's just an instructional class, right? No water involved?"

"Not a drop," Kaitlyn promised. She fought to suppress the smile that was itching at the corners of her mouth.

"All right," Gracie blurted out. "I'll go to the class, but I'm still not going anywhere near the water." Gracie shook her head as if accepting defeat.

"That's okay," Kaitlyn quickly reassured. "That's good enough for me."

\* \* \*

Amber turned on the shower, stuck her hand into the steady stream, and adjusted the temperature. When she had it just right, she stepped out of the bathroom to get a change of clothing and make sure that the cabin door was locked. When she returned to the bathroom, the mirror on the wall was completely steamed over. As Amber slid open the shower door, there was a noise from inside the cabin. It sounded like the low-pitched creak of a door being opened slowly. Amber whirled around to face the closed bathroom door. For several seconds she stood there motionless, waiting for the noise to come again, but there was nothing. All she could hear was the steady beating of the water on the shower floor. Once she thought that she might have heard movement in the room, but it was so faint that it could have been almost anything. Amber tried to slow her erratic breathing and remain calm. Then, in an instant surge of relief, it came to her—room service. She had ordered a bowl of chicken broth just before turning on the shower. They must have slipped the tray inside the door so that no one would bother it, she figured. Amber let the air escape from her lungs in several short gasps. She could feel a tingling sensation from the surge of adrenaline, and instantly her limbs turned to jelly. She sighed, a little embarrassed for getting so worked up.

Ten minutes later, Amber emerged from the bathroom in a white, terry-cloth robe with a fluffy towel wrapped around her head like a turban. She unwrapped the damp towel from her head and began brushing out her hair.

A knock on the door startled her. "Room service," a voice on the other side of the cabin door called out.

Amber immediately turned to face the door. She quickly tightened the robe about her and made her way across the room, but before she made it to the door, an eerie chill shot through her. The arctic blast seemed to freeze her feet solid to the floor. If room service was at her door now, then who had been in her cabin earlier? Worse yet, who might *still* be in the cabin? Amber could feel a scream emerging from deep within her lungs, but her throat was too constricted to give it life. A part of her wanted to dash out the door without once looking over her shoulder, but the other part seemed almost unable to resist the urge to look. Slowly Amber turned around to face the room. She could feel every muscle in her body tighten in anticipation of what would come next. Everything in their cabin seemed to be completely still. After just a moment she took a breath. *Of course, it's so obvious*, Amber chided herself as she shook the tension from her shoulders. *Kaitlyn and Gracie must have come back to the room to get something.* Amber shook her head for letting her imagination get the best of her twice in one night. Then she turned back to the door and collected her tray.

* * *

After dinner Kaitlyn and Gracie decided to return to the cabin to check on Amber. The movement of the ship had intensified considerably in the past half hour or so. Even Kaitlyn's stomach was starting to feel a little queasy.

When they arrived at the cabin they found Amber sitting up in her bed, reading. At first glance it was obvious that she was feeling much better. The color in her face had returned to normal and she greeted them with a smile.

"Hey, I didn't expect you two back for a couple more hours."

Kaitlyn walked over and sat at the foot of her bed.

"We just wanted to see how you're feeling."

"Much better. The motion-sickness pills kicked in a little while ago. Plus, I took a hot shower and ordered room service. Hopefully, tomorrow this storm will let up and we can do something fun. I would hate to spend all this money just to hug a toilet."

"Well, you didn't miss too much tonight. Just a bunch of plaid suits playing elevator music," Gracie lied.

Both Amber and Kaitlyn began to giggle over the mental image that Gracie's comment caused.

"Let me guess, green and mustard yellow," Amber offered.

"Exactly! Believe it or not, I've got a picture of me when I was little in those exact colors," Gracie confessed. "My mom insists that those were popular colors back then. Personally, I think that my parents knew full well what they were doing when they dressed me up like that and carted me off for pictures."

Kaitlyn tilted her head to the side and looked at Gracie with a curious grin. She was waiting to see what kind of bizarre conclusion Gracie could come up with.

"For blackmail, of course. If ever I get out of line, someone is invited over for a lovely dinner and a night of looking through family photos. Then, if that doesn't do the trick of scaring me into complete submission, there's always the family videos, not to mention the family stories. Like the time when I was five and Grandma and Grandpa Rose came to visit from Connecticut. I got up in the middle of the night and staggered down the hall to the bathroom, my eyes just barely open. A glass of water was sitting on the counter. I picked it up and drank it on my way back to bed. In the morning, Grandpa Rose asked me if I knew what had happened to the glass he puts his dentures in."

Kaitlyn and Amber were both laughing hard now.

"That is *so* gross." Kaitlyn cringed as she tried to catch her breath.

Amber set her book down on the nightstand next to her bed and rubbed her stomach.

"Well, I *was* feeling better until the two of you came back and got me laughing."

"Would you please behave yourself, Gracie?" Kaitlyn said, wagging an accusing finger.

"Me?" Gracie asked innocently. "I was merely pointing out a gross injustice that has been inflicted on me at the hands of my own parents."

"By the way, what was it that you came back for last time?" Amber asked as she absently adjusted the pillow behind her back.

Kaitlyn turned to Amber and wrinkled up her forehead.

"What are you talking about?"

"When you came back to the cabin, what did you need?"

Kaitlyn looked over at Gracie and then back to Amber in confusion.

"Amber, this is the first we've been back to the room."

"I heard a noise in the cabin when I was in the bathroom showering," Amber persisted. "I thought that it was room service, but they didn't come until after I'd gotten out of the shower."

The smile that had been on Kaitlyn's face only a second ago was gone.

"You didn't come back to the room?" Even as Amber said the words, she knew the answer by the look on their faces. "If it wasn't the two of you, then who was it?"

The three girls stiffened as an uneasiness filled the cabin. For a second no one moved. Their eyes quickly darted around, surveying the stillness of the room. Kaitlyn was the first one to get up. Apprehensively, she made her way over to the closet while Gracie and Amber reluctantly checked under the beds. Kaitlyn stopped right in front of the closet. She could feel the pulsating of her heart clear up in the nape of her neck. She took a deep breath and swung open the closet door. Other than Amber's neatly hung clothes, the little closet was empty.

Kaitlyn reached out and steadied herself with the closet door. "All clear in here," she said breathlessly.

"I found a buck fifty under my bed," Gracie announced triumphantly.

"Good, that will help pay for medications for my heart attack."

Kaitlyn shook her head and then her eyes fell on the dresser where she had left her purse. She hadn't wanted to take her purse to dinner, and since Amber was staying in the cabin, she had left it on the dresser. Her knees instantly grew weak. The dresser was empty. Her purse, with all of her money, was gone. Kaitlyn rushed over to the dresser and pulled it away from the wall to see if maybe it had fallen behind, but there was nothing there but lint and dust.

"Kaitlyn, what's wrong?" Amber questioned hesitantly as she walked over next to her friend.

"My purse! It's gone!"

"What do you mean it's gone?" Amber said, her voice rising.

"I put it right here before Gracie and I left," Kaitlyn said as she gestured toward the dresser.

"Are you sure you didn't put it in your suitcase or take it with you to dinner?" Amber persisted.

Kaitlyn shook her head. "Amber, I'm sure." Then she turned and slowly looked around the cabin. "They're not here now, but someone *was* in the room!"

Both Kaitlyn and Gracie watched as Amber's eyes seemed drawn toward the door. They watched in silence as she walked over to the door and ran her finger across the lock. Then she slowly turned around to face Kaitlyn and Gracie. "There's no sign of forced entry. Whoever it was, they have a key."

# CHAPTER 7

Kaitlyn looked absently down at the carpet as she walked down the corridor. A path in the center of the walkway was the only sign of wear. She followed the pattern of the carpet with her eyes in an attempt to occupy her thoughts. It had an intricate design in burgundy and cream with just a hint of royal blue. The effect was elaborate, yet tasteful. Kaitlyn looked up from the pattern. The combination of staring down at the carpet while walking and the constant movement of the ship was making her feel nauseated.

Kaitlyn had decided to go for a walk after giving her statement to the ship's security officer. The officer had assured her that every effort would be made to recover her purse, but she knew the likelihood of that happening was minute. Kaitlyn let out a heavy sigh as she continued walking. She had spent the last few hours wandering around the ship aimlessly. In a ship that size there was more than enough to occupy her thoughts. She could feel the sting of tears in her eyes, but she gulped hard and willed them not to fall. She needed something to keep her mind off what was really bothering her. It was more than just her purse being stolen; it was the combination of everything in the last few months—it was even more than her sister's death. Kaitlyn felt as if she'd lost herself somehow, and wasn't sure who she was or what she wanted anymore. Kaitlyn could feel a tear escape and make its way down her cheek. She pushed at it stubbornly with the back of her hand and then made her way to the double doors that led out onto the deck. As soon as she pulled the door open, a surge of wind enveloped her. Kaitlyn's eyes opened wide. The sky was alive and twisting. The clouds raced by, some of them so low that they skimmed the upper decks. Their presence was dark and threatening. Off in the distance, lightning etched its signature across the sky. Its flashes lit the darkness just enough for her to see the waves rising and falling like giants thrashing an unseen enemy below them. The whole scene caused an explosion of adrenaline through her body. Kaitlyn's eyes went to the lifeboats, which were swaying with each gust. Earlier that afternoon, on the other side of the ship, she had counted twelve lifeboats with motors. Each boat looked big enough to seat a hundred and fifty people. They were even equipped with food and water rations and GPS systems for quick recovery in the slim chance of an emergency. Or at least, that's what Kaitlyn had overheard one of the stewards telling a group of passengers. The lifeboats before her now were much smaller. Though they were metal, they looked like they could only seat around twenty-five people and they didn't have motors. The wind seemed to have no trouble moving these small crafts.

Kaitlyn could feel her stomach tighten. She quickly stepped back inside and made her way to the elevators. About halfway down the corridor, a sudden movement at the end of the hall, next to the elevators, caught her attention. Kaitlyn watched as a boy crept from around the door that led to the stairwell. An emergency-exit sign was posted in bold green letters above the door.

The boy appeared to be about ten, but it was hard to tell from that distance. Kaitlyn watched as he crouched quietly in the doorway, his head turned toward the elevator. He seemed oblivious to Kaitlyn's presence at the far end of the hall because he was so focused on the elevator. The elevator doors were shut, but the lit numbers above them indicated that it was on its way up to their floor. The boy scrambled out of his hiding place in an attempt to beat the elevator. About three-fourths of the way across the corridor he dropped something. He quickly bent to grab the object, but in his haste to pick it up, he dropped something else. Kaitlyn strained to see what it was, but she was too far away. The boy grabbed the closest object to him, but before he could reclaim the other, the bell on the elevator door rang. The boy hesitated for only a second and then darted across the corridor to what appeared to be a small utility closet. He closed the door just as the elevator opened.

Kaitlyn's curiosity was at a peak now, which put all her other problems momentarily on hold. She quickened her step down the hall toward the object the boy had dropped. A man and woman exited the elevator and walked right past the small item, so deep in conversation that they didn't even notice it. As soon as they passed, Kaitlyn looked down at the floor and frowned when she recognized the object as a small dinner roll. She looked over at the utility closet just as it began to creak and slowly open. A black head of thick hair was followed by two dark, round eyes. The second the boy saw Kaitlyn, just a few feet from him, he slammed the door shut, nearly pinching his nose in the process. Kaitlyn glanced back down at the roll that she held in her hand. She didn't know why the boy was hiding, but if he was hoarding food, he was probably hungry.

After a short tap, Kaitlyn slowly opened the door. It was dark inside, so she stood motionless in the door frame until her eyes adjusted. Once she could see, she recognized that the tiny room was definitely a utility closet. There was a mop bucket not two feet in front of her with a damp mop still in the bucket. Several brooms were propped in the corner next to a large commercial vacuum, and the whole room smelled of cleaning supplies. Kaitlyn let her hand explore the wall next to the door, searching for the light switch. When she flipped it on, she saw the boy crouched in the corner. She could see his shoulders rising with each breath.

"I saw you drop this in the hall," she said as she held up the roll and stepped toward him.

As the boy scrambled to move deeper into the closet, he bumped into a shelf holding stacks of toilet paper.

"Watch out!" Kaitlyn called out.

But it was too late. Twenty or thirty rolls of toilet paper came tumbling down on the young boy. Before Kaitlyn could even rush over to help, she saw his head pop up in the center of the pile.

"Are you okay?"

The boy tossed the tissue aside and stood. Kaitlyn eyed him closely. Now that she was closer, she guessed him to be more like eleven or twelve. From a distance his slim build had made her think him younger than he really was. His hair appeared as though it had not seen a comb in quite a while. His clothing was also soiled and ragged, but his eyes were what captured Kaitlyn's attention. They were big as saucers, with long, dark lashes—the kind of lashes girls would love to have, but that boys who couldn't care less usually ended up with.

"What's your name?" Kaitlyn asked, trying to keep her voice as soothing as possible.

The boy did not respond, but his eyes never left her. He seemed to be focusing on her hand. Kaitlyn looked down at the dinner roll she had forgotten was still in her hand. The boy eyed it hungrily but still did not move. Kaitlyn knew he wanted it, but she also knew that as long as she was in the room he wasn't going to take it. She slowly bent down and set the roll on a stack of towels and then turned to leave.

"You gonna turn me in?"

Kaitlyn turned back around to face the boy. She could see the pleading in his dark eyes. She hesitated for several seconds.

"No. I won't turn you in."

* * *

"What do you mean you're not going to turn him in?" Amber blurted out incredulously. "Kaitlyn, he's a stowaway."

"I know it doesn't make any sense. I just saw the fear in his eyes, and the words jumped out of my mouth."

"No, no, no. *You're* the levelheaded one," Gracie jumped in. "Words just jump out of *my* mouth. You make well-planned, mature decisions."

Kaitlyn turned to look at Gracie. "Oh, is that how it works?" she mocked, suddenly amused that this change in her character had Gracie flustered.

"Kaitlyn, with him being so young, I'm sure that nothing major is going to happen to him. The cruise line will probably just ship him back home when we get to the next port and have his parents pay for the ticket," Amber offered. "There is no sense in us getting into trouble."

"No, it was more than that," Kaitlyn persisted. "This kid was really scared."

"Of what?" Gracie exclaimed.

"I don't know," Kaitlyn admitted. "But I say we find out."

*"We?"* Amber began, still not sure that she wanted any part of this.

"But first we need to start by getting him something to eat," Kaitlyn suggested, totally ignoring Amber's hesitation.

"The midnight buffet starts in ten minutes," Gracie added eagerly as both she and Kaitlyn started for the door.

"All right, all right," Amber surrendered. "I'll come. But I'm warning you, I still think this is crazy."

Gracie turned to Amber with a broad smile. "I know. That's just what I like about it."

\* \* \*

Matthew could hear the music, laughter, and occasional clanging of dinnerware as he approached the Caribbean Room. He stood in the elaborate, arched entryway for a moment to scan the room; it really was incredible. On his downtime, he would find himself either in this room or on the top deck overlooking the ocean. However, tonight was not his downtime. He had been sent to deliver an urgent message to the captain.

It only took a moment to spot the captain. He was seated prominently in the center of the room. More than a dozen of the ship's most distinguished guests were seated around him, including the vice president of the cruise line, Mr. Warren Farthing, and his wife. Because of their special passengers, Captain Bridges had made it quite clear to the crew that this was to be a problem-free voyage.

Even though Matthew had not worked on the ship for very long, he had worked long enough to recognize that the captain was probably midway through one of the stories that he was famous for. His guests seemed to be hanging on his every word and laughing in all the appropriate spots. Matthew had learned early on that this was not a time to interrupt the captain. He would usually hold back just long enough for the captain's story to end and for the laughter from the guests to subside. Tonight was different though; his instructions had been explicit. Matthew looked down at the sealed envelope that he held in his hand. He was to deliver the message to the captain without delay. Matthew quickened his stride as he made his way down the steps and across the floor to the captain's table. He paused only long enough to clear his throat and make his presence known.

"Excuse me, sir," Matthew interrupted.

The guests, who were all engrossed in the captain's story—or who at least appeared to be—now looked directly at Matthew.

The captain stopped midsentence and turned to see the cause of the disruption. His expression clearly read, *This had better be important.*

Matthew could feel his face begin to flush with the attention as he extended the envelope toward the captain. Captain Bridges, who had always loved being the center of things, seemed totally oblivious to Matthew's discomfort. The captain took the envelope and opened it, read the message quickly, then turned to his guests.

"I'm afraid that I'll have to continue my story another time."

An audible sigh could be heard from several of his dinner companions, but if the captain was pleased by their reaction he gave no sign. He excused himself from the table and then headed toward the entryway. A quick motion of his hand directed Matthew to follow him. Once the two of them were out into the corridor, the captain turned to face Matthew.

"Whatever your previous responsibilities were for this evening, they've been canceled. For now, you are to stay here and make sure that my guests are as comfortable as possible." There was no mistaking which guests Captain Bridges meant. "If your duties change, you'll be notified. Is that clear?"

"Yes, sir," Matthew said.

\* \* \*

Captain Bridges scowled as he looked down at the weather fax in his hand. The "severe storm and strong winds" bulletin that they had received a couple of hours ago was now being replaced by one informing them of the undeniable formation of a full-blown tropical storm.

"I had a bad feeling about this one," the captain sighed. "All the weather reports before we left said that the storm would fizzle out and not amount to much, but apparently it's done just the opposite.

Another tropical storm over the equator, one that has intensified over the last few hours, is feeding it. Unless it changes course, by the time it gets to us, this storm is going to be a monster."

Captain Bridges traced the distance between the center of the storm and their position with a pencil. Then he sat back and rubbed his jaw thoughtfully as he so often did when he was thinking. The first mate stood by, watching him closely.

"Looks like we're in for a long night," he finally offered.

The first mate looked at him blankly, apparently not sure of their course of action.

"Sir?"

The captain looked back down at the fax without saying a word. He just sat there staring at the paper, as if it could speak to him. After what seemed like an eternity, he finally raised his head to meet the first mate's gaze.

"Lieutenant, in all the years you've known me, how many times have you seen me back down from a fight?"

The first mate gaped at the captain in disbelief. Surely he did not intend to go right through a storm system that was this unpredictable? After all, this was a pleasure cruise liner, not a warship. Lieutenant Lewis knew, better than most, that Captain Bridges was a little overly confident, but not until now had the lieutenant doubted his integrity as a captain.

"But I am backing down from this one," the captain admitted. "This could just be another storm like the hundreds we've been through before, but if it's not . . ."

"Captain Bridges, should I notify the Coast Guard that we'll be returning to port?"

"No, not yet. I have a few more options to think about before we make the call."

"Sir?"

"Either way you look at it, we're in for a rough ride. This storm is in front of us, but there are smaller storms forming all around. My biggest fear is that storms are going to combine."

Both men looked at each other as a chill seeped into their bones.

"I'm just not sure it would be wise to attempt turning this ship completely around and risk getting caught sideways." The captain paused as he considered the implications of his decision. He loved the ocean, but at the same time, he had seen it turn deadly.

"Give me five minutes on this, Lieutenant," the captain said, thumping the fax with his finger. "I'll work it out on the charts before we go to the crew. I don't want this leaking to the guests. The last thing we need is a panic."

# CHAPTER 8

The lieutenant watched the captain as he stared out the window at the vivid lightning display before him. The intensity of the waves were increasing by the minute. The captain winced as another clap of thunder shook the cabin. The strikes were getting dangerously close. Captain Bridges threw his itinerary down on the desk in front of the lieutenant.

"It looks like the safest thing to do is to veer off and go the long way around. We'll have some stormy seas, but we'll miss the brunt of the storm."

"If it makes any difference, Captain, I think you're making the right decision."

The captain nodded, though his eyes seemed fixed on the tossing of the sea outside the window.

"Would you like me to call in the change of course, sir?" the lieutenant offered.

"It's already been done. The sooner we get some distance between us and this storm, the better. Why don't you take the helm for the next few minutes and I'll inform Mr. Farthing myself. He's meeting me in the boiler room in five minutes for a tour."

The lieutenant looked down at his watch. "*A tour?* At this hour? Sir, it's almost one o'clock in the morning."

The captain shook his head. "Mr. Farthing isn't much of a dancer."

The lieutenant lowered his brow in confusion. "Excuse me, sir?"

"Apparently, *Mrs.* Farthing is," the captain said with a smile. "Warren said that business would be the only excuse that his wife would accept. With her being twenty years younger than him and capable of dancing until dawn, he's opted to take a tour of the boiler room."

The lieutenant shook his head and smiled.

"As soon as I advise Mr. Farthing of our situation, I'll be back. I won't be longer than fifteen minutes."

The lieutenant took his place at the helm and then watched as the captain disappeared through the door. As soon as he was gone, his attention went back to the window before him. An enormous bolt of lightning threaded its way across the sky, while the thunder that followed it was so close that it rattled the bridge. The lieutenant took a deep breath. He would feel a lot better when they had put some distance between themselves and this storm.

The lieutenant stayed at the helm for the next ten minutes, anxiously awaiting the captain's return. Although he was fully capable of handling the ship, he preferred the role of second in command. With all the notoriety and attention that came with captaining a ship—all the things that Captain Bridges seemed to thrive on—also came the weight and responsibility of every life aboard. When the lieutenant was younger he had competed several times for just such a position, but now he was quite content with his rank and station.

He turned as a young woman in the cruise line's uniform entered the bridge. He recognized her instantly. She was young, no more than twenty-one, with a personality that seemed always to be bubbling over, very much like his own daughter. She was holding a tray with a pitcher of water, two empty glasses, and a couple of deli sandwiches.

"I thought you and the captain could use something to eat," she offered with a quick smile.

"Actually, that sounds great," he admitted, only now aware of his empty stomach. "Thank you."

"Can I get you anything else?"

"You wouldn't happen to have a big piece of chocolate cake stashed away somewhere?"

The young woman smiled. "No, but when I go back to the kitchen, I'll bet I could round you up a piece."

As she started toward the lieutenant with the tray of food, a loud noise from somewhere deep within the ship echoed down the corridor, followed instantly by a vibration than seemed to penetrate the entire ship. The woman stopped dead in her tracks. Her hands instantly began to tremble so that she almost spilled the tray.

"Was that thunder?" she asked anxiously.

"I don't know," the lieutenant said uneasily as the lights in the room began to flicker.

Lieutenant Lewis could feel his breathing quicken. He had heard that sound many times before in the rice paddies of Vietnam, and it wasn't thunder. The lieutenant turned toward the control panel where there was a phone attached to the wall. Before he could reach for it, the noise and vibration came again, only this time the force was strong enough that the lieutenant lost his balance. He found himself sprawled out on the floor. At the same time, the woman let out a shrill scream and dropped her tray. For a minute the lieutenant just sat there as if he were bolted to the floor. His mind was scrambling to grasp what had just happened. In stunned silence, he listened as the corridor echoed the groans of a wounded ship and watched as the lights in the bridge flickered and then went out. Though the lights were off, the bridge continued to be illuminated by the increasingly frequent flashes of lightning. The lightning and thunder seemed to be coming simultaneously. After a couple of seconds, the lights came back on. The lieutenant slowly looked around the bridge. The woman had a death grip on the control panel, and her eyes were round as moons. Several controls along the wall were flashing and sounding with alarms.

"What's going on?" she screamed.

The lieutenant immediately grabbed hold of a table to pull himself to a kneeling position. As he did, he could feel a stray piece of glass from the dropped pitcher embedding into his flesh. By the time he was able to pull himself to a standing position, a warm trickle of blood was making its way down his leg. The lieutenant ran to the control panel, only vaguely aware of the pain in his knee. Before he could even check the readings, a member of the crew raced into the room, his face drained of all color.

"Lieutenant, there's been an explosion in the boiler room."

"The boiler room?" the lieutenant asked, staring at the man blankly.

"Yes, sir."

"Are you *sure* it was the boiler room?"

The young man nodded his head in the affirmative. "Yes, sir. That's the report we've received from the engine room."

The lieutenant grabbed hold of the counter to steady himself.

"I need to notify the captain, sir," the young man insisted.

"He was in the boiler room," the lieutenant said, his voice barely a whisper.

"What did you say?" the woman broke in.

The lieutenant's eyes flashed between the two of them. "The captain was giving a tour to Mr. Farthing in the boiler room."

Both the woman and the young man stared at him in horror.

"Are you sure?" the woman finally asked, her voice revealing more of the girl in her than the woman she was.

"I don't know," the lieutenant barked in frustration. "Go find out."

As the two of them scrambled out of the room, the lieutenant glanced back out the window at the building storm. He could feel every muscle in his body go taut. "Please let him have been on his way back to the bridge," he prayed breathlessly.

* * *

Kaitlyn, Amber, and Gracie were making their way down the corridor with a plate of food for the stowaway when the noise came. Gracie was so startled that she bumped into Kaitlyn. In turn, Kaitlyn jumped straight into the air, sending the glass of milk that she held flying. Amber, who was next to Kaitlyn, let out a scream that seemed to rival the thunder.

"Did lightning hit the ship?" Gracie gasped as she grabbed Kaitlyn's arm.

Kaitlyn looked around at the other passengers that were scattered across the hall. They were having much the same reaction as the three of them. Everyone watched anxiously as the lights in the hall flickered and dimmed. A little girl not far from them buried her head in her dad's chest and started whimpering. He was trying to reassure her, but at the same time he had his own head low on his shoulders in anticipation of another strike.

"No, I think it was just a near miss," Kaitlyn offered weakly, not convinced herself.

"I don't know, Kaitlyn," Amber cried. "That sounded awful close to me."

Kaitlyn turned to look at Amber. When she did, she had to do a double take. Amber's hair was plastered to her head, and droplets of milk were falling from her bangs. Kaitlyn was not quite sure what the lightning had struck, if anything, but apparently the glass of milk that she had thrown was a direct hit.

As Kaitlyn handed Amber one of the napkins intended for the boy, there was another loud rumble deep within the ship, followed by a sharp jolt. Kaitlyn stumbled toward the wall. Just before she hit, the lights went out completely. Kaitlyn's body took a sharp blow, but she was able to keep on her feet. Several screams rang out across the hall as another clap of thunder echoed down the corridor. Fear fell over them, silencing the passengers. As Kaitlyn stood there, leaning against the wall, she could hear her own sporadic breathing amplified in the darkness.

"Is everyone all right?" Kaitlyn finally managed to call out amid the thundering of her own heart.

Before anyone could answer, the low hum of the backup generator kicking on interrupted the silence. To her relief, it brought the lights back to full force. Kaitlyn, along with almost everyone else in the corridor, blew the air out of her cheeks in a long sigh. Then Kaitlyn's focus went to Gracie who was sprawled out on the floor. The contents of the boy's dinner were strewn around her.

"Are you okay?"

"I'm fine," Gracie said as she picked up the sandwich next to her, blew on it, and then placed it back on the plate.

Amber wrinkled her nose and then reached out her hand to Gracie.

"Thirty-second rule," Gracie said adamantly. "Sesame seed, fuzzy hall lint, it's all the same."

"Definitely a head injury on this one," Kaitlyn said as she helped pull Gracie to her feet.

"So, do you think *that* was just a near miss?" Gracie asked sarcastically.

Kaitlyn glanced down the corridor at the other passengers and then back to her friends.

"I don't know. All I know for sure is that there's a scared little boy huddled in a closet who needs our help."

Gracie nodded. "Come on. Let's get out of here."

# CHAPTER 9

Thick, black smoke was now pouring out of the boiler room. The heat around the door was so intense that the men fighting the blaze had to back up. Matthew wiped at the sweat that ran freely down his forehead and into his eyes. He was having a hard time seeing through the sweat and the smoke, but he continued to spray the fire extinguisher in the direction of the fire.

Matthew had been in the Caribbean Room when the lightning struck, but he'd immediately run to the navigation room to see what had happened. It was then he was informed that there had been an explosion and the boiler room was on fire. While he was there, confirmation came that the captain as well as several others had been killed in the blast. The command of the ship was now in the hands of Lieutenant Roger Lewis. The lieutenant immediately sent Matthew down to help battle the blaze.

Matthew tried to edge closer to the door, but the heat from the searing flames forced him back. The flames were now shooting out from the doorway and scorching everything in reach. He could feel the heat singeing his uniform. If he went any closer he would be putting his own life in jeopardy. Matthew fell back a step, and as he did another explosion shook the ship and sent him flying face first into a wall. He stumbled to his feet, a little dazed and with the taste of blood in his mouth. The heat was so intense that he could feel the rubber on the soles of his shoes beginning to melt. Matthew scrambled down the hall, bumping into the walls and other crew members as he went. When he reached a safe distance down the hall, he flung off his shoes so that his feet would not get burned.

Once his shoes were off, his attention went directly back to the fire. The flames were now climbing the walls and ceiling unrestrained.

"Are you okay?"

Matthew turned to the crew member next to him. From the color of his uniform, Matthew knew that he worked the lower decks. His face was black from smoke, and his shirt stretched over shoulders almost as broad as Matthew was tall.

"I'm fine," Matthew lied as he wiped the blood from his lip. "What caused the explosion?"

The man turned back to the crew members who were still fighting the fire. "Everyone get back. You're too close," he called. Then he looked back down at Matthew, who was still sitting on the floor. "I don't know. The only people who might have known are in no condition to tell us." He gestured to the still, dark shapes on the boiler room floor.

Matthew looked briefly at the bodies and then glanced up at the fire sprinklers placed sporadically across the ceiling. They were completely dry. He knew that a crew of about nine hundred Coast Guard thoroughly inspected all safety equipment before a cruise ship was allowed to leave port.

"Why aren't the sprinklers working?"

The man shook his head. "I don't know for sure, but I'd guess the force of the blast and the fire must have eliminated the water pressure."

"How are we going to stop the fire without water?" Matthew blurted out.

The man looked at Matthew. His chiseled features looked as solid as the large metal machinery that he worked on daily.

"We're not. If we're lucky we can slow it down long enough to save a few people."

Matthew felt sick. He looked back at the scarred boiler room, diverting his eyes from the figures that lay motionless on the floor. He swallowed hard and then looked back at the flames. They seemed to be increasing by the minute. Without sufficient water, the whole room would be a fiery inferno in a matter of minutes.

"We've got to tell the lieutenant," Matthew insisted, somewhat frantically.

"Our communication is down. You're gonna have to go to him yourself," the man answered decisively.

Matthew quickly tied his shoelaces together, slung the still-smoldering shoes over his shoulder, and got to his feet. Just before he made it to the stairs, he shot a glance back over his shoulder. Thick, black, toxic smoke billowed out of the boiler room, while the flames within devoured everything that they came in contact with. The man that Matthew had just been talking to, along with several other crew members, stood with their fire extinguishers, boldly fighting the blaze. Several of them coughed violently as the smoke filled their lungs and painted their features as black as soot. Matthew could tell by the look on their faces that they knew what the end result would be, just as readily as he did, but they seemed resolved to keep on fighting.

* * *

"We're not going to be able to contain this, sir."

The lieutenant didn't say anything. He just looked at Matthew blankly as if his mind were a thousand miles away.

"Sir, in a matter of minutes the entire bottom deck is going to be in flames," Matthew urged.

"Under any other circumstances, an evacuation would have already been started, but . . ." the lieutenant hesitated.

"But what?" Matthew asked, not sure that he really wanted to hear the answer.

Lieutenant Lewis looked Matthew straight in the eye. "We've got a tropical storm coming straight for us."

Matthew felt like he had just been slugged in the gut. He reached out for the wall to steady himself.

"But," the lieutenant continued, "I don't see any other choice. We're going to have to prepare to evacuate."

Matthew's eyes seemed immediately drawn to the scene outside the window. In that second he felt fear rush through him like he had never felt it before.

"I've notified the Coast Guard of our position," the lieutenant offered. "But if we wait for them it will be too late."

Matthew had been on the bottom decks. He had seen the fire firsthand. Deep down he knew the lieutenant was right, but somehow he just couldn't accept it.

"There's got to be another way," he blurted out.

The lieutenant narrowed his brow in warning at Matthew's insubordination.

"We could fight the blaze until the Coast Guard made it to us," Matthew rushed on.

Lewis turned on Matthew, frustration, fear, and anger evident in his face.

"There *is* no other way." The words were shot out with such fury that Matthew fell back a step. "If you want to stay on a burning ship, then stay, but it's my responsibility to save as many of these passengers as I possibly can. I don't like the alternative any more than you do, but right now it's the only one we've got."

Matthew studied the lieutenant's face. He had liked and respected Lieutenant Lewis from the start. He had the skill and knowledge of the captain, but he also had a genuineness about him that reminded Matthew of his own father.

"What do you want me to do, sir?"

Lewis put his hand firmly on Matthew's shoulder. "Let's get to work."

\* \* \*

"It's that one there," Kaitlyn said, pointing to a door just a few feet away.

Kaitlyn glanced around the hall to ensure that no one was watching, then she turned the knob and the three of them started in. This time the light in the utility closet was on. Once Kaitlyn was all the way inside the closet, she stopped and fell back a step. A man stood on the far side of the closet next to the boy. His hand was firmly wrapped around the young boy's arm. From the look on the man's face, he was just as startled to see them as they were to see him. Kaitlyn's eyes fell on the nametag and uniform that he was wearing. It was not the white uniform that Matthew wore, but a royal blue maintenance uniform. He must have discovered the boy hiding in the closet and was now about to turn him in.

"Can I help you?" the man asked, his voice still showing the effects of being startled.

"No," Gracie jumped in. "We must have made a wrong turn somewhere, that's all."

"That's easy to do in a ship this size," the man agreed.

Kaitlyn looked down at the boy standing motionless next to the maintenance worker. His eyes seemed to be pleading with her not to go.

"Your ship recruits are getting kinda young, don't you think?" Kaitlyn said with a smile.

The man shook his head and then looked at the boy next to him.

"I don't think work is what this one had in mind. I found him hiding here. Seems he planned to catch a free ride to the Caribbean."

Just then a siren began blaring in the hallway, catching them all off guard.

"What is that?" Gracie cried, cupping her hands over her ears.

All of them turned instinctively to the maintenance worker. He let go of the boy and then rushed out into the hall with the rest of them close on his heels. Several other passengers had gathered to look up at the flashing light on the wall.

"What's happening?" Kaitlyn yelled over the deafening screech of the high-pitched alarm.

"It looks like we're evacuating," the maintenance man hollered back.

"Are we sinking?" Gracie shrieked, her voice high and panicked.

Kaitlyn could feel the fear begin to well up inside her, but she forced herself to remain calm.

"Gracie, we're not sinking! It's probably just a precaution because of the storm."

They all watched in horror as two passengers rushed out of their cabins wearing their life jackets. Kaitlyn whirled back to the maintenance worker.

"What are we supposed to do?"

"Go back to your cabin and get your life jackets." Then the man turned and eyed the boy next to him. "Boy, it looks like this was the wrong ship to stow away on. Stay out of trouble and we'll forget this ever happened." The maintenance worker narrowed his eyes in warning. "Do you understand?"

The boy nodded. "I understand."

The four of them watched as the maintenance worker raced down the corridor toward the stairs. Kaitlyn reached over and grabbed the boy's hand, then turned to Gracie and Amber.

"We need to get out of here."

Five minutes later, Gracie and Amber grabbed the life jackets they had hung in their closet. Gracie immediately put hers on and fastened it tight. Amber put on her own jacket and then hurried over to hand Kaitlyn hers. Kaitlyn was at the door snapping on her backpack. Amber held Kaitlyn's jacket out to her, but Kaitlyn only gestured toward the boy.

"He doesn't have one, and I'm a lifeguard," Kaitlyn insisted.

"Oh yes, I forgot. You're the lifeguard at a community pool where the largest wave comes from the occasional cannonball plunge. Have you seen the waves out there?"

"Just give him the jacket," Kaitlyn said flatly.

Kaitlyn looked at the boy she was about to give her life jacket to. He had barbecue sauce from the sandwich they had brought him smeared all over his face. Eating while running down the hall or not eating at all had been his only options.

"By the way, what's your name?" Kaitlyn asked the boy.

"Pete, but you can keep your life jacket. I can handle myself."

Kaitlyn took the life jacket from Amber and handed it to Pete. "We don't have time to argue. Just put it on."

They all turned as a loud voice, followed by several sharp knocks, rang out from the other side of the cabin door. "Open up! Open up!"

Kaitlyn quickly yanked the door open to see a man in uniform standing in front of them.

"We're preparing to evacuate the ship, ma'am. Everyone is to meet at the lifeboats."

Kaitlyn could feel her knees grow weak.

"Why? What's going on?" Kaitlyn asked anxiously.

"Did lightning strike the ship?" Amber broke in. "Or was that some kind of explosion?"

"Once you get to the lifeboats, everything will be explained."

Kaitlyn watched as he rushed to the next cabin and began pounding on the door. The corridor was filled with people scrambling in different directions. Some of them appeared to remain levelheaded, while others were clearly terrified. Kaitlyn could feel herself going on autopilot as she turned back to face her friends. Amber seemed to be in control, for the moment at least. Gracie, on the other hand, was way past the point of any rational thinking.

"We're all going to die!" Gracie mumbled to herself as she began pacing back and forth in the room.

Kaitlyn walked over and put her arm around Gracie. She could feel her whole body trembling.

"It's going to be all right, Gracie. I promise."

Gracie looked up to face Kaitlyn. "I can't get on one of those little boats! I just can't." Her eyes were glassy, as if her body was there but the rest of her was back at the lake watching the rescue workers trying to save the man who had drowned. A part of Kaitlyn completely understood Gracie's fear. Even Kaitlyn had been haunted by the man's lifeless face for months after it happened. Kaitlyn reached out and grabbed Gracie's hand.

"I'm not leaving," Gracie screamed, yanking her hand away.

"What are you talking about?" Amber jumped in. "You just heard what he said, we're evacuating."

"I don't care what he said," Gracie said defiantly. "I'm not going."

"Gracie," Kaitlyn said, her voice beginning to show the strain of the situation. "You're coming with us."

"No!" Gracie screamed, her face twisted in fear. "I can't. I just can't."

Kaitlyn wiped at the tears that were streaming down Gracie's cheek. For several seconds neither girl spoke, then slowly Kaitlyn turned back toward Amber.

"You and Pete go to the lifeboats."

*"What?"* Amber exclaimed, clearly shocked. "Kaitlyn, we're evacuating!"

"I know," Kaitlyn began as she walked toward Amber.

Amber opened her mouth, but Kaitlyn rushed on. "Just give me some time to calm her down."

"This is crazy," Amber said, flinging her hands above her head in frustration.

"What do you want me to do, carry her?"

Amber looked over Kaitlyn's shoulder at Gracie. Gracie's eyes were glued on the storm raging outside the porthole.

Amber closed her eyes and shook her head. "I can't believe this is happening."

Kaitlyn reached out and hugged her friend. "We'll catch up, you'll see."

Amber shook her head with tears in her eyes. "You better."

\* \* \*

Kaitlyn handed Gracie a glass of water and then sat her down on the edge of the bed.

"I'm going out in the hall to see if I can find out anything."

Gracie reached out and grabbed Kaitlyn's arm. "Please don't leave me."

"I'm just going out in the hall. I won't leave you. I promise."

Gracie still clung to Kaitlyn's arm, a haunting look of desperation etched on her face.

"You're going to have to trust me," Kaitlyn continued. "We can't just sit here in this room."

Gracie nodded her head and then reluctantly let go of Kaitlyn.

"I'll be right back," Kaitlyn promised as she turned to leave.

Once Kaitlyn was out in the hall she looked around, searching the crowd for the man who had knocked on their door to warn them, but she couldn't see him anywhere. She started down the hall in the direction of the elevators. A large man with a bright orange life jacket cinched tightly around his waist came running down the hall at full speed. Kaitlyn tried to get out of the way, but he was coming too fast. Kaitlyn lunged forward, but he plowed right into her. She stumbled toward the wall, but somehow managed to stop herself just before she hit. When she had her balance again, she looked over her shoulder at the man that had knocked into her, but he had blended into the mass of passengers that were now stampeding toward the lifeboats. Kaitlyn rubbed at her now-tender shoulder, sure that she would be bruised by such a hit.

Before Kaitlyn could start toward the elevator again, a woman carrying several bulging suitcases smashed right into her. This time they both went flying. Though a little dazed, Kaitlyn pushed one of the heavy suitcases off of her and sat up. The woman who had knocked into her frantically began collecting her possessions. She seemed completely oblivious to Kaitlyn's presence on the floor in front of her. Kaitlyn glanced around the corridor at the other passengers. She could tell by the expressions on their faces that they were all starting to panic. With the siren on the wall still blasting its warning, Kaitlyn struggled to her feet. Things were getting dangerous. Kaitlyn turned back in the direction that she had come. She needed to get Gracie and get out of there fast.

# CHAPTER 10

The lightning had subsided considerably, but the rain was now coming down in sheets. Matthew held a small boy in his arms as the child's mother climbed aboard the lifeboat. The child, who had been snatched from his warm bed in the middle of the night to come out in the pouring rain, was terrified. When the little boy saw that the crying and squirming was not working, he began screaming and kicking. Once the mother was safely seated in the boat, Matthew eagerly handed the child over to her, then he turned to help the next person. As he turned, he noticed a frail, elderly woman across the deck. She was futilely trying to make her way through the crowd. Matthew shielded his eyes from the rain to see better. He watched as she was bumped and tossed in the crowd. He knew that if someone didn't help her soon, she would likely be trampled. Matthew grabbed the man next in line.

"Would you help the others board while I go help that lady?" Matthew gestured in the direction of the tiny woman. The man nodded his head and then began helping the others board.

"I'll be back to lower the boat," Matthew assured him.

Matthew's orders had been to fill the lifeboats, but to wait until the last possible minute to lower them; the last seemingly fruitless efforts were being made to put out the fire. Lieutenant Lewis had stressed the fact that only he would give the orders to lower the boats.

As he thought on their predicament, Matthew made his way across the deck in four quick strides. Then, without a word, he reached out and picked the frail woman up in his arms. She jerked her head around, startled to have someone picking her up. The minute she saw Matthew in his uniform, her whole body relaxed.

"Thank you," she whispered, too exhausted to say more.

Matthew looked down at the tiny woman. Her clothing was soaked through and her body was trembling.

"Where were you trying to go?" Matthew asked.

She gestured toward a large group of people waiting to get onto one of the lifeboats.

"I was separated from my sister, Bethann, in the crowd."

Matthew looked in the direction that she was pointing. Another small elderly woman stood across the deck waving frantically at them. Matthew made his way through the crowd to the sister. Bethann covered her mouth with her hands as she tried to control her tears.

"I was so worried," she began, her voice giving away the depth of her fear.

"Follow me," Matthew said to Bethann as he carried her sister to the front of the line.

Once they reached the front, Matthew gently set the older woman down.

"God bless you," she said sweetly as she reached out and squeezed his hand.

Matthew paused to squeeze her hand in return, genuinely touched by her gratitude.

A young woman at the front of the line reached out and steadied the older woman. Then she turned to Matthew. "Don't worry, I'll help them," she said.

Matthew nodded his head appreciatively, then stood back to let them board. Once they had boarded, Matthew turned back toward the ship. His eyes quickly assessed the scene before him. People were running around frantically. The air seemed filled with the frenzied screams of people calling out to loved ones that had been lost in the crowd. Some of the passengers were reaching out and helping those around them, while others were scrambling over the top of people to save themselves. Matthew's eyes seemed drawn to the frightened passengers suspended over the edge of the ship in lifeboats. An eerie hush had settled over them as they sat helplessly waiting to see what would happen next.

\* \* \*

Amber and Pete joined the throng of people pushing and shoving their way toward the lifeboats. Crew members were scattered across the deck, trying to subdue the crowd. Amber held tight to Pete's hand as they made their way across the deck.

A flash of lightning cut through the night sky. Amber lowered her head in anticipation of the sharp clap of thunder that quickly followed. The rain was coming down so hard that it was difficult to see. Amber stood up on tiptoe, but all she could see were large groups of people crowding around each lifeboat. Some of the boats were already loaded and just sitting at the edge of the ship, hovering over the water.

"Let's go to the far end of the deck. Maybe there'll be less people down there," Amber suggested as she continued maneuvering her way through the crowd.

As the two of them made their way down the deck, Amber's eyes fell on a man who seemed to be fighting against the current of the crowd. Something about him seemed familiar, but he was still too far away for her to see him clearly. As the man neared, Amber's heart began to race. It was Matthew, the ship's steward they had met when they'd first arrived. Amber lunged in Matthew's direction, dragging Pete along with her.

"Matthew! Matthew!" she yelled as she raised her free hand above the crowd and waved frantically.

Matthew, who was now a few hundred feet away, turned his head toward them. His eyes first fell on Amber, but then quickly went to the boy. Amber could tell by the look on his face that he wasn't registering who she was.

"I'm Kaitlyn's friend," she hollered over the noise of the crowd.

As soon as she mentioned Kaitlyn, Matthew nodded his head in recognition and motioned for her to get out of the stream of passengers. Fighting against the flow of people was becoming increasingly difficult. Amber and Pete slipped out of the grip of the crowd and made their way over to the railing. Amber grabbed hold of the railing and held on tight. She stared out across the ocean, her eyes growing round with fear. Gigantic waves slapped against the sides of the ship, sending enormous sprays of water over the railings onto the already-soaked deck. Amber swung around as a hand came down on her shoulder.

"I'm sorry," Matthew began. "I was trying to get over to you, but it's almost impossible to move with all those people." Matthew's eyes suddenly grew concerned and he began frantically scanning the deck. "Where are Kaitlyn and Gracie?"

Amber's throat caught. "Gracie was afraid to get on the lifeboats, so Kaitlyn decided to stay with her until she calmed down."

Even as Amber said the words, they sounded completely ludicrous. They never should have split up.

"She *what?*" Matthew shouted, his resolve to remain calm temporarily forgotten.

"I know. I told her it was a bad idea, but she was afraid that Gracie would panic."

Matthew blew the air out of his cheeks as he tried to think the situation through.

"Where did you leave her?"

"They were still in the room when we left—318."

Matthew reached over and grabbed Amber's arm. "I'm going to go get them. I want you to get on that lifeboat." He turned and pointed to a lifeboat not far from them. It looked capable of holding over a hundred people. "Do you understand me? Go right now and stay there," Matthew commanded.

Amber bobbed her head as she fought to control the terror inside her.

"I mean it—get on the boat," Matthew shouted over his shoulder, his voice rising in intensity.

Amber watched as Matthew slipped into the crowd and was gone.

# CHAPTER 11

The hallway that had only minutes ago been filled with passengers was now completely empty. Kaitlyn paused in the doorway as an overwhelming panic seized her. The stillness of the scene sent a shiver up her spine. She could feel the ship swaying beneath her as the storm continued its assault, but it was what she didn't hear that bothered her the most. A couple of hours before, the whole ship had been alive with activity as excited tourists explored their temporary home. Now only a groaning from somewhere within the ship permeated the hall.

Kaitlyn could feel her stomach tighten. She never should have insisted that Amber go on without them. Not only did they have to face all of this, but now they were separated. Kaitlyn turned to look at the figure that stood silently next to her. After Kaitlyn had made it back to the cabin, it had taken a good five minutes to talk Gracie into leaving. Finally Kaitlyn had resorted to threatening to leave her and go to the lifeboats alone. Gracie was afraid of going, but she was even more afraid of being left. Kaitlyn felt a little guilty, but after seeing the empty hall, she was glad that she had used such drastic measures. Kaitlyn watched as a straggler, a man in his late thirties, bolted out of his cabin and raced down the hall toward the stairs.

"Come on, Gracie, we need to hurry."

Kaitlyn and Gracie started toward the stairs at a fast walk. By the time they were halfway down the corridor, they were closer to a run. As they neared the stairs Kaitlyn came to a dead stop. A light haze was coming from under the door to the stairs. Kaitlyn started forward to get a better look, but as she did, the door to the stairwell flew open. She fell back a step or two, startled by the man that now stood before her. It was the straggler who had raced down the hall just seconds before them. Kaitlyn watched helplessly as the man struggled for air. She reached out to help him, but as she did, a smell hit her that stopped her cold. The odor was strong and undeniable. Kaitlyn reached out and grabbed the man's arm, her fingernails digging deep into his flesh.

"Fire!" she whispered, her throat too tight to scream.

The man looked up to face her; his expression was all the confirmation she needed. Kaitlyn could feel her whole body begin to shake.

"I couldn't get through," he began between coughs. "The fire's blocked the stairwell."

Kaitlyn's eyes shot to the open door. The haze was quickly changing to dark, foreboding smoke. Kaitlyn could hear a loud, penetrating scream. She began to turn toward Gracie before she realized that the scream was not coming from Gracie, it was coming from her. The man quickly pushed the door shut and then turned to Kaitlyn and Gracie.

"We need to find another way out of here."

Gracie started toward the elevator, but the stranger reached out to stop her. "We can't use the elevator. It's not safe. It could end up taking us right to the floors that are on fire."

"There's a second set of stairs down at the other end of the corridor," Gracie offered.

The three of them raced down the hall. As they neared the other side, they could see an exit sign and another set of stairs. Kaitlyn threw open the door, and as she did, a massive explosion rocked the ship. The three of them struggled to keep on their feet as the floor beneath them shook violently. Kaitlyn turned to look behind her. An enormous ball of flames had erupted from the stairwell on the far side of the ship and was coming straight for them. The man gave Kaitlyn and Gracie a giant shove, sending them both flying into the stairwell. Then he jumped in and slammed the door behind him.

"Run!" he screamed.

The three of them flew up the stairs two at a time. Kaitlyn could feel her heart beating with such force that she was sure it would burst. The intense heat from the inferno was consuming everything it came in contact with. They could hear the ball of flames roaring behind them like a ravenous beast. The fire seemed to be picking up momentum as it sucked the oxygen out of the corridor. Gracie was first to reach the door to the next level and she flung it open. As the three of them slammed the door shut and dove for cover, they could hear the glass on the bottom-level door shatter. Kaitlyn put her hands over her head—she didn't have time to do anything else. The force of the blast took the door they had just come through right off its hinges. Kaitlyn watched as it sailed through the air, just barely missing the man who had helped them. She immediately jerked around, anticipating the enormous ball of flames that had engulfed the floor below them. Thick black smoke was followed closely by scorching hot flames, but something about the stairwell had temporarily hindered the fireball's force.

When the three of them saw that it was safe to stand up, they started picking their way cautiously toward the opening to the deck. Kaitlyn's legs felt like jelly, and her head was dizzy from the thick, suffocating smoke, but somehow she was able to make it down the hall. The smoke seemed to be enveloping them, making it harder and harder to see. As she neared the door to the deck, Kaitlyn could make out the silhouette of a man. He was running toward them and shouting something, but she couldn't make out what he was saying. All she could hear was the fury of the fire. Her lungs were burning from the smoke. Everything seemed to be swirling inside her head, and then suddenly there was nothing—everything went black.

\* \* \*

Kaitlyn's eyelids began to flicker as a steady stream of rain fell on her face. She blinked hard as she tried to open her eyes. She could hear someone speaking to her, but she couldn't make out what they were saying.

"Kaitlyn! Kaitlyn!" came the voice again.

Kaitlyn knew the voice, but she still couldn't place it. She tried to move, but quickly learned that someone was holding her.

"You're going to be fine," the male voice reassured her. "You just passed out."

Kaitlyn wanted to close her eyes and rest; her whole body felt so heavy. Then, in a horrifying instant, it all came back to her—the explosion, the fire, the evacuation.

"Gracie?" Kaitlyn mumbled. "Where's Gracie?"

"She's right here," came the voice again.

Gracie placed her hand on Kaitlyn's shoulder. "I'm here."

Kaitlyn struggled to focus her eyes as she looked up at the man who held her in his arms.

"Matthew?" she whispered.

Matthew smiled down at her. "I thought for a minute you weren't going to make it out of there."

"You weren't the only one," Kaitlyn uttered weakly.

"We need to get to the lifeboats," Matthew began. "This ship isn't going to last much longer."

"No, I can't," Kaitlyn snapped. "I need to find Amber and Pete."

"It's okay. I had Amber and the boy get on one of the lifeboats. I'll take you to them. Are you steady enough to walk?"

"Yes. I'm fine."

As Matthew set her down, Kaitlyn looked past him to the ocean. Her mouth instantly dropped open. The sea looked like a boiling pot of water, erupting and then plummeting, only to rise again with greater intensity.

"We're evacuating into *that?*"

"Kaitlyn, there's no other option," Matthew began. "Believe me, I wish there were."

The deck was empty now. Except for a handful of the ship's crew who were still rushing about, everyone had been safely placed in lifeboats awaiting the signal to be lowered into the ocean. Matthew held tight to both girls' hands while the three of them ran toward the lifeboat. As they neared the boat that Matthew had instructed Amber to get on, Kaitlyn began frantically searching the faces of the passengers. A boy stood and began yelling in their direction, but the man who was loading the boat pushed him down hard.

"Do you want to tip the boat over?" he growled.

Kaitlyn instantly recognized the man. It was the maintenance worker who had found Pete in the closet. Kaitlyn let go of Matthew's hand and ran to the boat.

"Pete, where's Amber?"

"Isn't she with you?" Pete questioned back.

"What do you mean? She was with you."

"When it took you so long, Amber got worried," Pete began hesitantly, not wanting to tell her the rest. "She went after you."

"No!" Kaitlyn screamed.

They all turned back to look at the ship. All the windows were shattering from the heat of the fire, sending a shower of glass across the deck. Black smoke was billowing out of the double doors that led from the decks back to the corridors. The only thing hindering the flames from consuming the deck was the rain. They all watched as a large man in uniform, with blood smeared across one knee, came running out on deck with four or five other men close on his heels. It was the man that they had met on their tour of the navigation bridge, Lieutenant Lewis.

"Evacuate!" yelled the lieutenant. "Lower the lifeboats *now!*"

Matthew turned to Kaitlyn and Gracie, who were both sobbing.

"I'm sorry, but we've got to evacuate."

"No!" Kaitlyn yelled. "We've got to find Amber. We can't just leave her here to die."

Kaitlyn lunged toward the burning ship, but Matthew grabbed her.

"It's my fault," Kaitlyn sobbed as she buried her face in Matthew's chest. "It's all my fault."

"You've both got to get in," Matthew pleaded. "I've got to lower the boat."

"I can't," Gracie cried in panic.

Matthew turned to look at Gracie. Then he reached over, scooped her into his arms, and placed her on the lifeboat.

"What about you?" Kaitlyn insisted, her voice filled with emotion.

"I'll get on one of the lifeboats," Matthew said as he picked Kaitlyn up and placed her on the boat next to Gracie and Pete. "Don't worry about me."

Kaitlyn reached over and grabbed Gracie's hand. She could hear Gracie's muffled cries as she buried her head in her hands. Kaitlyn glanced back at Matthew as he began to turn the crank to manually lower the lifeboat. At first the lifeboat began to move, but then almost instantly it jerked to a stop a foot below the deck. Matthew grabbed the crank with both hands and pushed with all he had. Kaitlyn could see the veins on his neck bulging.

"What's the matter with it?" the maintenance worker barked.

"It's jammed," Matthew called back in frustration.

Kaitlyn knew that there were easily over a hundred people crammed into their lifeboat. The other lifeboats around them were mostly filled to capacity. Kaitlyn watched as Matthew futilely tried several more times to lower the boat, but it didn't budge an inch. He glanced over at the other lifeboats. Some of them were already being lowered. As he turned back to them, his face was unable to mask his fear. Matthew's eyes locked on the maintenance worker.

"Get them off as quickly as you can. I've got to stop the other stations before they lower their boats."

The maintenance worker stood and began helping the passengers out. Kaitlyn's attention stayed on Matthew as he raced over to the lifeboat next to theirs. Matthew said something to the crew member that was assigned to that station and then pointed back at their lifeboat. After a quick nod of his head, Matthew turned on his heels and ran back to them.

"They'll wait for us," Matthew began anxiously. "But we've got to hurry."

As Matthew and the maintenance worker stood on the deck and helped each person climb from the suspended lifeboat, Kaitlyn put her arm around Gracie.

"Come on, Gracie. We've got to go."

Gracie lifted her head and looked out across the water.

"No! I can't," she cried, burying her head back in her hands.

Kaitlyn looked around the boat. It was already half empty. Kaitlyn could feel the desperation within her rising.

"Gracie, *please*," she begged. "The lifeboats are almost full."

Kaitlyn looked up as Matthew climbed into the boat. Without saying a word, he picked Gracie up in his arms again. Almost as quickly, he climbed back onto the deck. Kaitlyn and Pete followed right behind him. The lifeboat next to them was already over its loading limit, so only a couple of passengers were allowed to board. The rest of them hurried to the boat on the other side of it but were just seconds too late. It was already being lowered. Everyone from their lifeboat was beginning to panic as they scrambled across the deck. Kaitlyn stared in horror as one man dove toward a lifeboat that was in the process of being lowered. He crashed down on three or four people who were already seated. There were several screams, but it didn't appear that anyone was seriously injured. Kaitlyn didn't watch long enough to be certain. Her eyes were frantically searching each lifeboat, looking into each face. Then she scanned the decks. She tried to keep her eyes off the ship. She wouldn't allow her mind to even consider the possibility that Amber was still in there. Finally her eyes fell on the ocean. Several lifeboats were already battling the raging sea. Their fate was no more certain than Amber's.

As they continued to race across the deck, they passed several lifeboats that were completely empty. They were much smaller than the other lifeboats, with a capacity of about twenty-five people, and did not come equipped with a motor or the safety features that the larger boats had. Kaitlyn saw Matthew glance at them from the corner of his eye, but that only made him quicken his step toward the larger lifeboats. The four of them, along with several other people from their first lifeboat, came to an abrupt stop in front of the last of the larger lifeboats. The crew member that was stationed there was just about to lower it. The man turned to the crowd that was quickly forming around his station.

"We have room for four more people."

Kaitlyn stepped forward just as a woman leaped to the front of the crowd. She was dragging two little children behind her.

*"Please,"* she begged. "Put my children aboard." She quickly turned back to the crowd. Her eyes were damp and her voice choked with emotion. "They're too little to . . ." Her voice caught.

Her husband came up beside her and took her by the shoulders. Kaitlyn quietly stepped back into the crowd. She could feel her heart forcing blood through her arteries in giant surges. There was only one option left and she knew it. Kaitlyn's eyes met Matthew's. His expression was the same as her own. Silently they turned and quickly started back across the deck.

"We're getting on *that?*" Pete exclaimed as he pointed down at the small lifeboat and then glanced out at the turbulent ocean. "We'll be smashed to bits."

"We don't have time to debate this," Matthew began as he picked Gracie up and set her down on one of the benches.

Kaitlyn sat down right next to her while Pete took the seat just to her left. Several other people, including the maintenance worker, hesitantly climbed aboard. Matthew grabbed ahold of the maintenance worker's arm.

"Watch over them for me."

The man extended his hand to Matthew. "You have my word."

"You're not coming with us?" Kaitlyn cried.

Matthew turned to scan the deck. Then he looked back at Kaitlyn.

"I can't. Not yet."

Kaitlyn started to protest, but Matthew had already begun to lower the boat. Kaitlyn glanced from Matthew to the ship, then back at him as tears streamed down her face.

"Find her, Matthew. *Please* find her."

\* \* \*

The ocean seemed to pick up the tiny boat and toss it effortlessly on its gigantic waves as Kaitlyn clung to the edge with all her strength. She tried to look back in the direction of the ship, but it was taking all of her energy just to hold on and remain in the boat. She was vaguely aware of the other passengers around her, though at this point it was an individual fight just to survive. She could hear a few of the passengers praying out loud over the howling of the wind. Kaitlyn believed in God, but after Leslie's death she had been so angry that she had completely turned away from religion. And here, now, at this second, when she wanted to call out and plead for life, the words just would not come.

Kaitlyn tucked her head low in the boat in an attempt to shield herself from the pounding waves. She tried to ignore the burning in her eyes and throat from the salt water and concentrate on holding on. Her clothing was completely drenched, and she could feel her body trembling from both exposure and fear. She could see Gracie and Pete in the seats in front of her. Both of them were struggling to hold on. The waves were constant and relentless, the swells more terrifying than anything Kaitlyn could ever have imagined. Several of the waves completely covered the lifeboat, threatening to drag it and all its passengers down into a watery grave.

Kaitlyn's head shot up as another clap of thunder echoed across the water. As she lifted her head, a huge wave nearly covered the lifeboat. Kaitlyn choked as she gulped in the pungent water.

"Hold on, here comes another one," one of the passengers yelled.

Kaitlyn stared in horror at the wave that towered above them. It continued to rise out of the depths of the sea like a hideous sea monster. Before she could even react, the wave came thundering down upon them. The force of this wave sent Kaitlyn flying to the other end of the small craft. She was scrambling to grab hold of something as she was tossed end over end, but she was completely out of control. The force of the wave was pulling her with it. Kaitlyn started to scream as she neared the end of the boat and the immense ocean beyond it. As she reached the edge, the wave seemed to lessen just enough that she slammed headfirst into the side of the boat instead of being swept overboard. Kaitlyn crumpled to the floor of the lifeboat. She tried to move, but her body remained motionless, facedown in a pool of water. She could taste the combination of salt and blood in her mouth. Just as she was about to surrender all coherency, a hand reached down and pulled her up. Kaitlyn was too weak to do anything. The man who held her shielded her face from the next assaulting wave.

"Don't give up! You're going to make it," he screamed over the roar of the waves.

Kaitlyn couldn't respond. She just stared up at his face until she could no longer hold her eyes open.

# CHAPTER 12

The sun struggled to send the first rays of morning down, but the gray clouds that still monopolized the sky only allowed little slivers of light to break through. One of the streams of light fell on a small lifeboat floating aimlessly on the ocean. Kaitlyn lay motionless in the boat, her head resting on Gracie's lap. She had been unconscious since her head had slammed into the side of the boat the night before. Gracie gently pushed Kaitlyn's hair back from her face. It was tangled and matted with blood. Then Gracie straightened the strip of cloth that had been used to bandage Kaitlyn's head. One of the men on the ship had offered his shirt to help bandage those who had been injured during the storm.

Gracie glanced around the small lifeboat. The metal craft looked to be twenty feet long and approximately six feet wide at the middle, but narrowing toward the ends so that only two people could sit comfortably side by side near the stern and bow. The seats were foot-wide slats that stretched across the width of the boat with a two-foot space between each bench, allowing just enough room for a person to lie down on the floor of the boat widthwise between the benches. There was also seating along the boat's edge that butted up to the seating in the middle. The boat was deep enough that while sitting on the seats, the edge would come to an average adult's waist. She guessed that it accommodated approximately twenty-five passengers, so, fortunately, the thirteen of them did not have to sit shoulder to shoulder. Gracie shook her head in wonder. She still had a hard time believing that no one on their lifeboat had been killed during the night. Gracie looked down at Kaitlyn's pale face.

"Please," she whispered softly, "don't be the first."

"She doesn't look very good," Pete said with a frown.

Gracie glanced over at the dark-eyed boy next to her. "She's a fighter."

Both Gracie and Pete turned as a woman at the far end of the boat cried out in pain. Her leg had been broken, and the same man who had offered his shirt to the injured was now trying to set the bone back in place. Gracie quickly turned away as the man twisted her leg. The woman immediately let out a chilling scream that sent a shiver straight up Gracie's spine. She glanced around at the other passengers. Even the grown men turned away as the woman screamed in agony. Then the woman slumped back against the side of the boat, too exhausted to do anything else.

Gracie closed her eyes. Why was this happening? They were stranded out in the middle of the ocean with no idea of how long it would take for a rescue ship to find them. One of her friends lay unconscious in her arms, and the other one . . . Gracie could not even bring herself to think it. She looked out across the endless ocean. Her free hand instinctively reached out to grab hold of the side of the boat as soon as her eyes met the water. She bit down hard on her lip as the warm tears that filled her eyes began to spill over. Gracie shook her head vigorously, angry at herself for allowing her fear of water to hold such control over her.

"Don't cry," Pete began. "Someone will find us." He reached out awkwardly and touched her shoulder.

Gracie nodded, though she did not look at him.

"Are you two close?"

Gracie jerked her head around, startled by the woman who sat across from her. The woman smiled kindly as she gestured toward Kaitlyn.

"We've been friends since we were little," Gracie said as she looked back down at her friend.

"I wish there was something we could do."

"Me too," Gracie said weakly as she lifted her head to meet the woman's gaze.

The woman appeared to be in her late thirties. She was exceptionally thin and sounded like a smoker. Her short blond hair was tousled, and a trail of black mascara was smeared beneath a pair of dark-rimmed glasses. Gracie guessed that at this point her own appearance was probably no better.

"By the way, I'm Morgan, and this is my husband Sam," she offered, gesturing toward the man next to her.

Even in a sitting position, Sam towered over Morgan's gaunt frame. He looked like a blocker for the NFL. His neck was thick, his shoulders were broad, and he had a generous spread around the waist. A freckle-faced boy sat contentedly on his lap.

Gracie introduced herself as Sam reached out his enormous hand.

Then the young boy, mimicking his father, extended his own small hand. "I'm Benton."

Gracie smiled. "Nice to meet you, Benton."

"And this is my mother, Eleanor," Morgan added, turning to the woman on the other side of her.

The older woman smiled broadly, the warmth in it making Gracie feel as if she were an old friend from church bingo, not a stranger introduced for the first time on a lifeboat in the middle of the ocean. Then Eleanor gave a quick squeeze to the little two-year-old on her lap. "And this is Madison."

Madison turned and buried herself in her grandma's arms. Eleanor chuckled softly. "She's not big on strangers."

"Look!" Pete shouted as he pointed down at Kaitlyn. "Her eyes flickered."

Gracie's eyes immediately shot back to Kaitlyn. Kaitlyn's forehead was furrowed, as if she were struggling to open her eyes.

"Kaitlyn, can you hear me?" Gracie shouted, using every ounce of restraint left in her to keep from shaking the life back into her friend.

After a moment, Kaitlyn's eyes began to flicker and then slowly opened.

"Kaitlyn, are you okay?"

Kaitlyn tried to speak, but it came out as more of a croak. "I think so."

"You had me so scared," Gracie rushed on. "I thought for sure that you were a goner." Gracie let out a huge sigh of relief and then relaxed back against the side of the boat.

Kaitlyn winced as she reached up to feel the cloth that was wrapped around her head.

"You've got a pretty big cut," Gracie offered.

"That explains the throbbing."

"You've also lost a lot of blood, but at least you're awake."

Kaitlyn moaned as she struggled to sit up. Pete reached out to help her.

"Hey, it's Pete," Kaitlyn said as she slowly leaned back against the boat.

Pete beamed down at her. "I'll see if I can get you some water."

Gracie and Kaitlyn watched as Pete made his way to the far end of the boat. Then Kaitlyn looked out across the ocean. Her eyes slowly surveyed the emptiness in every direction.

"It's gone," Gracie said, knowing full well what Kaitlyn was searching for.

"Did it sink?" Kaitlyn's face went instantly somber.

"I'm not sure. When it first started getting light, we saw a few objects off in the distance, but they were too far away to make out. It could have been a part of the ship or the other lifeboats. I just don't know. Since then we haven't seen anything." Gracie lowered her eyes. "If something happens to Amber . . ."

Kaitlyn reached out and grabbed Gracie's hand.

"She'll be okay."

"I hope you're right."

Kaitlyn glanced over at Pete. He was toward the bow of the boat, bent over, talking to a guy who looked to be in his early twenties. The man had bleached-blond hair and a dark, even tan, but Kaitlyn could not see his face well because he was bent down helping one of the passengers. The woman he was helping was squirming in pain. As Pete talked, the man turned to look in Kaitlyn's direction. Kaitlyn instantly looked away, strangely embarrassed to have them so obviously discussing her. Her eyes then fell on a man a few seats away from her. She did not have to take a second glance to recognize him. It was the maintenance worker who had discovered Pete hiding in the closet. When he saw her looking in his direction, he smiled.

"How are you feeling?"

"Okay, I guess."

He got up to make his way over to her. As he did, the lifeboat began to gently rock back and forth. Gracie reached out in a panic, grabbing hold of the edge of the boat.

"Just take a deep breath," Kaitlyn whispered as she leaned over and put her hand on Gracie's shoulder.

"I was afraid that your boyfriend was going to have to hunt me down," the man said as he sat down next to the two girls.

Kaitlyn looked at him blankly. "My *boyfriend*? What are you talking about?"

"I promised him back on the ship that I would watch out for you. You getting your head smashed into the side of a boat and nearly dying isn't exactly a fulfillment of that bargain."

Kaitlyn nodded as the realization hit her.

"Matthew isn't my boyfriend. I just met him this weekend."

"Could have fooled me," the man said with a wry grin.

Kaitlyn smiled uncomfortably. "I'm Kaitlyn and this is my friend Gracie."

"Gary Sanders," he offered back.

Kaitlyn glanced at Pete, down at the far end of the boat. "What's going to happen to him?"

Gary shrugged. "If the kid is stupid enough to stow away on a boat that sinks, I figure he's probably harmless enough."

Kaitlyn tried not to look offended by Gary's flippant remark.

"Don't worry about it," Gary continued. "I'll take care of him."

The three of them looked up as the boat again began to rock. The man Pete had been talking to was making his way over to them with Pete close behind.

"I better get back to my seat," Gary began. "If you need anything, just let me know."

"I will. Thank you."

Gary nodded a greeting as he passed the first man, but when he got to Pete he stopped and stared him straight in the eyes. Pete glanced up at Gary but then quickly lowered his gaze. Gary shot a glance back at Kaitlyn and winked.

"How's the head?" the young man with Pete asked as he approached Kaitlyn.

"Sore, but I'll be okay."

"You took quite a hit."

Kaitlyn first looked hard at the man's face, then her eyes fell on the bloodstains that were smeared across his undershirt before she glanced back at his face. He smiled as the realization hit her.

"You were the one last night that picked me up after I hit my head!" Kaitlyn exclaimed.

The man before her nodded and then smiled.

"You saved my life," Kaitlyn admitted frankly. "I was so weak I couldn't even pull myself up out of the water at the bottom of the boat. I really thought I was going to die."

Kaitlyn reached up and felt the cloth that was around her head.

"I guess this is yours, too?" she asked.

His face reddened. "I'm just glad you're doing better."

Kaitlyn watched as he glanced over at Gracie.

"I'm sorry," Kaitlyn began. "This is my friend Gracie. We came on the cruise together."

He smiled. "My name is Garret, but you can call me Flip."

"Flip?" Gracie asked, crinkling her nose in curiosity.

"It's short for Flipper. I'm going to school to be an oceanographer," he offered as though it explained everything.

Gracie stared at him blankly.

"I do a lot of diving," he continued. "You know . . . flippers." He pointed down to his feet.

"Any chance of you putting on a pair of flippers and going for help, Mr. Oceanographer?"

"Sure, why not?" Flip began. "And while I'm swimming past the tip of Cuba, would you like me to stop in at the nearest convenience store and pick you up a pint of chocolate-chip cookie dough ice cream, or is mint chocolate-chip more your style?"

Gracie cocked her head to one side, a little taken aback by his quick wit after such a long night.

"Make it rocky road and you've got yourself a deal."

Flip smiled. "Now you're talking. Actually," he continued hesitantly, "I may not be able to swim for help, but I do have a couple of ideas that might come in handy while we're here."

"Like what?" interrupted Sam, the husky NFL look-alike. "I'm getting a little tired of just sitting around waiting to be rescued. I've got a family to think of."

"The first thing we need to do is to get organized," Flip suggested. "We need to pool our resources together and find out who everybody is and what special skills they might have that could help us."

All heads aboard were now turned toward Flip. They had all over-heard and were anxious to do something. Everyone seemed content to let Flip take the lead, at least for now.

"Why don't we start with you," Flip said, gesturing to Kaitlyn.

After Kaitlyn had said who she was, she unzipped the backpack that lay beside her.

"I still have a few things I picked up in the airport gift shop." She reached her hand into the pack and pulled out a magazine, a candy bar, and a small package of spicy beef jerky. "Sorry, it's not much."

"Every little bit will help," Flip assured her.

Sam went next. Kaitlyn watched him as he spoke. His hair had just enough auburn in it to make Kaitlyn think that he might have been a redhead as a boy.

"I'm a used-car salesman. I won this trip for selling more used cars than anyone in Miami," Sam boasted. Then his face fell. "Some prize. I would have been better off choosing the snow blower and the designer ski parka. Next year I'm volunteering for the prize commission so I can give the winner snorkel equipment."

Then he dug deep into his pocket and pulled out a pack of gum and a handful of loose change. He set his items down next to Kaitlyn's on one of the empty bench seats. Then, one by one, the rest of Sam's family introduced themselves. Kaitlyn felt an immediate affinity for Eleanor, who was holding her sleeping granddaughter on her lap. She smiled warmly at the other passengers as she ran her fingers through the little girl's silky blond hair. To Kaitlyn she seemed to be the kind of grandma who believed you couldn't bake too many homemade cookies or give too many hugs.

"After forty-five years of cooking for one man and four children," Eleanor began, "I think I qualify as a cook. Unfortunately, I don't see any steak and potatoes out here."

Everyone nodded their heads at that. It was close to nine o'clock in the morning now, which meant that for most passengers, it had been at least fourteen hours since their last meal aboard the ship. Kaitlyn could feel her own stomach growling. Then Eleanor added a small, pink, beaded purse and matching necklace to the pile.

Benton, Eleanor's grandson, jumped off his dad's lap and made his way over to sit next to his grandma. He was probably about four.

He had flame-red hair, freckles, and deep blue eyes. He was the kind of kid that needed to be in commercials. He began playing with a little red car. Flip bent down to admire the car and ask him if he had any special talents that could help them.

"How's a snot-nose kid going to help us?" Gary mumbled under his breath.

If Flip heard the comment, he gave no indication. Kaitlyn, however, heard him loud and clear. The remark seemed completely out of character for Gary—or at least what Kaitlyn had seen of him. She frowned. Then again, how well did she really know him? Kaitlyn quickly shot a glance over at Morgan and Sam, Benton's parents. Apparently Gary's comment had not escaped Sam either; his eyes seared through Gary like a welder's torch.

"How can you help us, big guy?" Flip repeated with a broad smile.

Benton's eyes lit up. "I could catch a whale or a shark," he offered confidently.

Flip laughed. "I'll tell you what, if I can put something together to make a fishing pole, then we might take you up on that. But how about if we skip the shark and just stick to catching fish?"

Benton bobbed his head, apparently pleased. Then Flip asked if the little boy had anything to add to the pile. Benton's eyes instantly went to the shiny car clutched in his hand. It was a tiny sports cars with little doors that opened and shut. The boy looked down at the assortment of items on the bench seat, then back to his red sports car. As quickly as his little hand would go, he thrust his prized possession deep into his pocket. Kaitlyn couldn't help but laugh. Instead, Benton pulled out a pocketknife. His mother, who was apparently unaware of the knife, instantly narrowed her eyes and looked sternly at her husband. Sam avoided his wife's glare and continued watching his son. Flip tousled the boy's hair affectionately as he thanked him for his generous contribution.

"This just might save our lives," Flip admitted. Then he glanced up at Gary with a smirk.

The girl next to Eleanor had her arm propped up on the edge of the boat and her head resting in her hand. She did not appear to be at all interested in what the others had to say. Kaitlyn gave the girl a quick once-over. Her hair was sandy brown with subtle blond high-lights. It was cut short with a little flip at the back. Her skin was flaw-less with a beautiful, even tan. Plus, she also just happened to be one of those incredibly lucky people who look gorgeous without a stitch of makeup. When it was her turn, the girl straightened up and intro-duced herself as Rhonda Herring. She had come on the ship to cele-brate her twenty-first birthday. She said that her father, Robert Herring, was a wealthy businessman who owned a string of hotels across the Northeast. She didn't even try to hide her arrogance.

"I really don't see the need for all this. The instant my father is aware of our situation, the entire Miami Search and Rescue will be on their way."

Kaitlyn glanced over at Gracie, who was shaking her head.

The man sitting next to Rhonda went next. He looked to be in his mid-twenties. He said his name was Donald and that he was from New York. He had thick, curly brown hair that needed a trim, and a week-old beard and mustache. He wore a simple pullover and a pair of faded blue jeans. The trendy, thin-rimmed glasses that sat on the bridge of his nose looked out of place with his casual attire. He also had a strip of bloody cloth wrapped around his right arm.

"I'm into computers, but I'm kind of taking some downtime right now," Donald admitted as he tossed a gold chain into the pile.

"Translation: *unemployed*," Rhonda muttered softly.

Kaitlyn glanced distastefully at Rhonda. She couldn't help but wonder if Rhonda Herring would be able to make it one day on her own without *daddy's* money.

After Donald, Flip turned to Gary, the maintenance worker. Kaitlyn glanced over at Pete while Gary took his turn. Pete's head was lowered, and his big brown eyes were staring down at his feet. He glanced up once or twice but then quickly lowered his head. Kaitlyn decided right there and then that she needed to talk to Pete and tell him that Gary really had no intention of turning him in.

After Gary, everyone turned their attention to the woman whose leg had been broken. She had finally fallen into a fitful sleep and was lying at the far end of the boat. She was heavyset, in her early thirties, with shoulder-length brown hair. Besides the broken leg, she also had a deep, four-inch gash across her right shoulder.

"Her name's Karen. I don't know too much more than that," Flip offered. "I do know that she's going to need our help."

Kaitlyn noticed Rhonda rolling her eyes. It didn't take a brain surgeon to realize that the only person that Rhonda Herring planned on helping was Rhonda Herring.

Sitting quietly next to Karen was Pete. He bent down to play with his shoelaces. Pete had mastered going completely unnoticed, even in a small group of people. Flip asked Pete about himself, but before the boy could answer Flip shot up out of his seat, sending the small boat rocking. Gracie grabbed desperately for the side of the boat, while everyone else stared at Flip like he had just lost his mind.

"*That's it!* The shoelaces!" Flip exclaimed as he bent down and began untying Pete's sneakers.

"What do you want his shoelaces for?" Donald asked, tilting his head to the side and crinkling up his forehead and nose.

"Not just *his* shoelaces," Flip began excitedly, "I want *everyone's* shoelaces."

Everyone with laced shoes hesitantly bent down and began removing their laces. No one was quite sure what it was that he had in mind, but they were curious enough to at least make the effort.

"Benton!" Flip exclaimed. "You just might get the chance to catch that fish after all."

# CHAPTER 13

The clouds were quickly dissipating, and the sun was now beating down unrestrained. The dampness of the morning was being replaced by a hot, summer afternoon. Kaitlyn could feel the dryness in her mouth, but she tried to push the thought from her mind. They had all been given a small drink of water a couple of hours before from their limited water rations. Flip had retrieved a five-gallon jug of water that had been placed in an emergency storage compartment under one of the bench seats.

Kaitlyn glanced toward Flip. After collecting all of the shoelaces, he had gone to work making a fishing pole. He tied all the laces together, then one by one he added Eleanor's necklace and Donald's chain for weight. With the seven pairs of laces that he had collected, along with the two necklaces, his fishing line stretched out to about twenty-eight feet. Kaitlyn, along with most of the other women aboard, were wearing sandals. She wished now that she'd had on a pair of sneakers so she could have added a little more length to the fishing line. When Flip was done, he used a dangling earring that Rhonda had reluctantly given up for use as a lure. Then he tied the string to one of the oars to use, as a pole. It was a creative—or maybe desperate—effort, but at this point they were all just praying that it worked. That had been over an hour ago, with no luck still.

A look of concern was starting to crease the faces of almost everyone aboard. Benton, on the other hand, had his feet dangling over the edge of the boat and looked as if he were having the adventure of a lifetime. Flip and Pete sat next to him, patiently listening as the boy rattled on about pirates, buried treasure, and sea monsters.

Kaitlyn had spent the past hour and a half straining her eyes to see any sign of a rescue boat off in the distance, but there was nothing. Her fears were beginning to run wild. Maybe the storm and the current had caused them to drift too far away. With hundreds of miles of ocean to search, the Coast Guard might never find them, or they might find them after it was too late. With the intensity of the storm, everyone might just assume that they had all drowned. Then, in one awful moment, it hit her—her parents must have been notified as to what had happened. Kaitlyn wanted to cry. That thought was almost as horrifying as the realization that they might not be rescued. Her parents were already struggling; their marriage would never be able to withstand losing another child. Kaitlyn shook her head and tried to force her mind not to think like that. She needed something to occupy her time. She quickly looked around the boat for something to keep her busy. It only took a glance to see where she was needed. Karen was awake now, and it was evident from the look on her face that she was in a lot of pain.

Kaitlyn sat down on the bench next to Karen, who was lying on the floor of the boat with her leg propped up on a life preserver. Another life preserver had been gently placed beneath her head. Kaitlyn also noticed the blood-soaked rag wrapped around Karen's arm and shoulder.

"Hi," Kaitlyn began softly. "You were asleep when everyone was giving their names. I'm Kaitlyn."

Karen attempted to speak, but then flinched as another surge of pain raged through her body.

"Where are you from?" Kaitlyn asked, attempting to get Karen's mind off the pain.

"I've been living in Chicago for the past thirteen years," Karen said breathlessly. "But I grew up in Iowa."

"Is your family still there?"

Karen nodded her head and then gritted her teeth.

"Do you get to see them very often?" Kaitlyn rushed on.

"I haven't seen my mom and dad—or any of my family—since I left."

Kaitlyn must have had a look of surprise on her face, because Karen went on to explain.

"I got pregnant when I was seventeen."

Karen shut her eyes and clenched her teeth. Kaitlyn wasn't sure this time if it was because of the physical pain or the memory.

"News like that spreads like fire in a small town. I just couldn't stick around and put my parents through that. So I left without telling anyone."

"They didn't know that you were going to have a baby?"

Karen shook her head as her chin began to quiver. "No one knew."

"Not even the father?" Kaitlyn asked gently.

"Oh, he knew. But he was the star quarterback of our high school and had his pick of colleges. A baby—and a wife—didn't quite fit into his plan." Karen winced as the pain intensified.

"Just try to relax," Kaitlyn said softly.

Karen swallowed hard and then motioned toward her stomach. "My stomach is killing me," she moaned.

"Do you mind if I take a look?"

Karen nodded her head and then reached over and grabbed ahold of the bench seat next to her. Kaitlyn gently reached down and slowly began to lift the bottom of Karen's shirt, exposing only her stomach. She was careful to block the view from others. Kaitlyn visibly flinched when she saw Karen's injuries. They were far more serious than she had ever imagined. Karen had numerous dark purple bruises the size of grapefruits across her abdomen. Several ribs were visibly broken, bulging oddly against her skin, while the rest of her stomach was bruised and swollen. Though the extent of Kaitlyn's medical training consisted of a couple of CPR and first-aid classes she'd taken to certify as a lifeguard, it didn't take more than a glance to see that Karen was in serious shape.

"I was knocked down on deck," Karen offered weakly. "I tried to get up, but people kept pushing."

Kaitlyn could feel her stomach turn. Karen had not received her injuries from the cold, unfeeling rage of last night's storm; she had been trampled. Kaitlyn gently lowered Karen's shirt. She tried to keep her face as passive as possible, although inwardly she was horrified.

"Let me see if anyone has anything for pain," Kaitlyn said softly as she started to stand. "I'll be right back."

Karen swallowed hard and then closed her eyes to rest while Kaitlyn quickly made her way over to Flip.

"Have you seen Karen's ribs?"

Flip's face grew instantly serious. "Yeah, she's pretty banged up. I wish there was something more we could do until a rescue ship gets here. We don't have any pain medication or anything."

Kaitlyn looked over her shoulder at Karen and then back at Flip.

"Don't you mean *if* a rescue ship finds us? Who knows how far away we drifted in the storm."

Flip shot Kaitlyn a warning glance and then looked down at little Benton, who sat watching the fishing line next to him.

"They'll find us," Flip offered firmly.

"What's left of us, anyway," Kaitlyn blurted out a little more intensely than she had intended.

"Hey, you're alive, aren't you, right here, right now?"

Kaitlyn knew that he was right, but the gash on her head was throbbing, and she was too frustrated and tired to stop herself.

"What good is being alive if you slowly starve to death?"

"Look, you could have been thrown overboard last night, or you could still be unconscious, or better yet, you could be the one sitting over there fighting for your life. But at least she's *fighting*. You're giving up! You're quitting, and there is nothing more cowardly than a quitter." Then he lowered his voice so low that it was barely audible, but his words hit her as if he had screamed them. "If you ask me, Karen has a better chance of making it than you."

Kaitlyn felt as if she had just been slapped.

"I'm *not* a quitter," she said adamantly, the anger within her rising.

Flip looked at her intently for several seconds, and then a smile slowly stole across his lips. "Good!" Without another word, he turned back toward his fishing pole.

Kaitlyn stood there staring at the back of his head. Her breathing was deep and her emotions whirling.

"You did that on purpose," she finally acknowledged.

Flip reached down and tugged on his fishing string to test the tension, then he glanced up at the cloth that he had wrapped around her head the night before.

"I knew last night that you were a fighter. You just needed a little reminder." Then he turned his attention back to Benton. "I'll bet the fish are down there right now arguing over who gets to bite this lure first."

Benton giggled and then leaned his head over the edge of the boat to look directly down at the water. Kaitlyn stood there watching the two of them. Benton's innocence sheltered him from realizing the seriousness of their situation, but Flip had no such luxury. He was fully aware of the gravity of their condition.

"I'm sorry," Kaitlyn began as her face flushed. "I guess I kind of . . . freaked out."

Flip shrugged and then smiled. "Don't sweat it. We'll just chalk it up to temporary insanity."

"How can you be sure it was temporary?" Kaitlyn said with a smirk.

Flip laughed. "Time will tell."

* * *

"What's taking them so long?" Sam bellowed. "Where's the Coast Guard?"

"We've got to be patient," Morgan consoled her husband. "They have several lifeboats to look for that are probably scattered across a hundred miles by now."

Sam raised his eyebrows, letting her know that her comment didn't help.

"I'm sorry," she continued, "but getting upset, especially around the children, isn't going to help them get here any faster."

Sam looked over at his two small children.

"I'm sorry," he sighed.

Morgan reached over and grabbed his hand, then leaned over to kiss him softly. Kaitlyn could see Sam visibly relax. When Morgan pulled away, Sam put one arm around her and the other around his little girl. Madison, who had just woken from her nap, was sitting groggily beside him. She quickly climbed onto her daddy's lap and laid her head on his broad chest.

"What *is* taking so long?" Gracie whispered, softly enough that only Kaitlyn could hear.

Kaitlyn shook her head. "I don't know." She had spent the last hour asking herself that very question.

Kaitlyn leaned against the side of the boat and closed her eyes. She could feel the gentle rocking of the boat and the warm sun on her face. If not for the growling in her stomach, she could have easily been lulled to sleep. She opened her eyes and looked across the boat to Pete. He was sitting next to Flip. Kaitlyn tried to wave her hand and get his attention, but he was concentrating on the fishing pole.

"Pete," she called out softly, trying not to disturb the others.

Pete instantly got to his feet and carefully made his way over to her.

"I've been wanting to talk to you about Gary," she began quietly as soon as he sat down.

Pete's eyes shot over to where Gary was sitting. Kaitlyn could feel his body tense.

"I know you're afraid that Gary's going to turn you in after we're rescued, but he already told me that as long as you keep in line, everything will be fine."

Pete looked her right in the eye. "Is that what he told you?"

"I promise. I'm sure Gary knows that you've learned your lesson."

"I've learned my lesson all right."

Pete's big round eyes turned back to where Gary was sitting. This time Gary also had his eyes on the two of them. He flashed a quick smile.

"See, I told you," Kaitlyn reassured him as she affectionately tousled the thick mess of hair on Pete's head. "I promise, there's nothing to be afraid of."

Pete pulled away. "I'm not afraid."

Kaitlyn had to refrain from smiling. Pete's bravado reminded her of her little brother Kenny. He usually announced that very same thing right after watching a scary movie. Then he would inevitably end up curled in a ball at the foot of their parents' bed in the middle of the night.

"Good," Kaitlyn concluded. "Then I guess we've got that all settled."

\* \* \*

Kaitlyn shifted restlessly in her seat. Her head was pounding, which only added to the nausea of her churning stomach. She closed her eyes for a moment, trying to concentrate on the smell of the salt air and the warm breeze that brushed gently across her face, but no matter how hard she tried, nothing seemed to help. She opened her eyes and glanced around the boat. Now that their meager rations had been appraised and their makeshift fishing pole had been pieced together, there was nothing left to do but wait. To Kaitlyn, it was the waiting that was proving to be the most unnerving part of this whole nightmare.

"What I wouldn't give for just one cigarette," Morgan mumbled.

Kaitlyn looked at the woman across from her. Morgan was fidgeting nervously with her hands. Sam put his arm around his wife's thin shoulders.

"Maybe this would be a good time to kick the habit," Sam offered with a shrug.

Morgan gave her husband a sharp glance. Sam immediately withdrew his arm and picked up Madison. Apparently he didn't need a second glare to know that this was not a good time to needle his wife. Rhonda, however, was not that astute.

"If you ask me," Rhonda butted in, "smoking is a disgusting habit."

Everyone aboard turned to look at Morgan. Her face went bright red. Kaitlyn felt sorry for her. Kaitlyn didn't smoke or enjoy being around anyone who was smoking, but Rhonda's blatant insensitivity to Morgan's feelings was irritating.

"Don't you care about your children?" Rhonda plunged forward. "Or the effects of secondhand smoke on everyone else around you?"

Morgan stared at the woman before her, obviously too embarrassed and shocked by Rhonda's bluntness to even respond. Though not a complete introvert, Morgan appeared to be a rather private and soft-spoken person, which made Rhonda's verbal attack even more appalling.

"The smell permeates everything," Rhonda continued. "We had a chauffeur once that reeked so strongly of smoke that Father had to fire him. I personally couldn't stand to be around him."

"Blah, blah, blah," Gracie mimicked as she opened and shut her hand like a puppet.

Kaitlyn saw Eleanor quickly lift her handkerchief to her face to hide a big grin. Sam was not as discreet. He laughed so hard that his whole body shook. Rhonda's mouth snapped shut as she turned and glowered at Gracie. Her pale blue eyes narrowed into tiny slits. Kaitlyn could almost see the wheels inside her head spinning as she struggled to come up with a cutting retort. Kaitlyn shook her head. This high-society snob didn't have a clue what she was up against. Gracie was the queen of quick comebacks. She could give a tongue-lashing that would leave even the most formidable challenger dumb-founded as they licked their open wounds.

Rhonda glared defiantly at Gracie for several seconds, then she clicked her tongue, folded her arms, and turned away. It was obvious that Rhonda was not in the habit of losing. Gracie just sat there, her face the epitome of innocence, as if she didn't have a clue why Rhonda was so upset, which only seemed to inflame Rhonda all the more. Rhonda might have surrendered in this minor battle, but Kaitlyn had a feeling that the war between Rhonda and Gracie was only beginning.

# CHAPTER 14

Kaitlyn wiped at the sweat that had beaded up on Karen's brow. Then she wiped at her own forehead with the front of her lower arm. The temperature was sweltering. Kaitlyn guessed that it had to be somewhere around ninety or ninety-five degrees. Her whole body glistened with perspiration, and she could feel the sting of sweat and mascara in her eyes.

Kaitlyn looked down at the woman beside her. Karen was at least ten years older than she was. Her face was round, and her features were all small and pleasant. Something about her reminded Kaitlyn of a porcelain doll. Kaitlyn watched as Karen began to squirm. Her muscles tightened, and her face distorted with each shock of pain. Earlier she had drifted off into a fitful sleep, but even then she moaned and mumbled restlessly, repeating one name over and over again until finally she woke herself up.

"When are they coming?" Karen asked. Her voice was strained as she fought to keep from coughing.

"Not much longer," Kaitlyn offered, trying to sound reassuring.

"How long have we been out here?"

Kaitlyn looked down at her watch, even though the grumbling of her stomach told her that it was well past noon. The glass face on her watch was misted over from a mixture of water and heat, but it was still readable. "We've been out here about twelve hours."

"It feels like forever," Karen said as she licked her lips.

Kaitlyn squinted up at the sun. "Maybe by this time tomorrow we'll be home."

"I don't know if I can make it till then," Karen moaned, her face showing the depth of her anguish.

Kaitlyn looked down at the woman before her. Her leg was swollen, her insides bruised and broken, and her whole body racked with pain. Kaitlyn was not sure herself how long Karen would be able to hold on.

"Tell me about your baby," Kaitlyn said with a gentle smile.

"He's not a baby anymore," Karen said, her eyes showing the tender feelings of a mother. "Trevor's almost thirteen now."

That was the name—the name that Karen had repeated over and over again in her sleep and in fits of delirium.

"What's he like?"

"He reminds me of my dad. He's pretty quiet. More of a thinker than a talker." Karen's voice started to crack. "I don't know what he'll do if something happens to me."

"Where is he now?"

"He's staying with a friend. I would have brought him with me, but he insisted that I get out and have some fun without him. I think he was hoping I would meet someone nice. He wants so much to have a dad."

Kaitlyn reached out and grabbed Karen's hand as she began to cough violently. After the coughing had finally passed, Karen clutched at her stomach in pain.

"I'm *so* sorry," Kaitlyn offered sympathetically. "I wish there was something I could do."

Karen fought to regain control of her trembling body, then slowly reached over and grabbed Kaitlyn's hand. "There might be," she admitted weakly.

"What? Just tell me and I'll do it," Kaitlyn whispered.

Karen shook her head and then bit her lip. "Not now. Maybe later."

"Okay. Whatever you want," Kaitlyn said gently. "But for now, why don't you try and get some rest."

Karen bobbed her head and then closed her eyes. Kaitlyn held Karen's hand for several minutes until finally her breathing deepened. Then Kaitlyn peered off into the distance, glancing in all directions. Her heart sank. There was nothing out there but rolling waves meeting and blending into a soft blue sky. She looked back at Karen and began to gently stroke her damp hair. She could not help wondering how much more suffering Karen would have to go through before this was all over. Kaitlyn reached up and wiped at the corners of her own eyes, no longer able to stop her tears from spilling over.

"Why don't you take a break and let me sit with her for a while."

Kaitlyn glanced up at the older woman who was carefully making her way toward them.

"No, I'm fine. Really," Kaitlyn insisted as she quickly wiped at her cheeks.

Eleanor smiled and then sat down next to Kaitlyn. "My grandchildren are asleep. This is a perfect time for me to help out. Besides, I think your friend has had enough of Rhonda." Eleanor glanced over her shoulder at Gracie, who had her arms folded and was glaring at Rhonda.

Kaitlyn smiled knowingly. "I gotcha."

Kaitlyn sat down next to Gracie with a long sigh. She had been so focused on Karen that she had apparently missed the latest exchange between Gracie and Rhonda. Judging by the looks of it, though, Rhonda had emerged victorious this time. She was sitting all prim and proper like a peacock, with an insolent grin spread prominently across her face.

"What happened?" Kaitlyn asked quietly so that Rhonda would not overhear.

"Don't even get me started," Gracie said dryly.

Kaitlyn let it go with a shrug. She was emotionally and physically drained. This verbal onslaught between Gracie and Rhonda was just one more thing that she really didn't need. Besides, she had confidence that Gracie could handle her own battles.

* * *

"Trim the sails and down the hatch. Throw a few fishes to the crew," Gracie ordered in a thick pirate accent. "And then . . . tickle the prisoners."

Gracie reached out and tickled Benton until he squealed with delight.

"Aye, aye, Cap'n," Benton squeaked out between giggles.

"Now off with ya before I getcha with me hook," Gracie ordered.

Benton scrambled into his father's arms.

"What? You're not going to make him walk the plank?" Flip teased.

Flip stood and began making his way over to Kaitlyn and Gracie. The two of them scooted over to make room for him to sit down.

"Is she always like this?" Flip asked Kaitlyn once he sat down.

"Don't even ask," Kaitlyn said, shaking her head at Gracie. "When we were little and everyone else was having lemonade stands, Gracie wrapped a scarf around her head, peered into her mood ring, and exclaimed to all the neighbor kids in our class that for fifty cents each she could foresee Monday's math quiz being canceled."

Flip laughed. "I'll bet the kids were pretty steamed come Monday morning."

"There wasn't a test," Kaitlyn said, with a smile. "The pet lizard that Gracie brought for show-and-tell that day mysteriously disappeared somewhere in Mrs. Cannon's classroom. Once the principal had talked Mrs. Cannon down from the top of her desk, we were all dismissed early for lunch."

"So she got away with it?"

"Not exactly," Kaitlyn began. "Someone squealed about Gracie's prediction, and when Mrs. Cannon got wind of it, she announced to the class that she *too* could read the future."

Flip raised an eyebrow.

"Mrs. Cannon said she could foresee several days of staying after school and cleaning chalkboards in Gracie's immediate future."

Flip folded his arms and looked at Gracie.

"I have a feeling you were one of those kids that got pretty tight with the principal."

"I'm still receiving Christmas cards."

Flip smiled, causing a dimple high on his left cheek to deepen. Kaitlyn quickly appraised the man before her. His hair was cut short on the sides, but his bangs had a gentle wave to them that, if left too much longer, threatened to fall into loose curls. He had light hazel eyes that lit with excitement and interest when he talked.

"So how's the fishing coming?" Kaitlyn asked, though she already knew the answer.

They had all been confined to a small lifeboat for hours now and were bored out of their minds; watching Flip fish had been their only real diversion of the day.

"Actually, I was kind of hoping one of you girls might be able to help me out with that," Flip said, glancing around the boat.

"So you didn't just come over to sit by us because of our charming personalities and drop-dead good looks," Gracie teased.

Flip's smile deepened. "I came for that *and* a barrette or a hairpin or something to use for the fishing pole."

"I've got one," Rhonda offered anxiously.

Rhonda had been sulking the last few minutes, but now she was all smiles. "You're welcome to use it," she offered, her tone sickeningly sweet.

Kaitlyn wanted to gag.

"Thanks, I really appreciate it," Flip said.

He stood up as Rhonda handed him the barrette, and then he quickly started back toward his pole. Then, almost as an afterthought, he stopped and looked over his shoulder at Gracie. He gave a quick wink and then smiled. Kaitlyn watched as Gracie's face lit into a huge grin.

# CHAPTER 15

It was close to three thirty in the afternoon; the sun had been relentless all day. Gracie could feel the skin on her nose and shoulders beginning to sting. She was sure her fair skin wouldn't hold up very long in these conditions. She suspected that by nightfall her skin would be badly burned and blistered. If she could just get some relief from the direct sun she might survive the day, she thought. But there wasn't a cloud in the sky. It was as if the sky were declaring a victory over the night's storm—the bright sun was its trophy.

Gracie looked across the boat at Kaitlyn, who had spent most of the afternoon with Karen. Flip and Pete, on the other hand, were still tinkering with their fishing pole. So far the only thing they had managed to catch were sunburns. Flip was still trying to put on a good face to keep everyone's spirits up. Gracie had even overheard him telling Pete a few jokes. They were some of the corniest jokes that Gracie had ever heard, but Pete had laughed so hard that Flip had to stop telling them for fear that he was scaring off the fish.

Rhonda had also gone over to join Flip, Pete, and little Benton. Gracie had noticed Donald scoot down next to Rhonda earlier and try to strike up a conversation, but she had shot him down before he even knew what hit him. It appeared that Rhonda had already branded Donald as loose change. So now she was sitting right next to Flip, hanging on his every word. She would giggle at all of his jokes and then slap playfully at his shoulder and tell him to stop. Gracie was getting a little sick to her stomach, and it was not from the movement of the ship. Did this girl not realize that they were stranded out in the middle of about a trillion tons of water, or did she see it as just a quaint little opportunity to pick up guys? Gracie tossed her head back in disgust. She knew that she was being petty, but Rhonda really irked her.

"Would you like to borrow my wrap for a while?"

Gracie turned to the older woman sitting directly across from her.

"I'm sorry," Gracie began. "What did you say?"

Eleanor smiled sweetly over at her. "I was just wondering, dear, if you would like to use my wrap for a while. I noticed that you're getting a nasty burn."

Gracie looked at the cream-colored wrap that Eleanor had draped across her own shoulders.

"No, I couldn't. Then you'd get a sunburn," Gracie insisted.

Eleanor ignored Gracie's refusal and began to take off her wrap.

"Please, I'd like you to wear it. Your skin is already so burned."

Gracie began to decline again, but Eleanor persisted.

"I'll tell you what, we'll share it. You wear it for a while, and then I'll take a turn. How does that sound?"

Gracie smiled over at the sweet woman across from her. She wanted to refuse altogether, but her shoulders were already red and tender, and there were still several hours of daylight left.

Eleanor handed Gracie the wrap and then turned her attention to her granddaughter. Madison lay sleeping on the floor of the boat. She was using one life jacket for a pillow, while two other life jackets had been draped from one bench seat to the other above her, making a shield from the sun. Madison was curled up into a little ball and seemed to be sleeping peacefully. Before she had fallen asleep in her father's arms, she had cried that she was thirsty and wanted to go home. Sam had looked helplessly down at her. He had nothing to give her. The sparse water rations were not to be given out again until evening.

Everyone was grateful when the little girl had finally fallen asleep. It was not that they minded the crying. It was just a scary reminder of how, with each passing hour, their situation was becoming increasingly more critical.

"Are they your only grandchildren?" Gracie asked as she placed the wrap across her tender shoulders.

"No, but they are my youngest. I have two teenage grandsons from my eldest son. Both of them tower at least two feet over me." Eleanor beamed proudly. "When they were little, every time they would visit me, they would stand right next to me to measure how tall they'd grown. Of course, it didn't take them long to pass me up."

Gracie smiled. Eleanor could not have been much over five feet tall, if that. Then Gracie looked out across the water. Her smile quickly faded.

"I hope I live long enough to be a grandma."

"I'm sure a rescue ship is on its way at this very minute," Eleanor said.

Gracie nodded and then looked back out across the ocean. "I hope you're right," she said, trying to force herself to believe it. "For all our sakes."

* * *

Pete sat down next to Gracie and then shrugged his shoulders.

"We've tried everything, but we just can't get the fish to bite."

Gracie looked across the boat to Flip. He was still sitting next to the fishing pole, but he looked noticeably discouraged.

"Maybe you'll have more luck in an hour, when the sun starts to go down," Gracie began. "I've heard my dad say that's when the fish really start biting."

"Well, I won't tell you what *I've* heard," Pete said, keeping his voice low.

"What?" Gracie asked, a little concerned by his tone.

"Once, when I was hanging around the docks, I overheard a few of the fishermen talking about a time when they were having trouble getting their catch. They said that one of the guys aboard thought it was probably because a shark was following them."

Gracie, who had been leaning against the side of the boat, shot out of her position like a bullet. Then she twisted around sharply to search the water around them.

"That night," Pete continued in a hushed tone, "they spotted three sharks in the water not twenty feet from them. They trailed them for most of the night, but in the morning they were gone. After that, the men were able to get their catch."

Gracie's eyes were wide, and the hair on the back of her neck was standing on end.

"But I wouldn't worry about it," Pete continued. "Just because we haven't caught a fish yet doesn't mean there are sharks around."

"I wouldn't be so sure of that."

Pete whirled around. Gary had slid in next to them unnoticed. He now scooted in so close to Pete that their shoulders were almost touching. He was staring Pete right in the eyes.

"You been telling this girl a bunch of stories about sharks?" Then he glanced at Gracie. "Sometimes young boys can get a little carried away with their wild tales when trying to impress the ladies. Besides, if there are any sharks out there, we could always do what the old sailors used to do. If they noticed that sharks were following them, they accepted it as a bad sign and they'd throw one of their own men overboard to satisfy the sharks."

If Gracie had been horrified before, she was reeling now. Both she and Pete stared at Gary with their mouths wide open. Gary threw his head back and laughed so loud that everyone aboard turned to look.

"Don't worry, Petey," he continued, his voice now so hushed that only Gracie and Pete could hear him. "I don't think there's going to be any need to toss someone in for bait, do you?" Then, without waiting for an answer, he turned to Gracie. "Looks like the cat's got his tongue."

Gracie and Pete watched as Gary got up and made his way back to the other end of the boat. Gracie had that same creepy-crawly feeling she usually got right after finding a big spider. She looked at Pete, but he wouldn't meet her gaze; he just stared out across the ocean.

* * *

Gracie huddled close to Pete. He seemed nervous, though he had relaxed considerably since Gary, who sat at the far end of the boat, had fallen asleep.

"What is it?" Kaitlyn asked, looking curiously from Pete to Gracie.

Gracie did not even look at Kaitlyn. She kept her eyes glued on Pete.

"He doesn't really work on the ship, does he?"

Kaitlyn's head jerked around to look at Pete.

Pete hesitated as he shot a frightened glance down to the other side of the boat. Then slowly he began to shake his head.

"I knew it!" Gracie exclaimed.

"What are you talking about?" Kaitlyn asked, still not grasping exactly what was going on.

"Gary doesn't work for the cruise lines," Gracie said flatly.

"*What?*"

Gracie put her finger to her mouth. "Shhh! You're going to wake him."

Kaitlyn scooted in closer, her eyes glancing between the two of them.

"Pete wasn't afraid that Gary was going to turn him in on the ship," Gracie whispered. "Gary was the reason that Pete was scared in the first place."

Kaitlyn looked down to the far end of the boat, still trying to put the pieces together.

"I don't understand."

"Gary works the docks, loading and unloading ships," Pete offered, keeping his voice low. "But he's really just a crook." The words were spat out with contempt.

Kaitlyn's mind immediately went to her stolen purse.

"How did you get mixed up with him in the first place?" Gracie asked, crinkling her nose in disdain.

"He found me hanging around the fishing boats. He accused me of stealing and threatened to turn me in to the police."

"Were you?" Gracie asked flat out.

"No," Pete blurted out. "I just like going to the docks. My mom used to take me there, and we would watch the fishermen unload their catch. She loved the ocean."

"What happened to her?" Kaitlyn asked gently.

Pete shifted his dark eyes toward Kaitlyn. "She died a couple of years ago. Now it's just me and my dad."

"I'm sorry," she said as she reached out and touched his arm.

"So what were you doing aboard the ship?" Gracie whispered.

"Gary threatened me. Said that if I didn't help him with a job he had, he'd say he caught me stealing. I didn't trust him, but I didn't think I had much choice." Pete quickly glanced around the lifeboat to make sure that no one was listening. "Gary hid me between a few crates of frozen desserts and wheeled me aboard."

"I wish I were hiding between crates of cheesecakes, chocolate eclairs, and pound cake about now," Gracie said as her own stomach rumbled.

"Gary wouldn't let me eat until the job was done," Pete grumbled.

"Your father has no idea where you're at, then?" Kaitlyn broke in.

Pete shook his head. "He knew that I went to the docks, but—"

"There's something out there!"

The three of them, along with everyone else aboard, turned to look at Donald.

"Look!" Donald shouted, pointing to what appeared to be a small dot off in the horizon.

All eyes turned toward the tiny object off in the distance.

"What is it?" Gracie asked.

"Maybe it's another lifeboat," Kaitlyn exclaimed, the adrenaline now surging through her.

"It's too far away to be certain," Flip admitted. "But I'll bet you're right."

Everyone instinctively began yelling and waving their hands in that direction. Benton stood up on one of the benches and began waving his arms frantically. His mother reached up and grabbed his arm to pull him down.

"If you're not careful, young man, you'll end up in the ocean," she gently scolded.

"Listen to your mother, little man," his father quickly agreed. Then Sam jumped up and began waving his own arms.

Flip quickly detached the fishing string, handed the oar to Donald, and pulled the line in from the water. Then he grabbed hold of another oar that had been placed across the bench seats.

"Come on, if we start rowing, maybe we can make it to them by nightfall."

* * *

Kaitlyn watched anxiously as their boat approached the other lifeboat. After two hours of rowing, they were still too far away to make out the people aboard. At least they were now sure that the object was definitely a lifeboat. The sun had gone down a short time ago, but thanks to a full moon and clear night sky, they were still able to make out the silhouette of the other boat.

A full day of being out to sea with very little to eat or drink, combined with the rowing, was definitely wearing them down. Gary and Sam were now at the oars. Kaitlyn could feel the tightness in her arms from her own twenty-minute turn. Kaitlyn had been paired up to row with Rhonda, who obviously was not accustomed to manual labor. First she complained that her arms hurt, then when that didn't earn her the response she wanted, she grumbled that the oars were making blisters on her hands. Finally, after about ten minutes of nonstop whining, Donald had chivalrously volunteered to take her place, even though he had already had his own turn. Kaitlyn shook her head just thinking about it. Usually Kaitlyn didn't let people get under her skin, but she was exhausted, and her own arms burned from overexertion. She looked down at the huge blisters now on her hands. This was a time when everyone who was able needed to do their share. Eleanor had even offered—or rather insisted—that she take a turn, although that had won her a unanimous *no* from everyone aboard. They might have been tired, but they were not about to let a sixty-year-old grandmother row.

"It looks like someone is waving at us," Donald said.

Kaitlyn looked out across the night, straining her eyes to see the figure, but could not make out anything other than the boat. They were still just too far away. They all stared into the darkness, waiting pensively as the gap between the boats lessened. Kaitlyn could hear Gracie pleading under her breath.

"Oh, please, let it be Amber. Let her still be alive."

Kaitlyn reached over and squeezed her hand.

"Gracie, don't get your hopes up. The chances of her being in that boat . . ." She let her comment trail off, not wanting to hear her own words, hoping herself that Amber was still somewhere out there alive.

"Hello!" Sam stopped rowing and called out. "Can anyone hear me?"

Everyone grew silent as they listened for any response over the lapping waves.

"Hello! Can you hear me?" Sam shouted even louder, cupping his hands around his mouth. Again, if there was an answer, the night breeze caught it and whisked it from them.

Sam turned to Gary. "Start rowing! We've got to get closer," he commanded.

Gary and Sam started digging their oars into the ocean with every ounce of strength that they had left, but since the sun had gone down, the wind had picked up and the waves had intensified, making rowing increasingly more difficult.

"The current is pulling us back. Row harder!" Sam barked to Gary, even though his own strength appeared to be slipping.

Flip quickly jumped in and switched places with Gary while Donald relieved Sam. But despite their efforts, the current was separating them. The lifeboat that only minutes ago had been within eyesight was now receding into the night.

Gracie buried her face in her hands and began to cry, while Kaitlyn stared numbly into the darkness. She watched helplessly as the boat slipped farther and farther from their view until it finally disappeared completely. Flip and Donald fought the current for another hour until they had to stop from exhaustion.

"We were so close," Flip cried as he dropped his oar to the floor.

Nobody said a word. There was nothing to say.

That night Kaitlyn curled up into a ball on the floor of the boat. She willed sleep to come so that she would not have to feel the gnawing pain enveloping her, but her mind would not slow down enough to allow it. Why had they seen the boat in the first place just to have it snatched away? It all seemed so cruel. Kaitlyn looked up at the stars above her. Her eyes seemed drawn to the North Star. It shone down lustrously, constant, immovable, seemingly oblivious to their situation. Kaitlyn shook her head. Somewhere out there her parents and Greg could see those same stars and maybe, just maybe, Amber was seeing them too.

# CHAPTER 16

"Wake up, wake up!" Gracie shouted.

Kaitlyn blinked her eyes as she tried to focus on the figure before her.

"It's the lifeboat," Gracie persisted excitedly.

Kaitlyn sat straight up, almost hitting her head on the bench next to her.

"Look!"

Kaitlyn turned to look in the direction Gracie was pointing. Kaitlyn could easily see that it was a boat, but it was still too far away to clearly make out the passengers.

"I spotted it first thing this morning," Pete broke in.

He had a grin on his face that, if it got any bigger, would risk bursting his cheeks. Kaitlyn threw her arms around him and kissed him on the cheek.

"Good job, Pete!"

Kaitlyn turned her attention back to the approaching boat. The waves that had separated them last night seemed to be pulling them together this morning, and Flip and Donald were at the oars giving it all they had. Streams of sweat trickled down their faces, and large patches of perspiration dampened the backs of their shirts and under their arms. They were not about to lose the boat a second time. Kaitlyn was amazed that they had the energy to do it; but if they felt like she did at this minute, they had enough adrenaline to swim halfway to China. Last night she had gone to sleep feeling that there was no hope of seeing the lifeboat again, and yet this morning, here it was, just like a brightly colored package on Christmas morning. Kaitlyn was just about to call out to the boat when she heard it. At first it was so soft that she thought it was the wind, but then it came again a little louder.

"They're calling to us," Kaitlyn said excitedly. "Shh, listen."

"Hello," came a faint cry from across the water.

Kaitlyn let out a cry of joy, but it only mixed in with all the other shouts and cheers. Kaitlyn leaned over to Gracie.

"Can you see her?"

Gracie shook her head.

Despite the sun in their eyes, they could see that the other lifeboat, though the same size as their own, was not fully loaded with passengers.

"Hello," came the voice again, now only a few hundred feet away. "Is everyone all right?"

Kaitlyn grabbed Gracie's shoulder as the realization hit her. "Gracie, it's Matthew!"

Gracie called out his name, and Matthew instantly began waving his arms.

"It *is* him," Kaitlyn shouted, the excitement within her almost more than she could bear. "He made it! He's alive."

The girls were crying and laughing, and everyone aboard was cheering. None of them knew Matthew; they didn't have to. After thirty or so hours at sea, this was a sweet victory for everyone.

Kaitlyn turned back toward Matthew. She was not sure that she was ready to ask the next question, but at the same time, she had to know.

"What about Amber?" she called out hesitantly. "Is she with you?"

Kaitlyn held her breath as she waited for Matthew's response. Everyone aboard was silent. They seemed instinctively to realize the importance of his answer. Just then a lazy cloud slid right in front of the sun. The blinding rays that had prevented them from seeing clearly were instantly gone, revealing the boat's contents. Matthew was standing at the front, and a couple of beat-up wooden boxes were lying on the bottom of the craft. Kaitlyn's eyes ran the entire length of the lifeboat searching for Amber, but she couldn't see anyone else aboard. Kaitlyn's eyes locked on Matthew. The tears now flowed unrestrained down her cheeks. All that was left was for him to confirm the obvious. Matthew's face was filled with compassion, but he had just a hint of a smile. He turned his head as if to look at the floor of the boat, then he looked back at Kaitlyn.

"Kaitlyn, I found her," he said.

\* \* \*

Kaitlyn dipped the cloth into the water and then wrung it out tightly. She wanted to get as much salt water out of it as possible so that it would not sting when she put it back on Amber's legs. They needed something cool to keep the swelling down. Both of Amber's legs had been crushed just below the knee. Though the bones were not exposed, she also had numerous gaping lacerations from the ship's ceiling caving in on her. Kaitlyn looked over her shoulder at Amber, who was lying lengthwise between the bench seats on the floor of Matthew's boat. She was in bad shape, but at least she was alive.

Kaitlyn squeezed the rag one last time and then made her way back over to Amber. Gracie sat beside Amber, holding her hand, while Matthew rummaged through a half-empty first-aid kit that had been stashed in a storage compartment under one of the bench seats.

Kaitlyn tried to smile and look as positive as possible when she sat down. Amber had lost a lot of blood and was very weak. Kaitlyn gently placed the wet cloth over the open wounds. Amber grunted and then clenched her teeth.

"I'm sorry," Kaitlyn said as she reached over and grabbed Amber's other hand.

Kaitlyn looked over to Gracie for help reassuring Amber, but Gracie was watching Flip. The two boats had been tied together by a rope at their bows, and Flip had just climbed from what they had all deemed the supply boat back into the main boat. When he climbed back into the supply boat, he was carrying Eleanor's purse. Kaitlyn had to admit he did look kind of funny. Here was this masculine guy toting a frilly pink purse. Kaitlyn and Gracie both watched curiously as he took the purse over to Matthew and then took something out of it. Kaitlyn couldn't tell exactly what the guys were doing because Flip and Matthew had their backs partially to them, but when they turned around, Kaitlyn's stomach fell. Flip was holding a needle and trying to thread it from a white spool he had taken from Eleanor's purse.

Kaitlyn looked down at the stained rags that lay across Amber's legs. She didn't even need to ask what Flip planned to do with the needle. They had to stitch Amber's wounds, or she would run a greater risk of infection. Kaitlyn also knew that they didn't have anything for pain. She looked over at Gracie, who also appeared very much aware of what was about to take place. Kaitlyn squeezed Amber's hand and then bent down to look her right in the face.

"I'm sorry, Amber," Kaitlyn began, "but this is going to hurt."

Amber's eyes were wide and her whole body was trembling. She swallowed hard, then closed her eyes and turned her head away. Matthew took his place next to Gracie, while Flip sat down next to Kaitlyn. The two men had already determined that Flip would do the sewing and the three of them would hold her down. Flip took a bottle of hydrogen peroxide out of the first-aid kit while Matthew tenderly took the damp rags off Amber's legs. The bleeding had stopped, but the wounds were oozing. Flip poured the peroxide over the needle and then poured the remainder over Amber's legs. The wounds immediately began to foam. Kaitlyn could see that Amber was biting her lip to keep from screaming.

"Just squeeze my hand if it helps," Kaitlyn whispered in her ear.

After Flip had cleaned the wounds the best he could, he looked at the three of them to signal that he was about to start the stitching. Kaitlyn and Gracie got a firm hold on Amber's arms, while Matthew held down her legs. When Flip saw that they had a good grip, he bent over to begin. Kaitlyn had to turn away, but she knew the second that Flip inserted the needle. Amber let out a blood-curdling scream and her whole body jerked forward. Kaitlyn and Gracie had to use all of their strength just to hold her down.

"Pete," Flip called out. "Get over here. We need your help."

Pete, who had been watching the whole thing from the main boat, jumped up as quickly as he could and climbed into the supply boat. Then he took his place next to Flip to help hold Amber's legs down. He did not seem as fazed by what was happening as they were. He bent his face right down to watch Flip work. Kaitlyn, on the other hand, was already feeling weak from not eating and only drinking a small cup of water, and she felt suddenly queasy. She leaned close to Amber and tried to speak as comfortingly and calmly as she could.

With each stitch Amber would grit her teeth and twist her face in pain. Kaitlyn wanted to do something, anything, but there was nothing that she could do. She just sat there helplessly and watched as Amber grew increasingly pale and finally passed out.

\* \* \*

After Flip had finished with both of Amber's legs, he decided to stitch up Karen's shoulder. Gracie agreed to help him, so Flip grabbed another needle from the sewing kit Eleanor carried in her purse while Gracie picked up the last bottle of hydrogen peroxide. Then the two of them climbed into the other boat. Pete had already left to go back and watch the fishing pole. This was their second day out to sea, and they were all getting desperate for something substantial to eat. Amber had not come around yet, so that left only Kaitlyn and Matthew in the supply boat. Matthew positioned himself to shade Amber from the sun while Kaitlyn finished bandaging her legs with a couple of Ace bandages she had found in the first-aid kit.

"You know," Kaitlyn began, "what you did was pretty incredible."

Matthew lifted a questioning gaze to hers.

"Going back into the ship and looking for Amber," Kaitlyn continued. "You risked your own life for someone you didn't even know."

Matthew's cheeks instantly flushed.

"I'm just glad that I found her," he replied.

Matthew looked right at her, and for the first time Kaitlyn noticed just how blue his eyes were. There was something almost penetrating about them.

"Where are you from?" Matthew asked.

"Minnesota. My mom and dad both grew up just north of St. Paul."

"Do you have any brothers or sisters?"

"I have one brother, Kenny. He's a mess."

Kaitlyn stopped, surprised that her emotions were suddenly at the surface. She turned away, not wanting Matthew to see her like this.

"Let me guess," Matthew offered with a tender smile. "He borrows things that he never returns, and if he does, it's stained, sticky, or has an unexplainable, nonremovable odor. He also has memory lapses. He has no idea where he tossed your forty-five-dollar calculus book after he used it as a coaster for a grease-drenched, super-sized hamburger, but he has a crystal-clear memory when it comes to the ding you put in the family car. Does any of this sound familiar?"

"Painfully," Kaitlyn giggled. "I take it that you have a brother?"

"I have three, and one sister."

"There are *five* children in your family?" Kaitlyn exclaimed. "That would definitely bring a whole new dimension to shared bathroom space. Fortunately, Kenny's idea of hair care is a ratty blue baseball cap, so I've never had to worry about sharing with him, but Leslie was a different story. She had to wash, gel, blow-dry, and then primp. On rare occasions—like a bad-hair day—the whole process had to be repeated and then reexamined."

Matthew laughed. "So you have a sister too?"

"I had one. Leslie was killed in a car accident a few months ago."

Matthew's face fell. "I'm sorry."

"So now there's just the four of us, unless you want to count my boyfriend Greg."

Kaitlyn felt a little uncomfortable even bringing Greg up, but at the same time, she was a little curious to see Matthew's response. His expression never changed. He just continued watching her, as if he were genuinely interested in what she had to say.

"So what brought you on the cruise?"

Kaitlyn smirked. "Spring break. But Amber got sick, I got robbed, and then we had to escape onto little lifeboats in the middle of a hurricane. Some break!"

Matthew threw his head back and laughed. "I don't think you'll have to worry about the cruise line using you for their travel brochures."

Kaitlyn began to giggle. "*What?* No commercial endorsements? No photo shoots with me and my life jacket?"

"Wait a minute, did you say you were robbed?" Matthew asked, just now absorbing that detail.

"When we were at dinner, someone came into our cabin and stole my purse with all my cash and traveler's checks."

"You're kidding!" Matthew shook his head. "Did you report it?"

"Yeah, but I think it got put aside so that we could evacuate a burning ship."

Kaitlyn leaned her head back and stared up at the cumulus clouds above them.

"What about you? Where are you from?"

"I'm from a little farther west than you. Vail, Colorado. It's a small town up in the middle of the Rockies. My family owns a bait-and-tackle shop up there. We have a little sign on the front door that I made a few years ago. It says, 'If you're gone fishin'; come on in, if not, we're out to lunch.' My dad was so proud of that homemade plaque. You would have thought I'd brought home a Pulitzer Prize." Matthew smiled and then shook his head. "The store itself isn't much, but I love it. My dad walks around all day with a fishing hat covered with fly hooks and fishing lures and he gets paid for it."

"Your dad sounds like a character."

Matthew laughed. "Well, let's just say my mom is definitely the more conventional of the two. Growing up in Salt Lake City, in Utah, she wasn't quite convinced she would like living in a small town. Now I don't think you could get her to leave. There's just something about that place."

"Maybe it's the people," Kaitlyn said softly.

Matthew smiled thoughtfully. "Maybe."

He was still sitting next to Kaitlyn, but his mind appeared to be hundreds of miles away, somewhere up in the middle of the Rockies. Kaitlyn glanced over at Amber. Though she was still sleeping, it didn't appear to be restful. She would moan each time that she moved and contort her face in pain. Kaitlyn reached over and picked up the cloth that she had used to wash Amber's legs. She dipped the bloody rag into the ocean and began to swirl it around. Matthew immediately reached over and grabbed the cloth from the water.

"What are you doing?" Kaitlyn asked, looking at him quizzically. "I was going to wash that out and put it back on Amber's legs to help the swelling."

"Blood attracts sharks."

Kaitlyn's eyes opened wide as she looked down at the wet rag Matthew had tossed on the floor. It still had traces of blood mixed with the draining water.

"I'm sorry," Kaitlyn said as she shook her head, disgusted with herself for being so careless.

"It's okay," Matthew said with a gentle smile. "We just need to play it safe."

Kaitlyn could feel her stomach knotting with tension as she looked out across the water. It looked so tranquil, yet there was a whole dangerous world hidden in its depths.

"So," Kaitlyn began as she turned back to Matthew, anxious to get her mind on something else, "is working in the family tackle shop what you plan to do when you grow up?"

"What do you mean 'when I grow up'?" Matthew asked sternly. Then he laughed. "This all probably sounds pretty dull to you," he said.

"Actually, it sounds nice," Kaitlyn admitted, a little surprised that she meant it. "Maybe one day I'll drop in. That is, if we ever get off this lifeboat."

Matthew studied Kaitlyn thoughtfully. Kaitlyn could see his mind racing, and she wished that she could eavesdrop for just a minute on his thoughts.

"Colorado is a long way from here," Matthew began soberly. "Besides, I don't think that a certain guy back in Minnesota would approve of that idea."

# CHAPTER 17

Kaitlyn watched anxiously as Flip passed the water jug to each person aboard the lifeboat. She licked her dry lips as each of them took their turn. Her stomach had been growling all day, but it was thirst that had occupied her thoughts. She couldn't help thinking about all the water that she wasted at home. Her father had lectured her several times about her long bubble baths, filled almost to overflowing, or about letting the tap water run down the sink while she brushed her teeth. If she could just have several gulps of that wasted water now . . .

Kaitlyn pulled her hair back from her face. The wind had picked up a lot over the last few minutes. She could feel the choppiness of the water below her. Kaitlyn turned to look at Morgan. Madison was crying as Morgan struggled to console her. The toddler had cried a lot that day; she didn't understand what was happening, except that she was hungry and thirsty and wanted to go home.

Kaitlyn turned her attention back to Flip as he handed the jug to Gary, who lifted the jug to his lips and drank as if there were an endless supply. Flip immediately reached out to grab the jug from him.

"Hey," Flip snapped. "That's enough. Not everyone's had a turn."

Gary just ignored him and continued to drink the water greedily. Sam instantly jumped to his feet and pulled the jug from Gary's lips. "What's the matter with you?" Sam growled.

Without a word Gary reached out and shoved Sam. Sam tripped over the bench seat behind him and fell awkwardly onto the floor. He missed hitting his head on the edge of the boat by just inches. Before anyone could move, Sam was back on his feet. He barreled toward

Gary fists first, landing a well-placed punch right in the center of Gary's face. Gary's nose looked like it had just sprung a leak. He wiped at the blood and then lunged at Sam. Everyone was scrambling to get out of the way. Gracie was shouting at them to stop rocking the boat. At that very minute the boat rocked just enough that both Gary and Sam lost their balance. With arms and legs flailing to try to stop the inevitable, the two of them toppled over the edge of the boat and splashed into the water.

Flip shook his head in disgust as he turned to Matthew and Donald. "Help me get them back in the boat."

As Kaitlyn watched Gary and Sam being pulled back into the boat, Pete walked over and handed her the water jug. She gratefully lifted it to her lips. She was the last to drink, so the remainder was hers—which was only one swallow. She held the water in her cheeks for a minute, savoring the wetness of the tepid liquid, before letting it slide down her parched throat. Her body longed for more. They had probably been at sea for close to forty hours now with very little water and only her candy bar and bag of spicy beef jerky to share. Reluctantly, Kaitlyn set the empty jug down and looked at the faces of the others aboard the main boat. This had been the last drop of water that they had, and now it was gone. She could tell from the expressions around her that they all knew their only hope was to be rescued soon.

Kaitlyn's head jerked around as someone from the other end of the boat jumped to their feet.

"A shark!" Pete screamed, pointing to a spot underwater not ten feet from their boat.

Kaitlyn sprang to her feet to look over the side of the boat. At first all she could see was the sparkling reflection of the sun on the water, then, as if coming out of a light fog, the dark figure rose to the surface. Kaitlyn stared into the dark, unfeeling eyes of the shark. She instinctively lunged toward the center of the boat just as the shark brushed the bottom. Everyone was screaming and scrambling to get as far from the edges as possible. Kaitlyn could feel her whole body tingling with fear and adrenaline.

"Stop screaming!" Flip yelled. "You'll only attract its attention." Then Flip turned to Pete. "Get over by Karen, *now.*"

As she sat next to Gracie, Kaitlyn was only vaguely aware of Karen's moans. Gracie was in a fetal position in the center of the main boat, sobbing like a child. Kaitlyn put her arm around her friend in an effort to comfort her, as well as to calm her own fear. As she did, the shark slammed into the bow of the boat, causing everyone to start screaming again, despite Flip's pleading to stop. Little Madison wailed as she clung to her mother.

"The shark punctured the boat," Pete called out as he pointed to a four-inch crack near the front of the boat where seawater was quickly trickling into the craft.

"We've got to stop that leak," Flip yelled.

He was teetering in the boat with an oar raised, as if to strike the enormous creature that was now circling their boat. Kaitlyn's eyes fell on a pile of wool blankets they had been using to shield themselves from the sun, but when she tried to stand, Gracie grabbed her, digging her nails deep into Kaitlyn's flesh.

"Don't leave me," Gracie screamed.

"Would someone shut her up?" Rhonda shouted.

Kaitlyn grabbed Gracie squarely by the shoulders.

"Gracie, if we don't stop that leak, we'll sink."

"It's okay," Donald said as he grabbed ahold of Kaitlyn's arm. "You stay with her. I'll try and slow down the leak."

Kaitlyn watched gratefully as Donald hurried to the bow of the boat, scooping up a blanket on his way.

"Look, there's another shark!" Sam yelled. He was holding Benton in one arm and pointing with the other.

Kaitlyn closed her eyes and began to pray. She could hear the words coming out of her mouth, but her voice sounded much higher than usual and there was a pleading in her words that she had not heard from her lips in a long time. Then, as if a light had just turned on in a dark room, a thought brought her to her feet. Gracie immediately reached out and clung to the tattered pieces of Kaitlyn's grass skirt.

"The flare gun," Kaitlyn said breathlessly. They had been saving it as a last resort, or if they saw anything in the distance that could miss them due to their small size.

After they had stitched Amber's legs, she and Matthew had gone through all the boxes that were left in the supply boat after the storm.

Most of the boxes were filled with extra life jackets, along with a few blankets. The lifeboat must have served as an emergency storage for the ship, because along with all the other supplies was a box with a flare gun and several flares.

Matthew must have had the same idea, because he was already heading to where the two boats had been tied together. Kaitlyn's eyes went to Amber, who was still unconscious. Even if they could wake her, there was no way she could protect herself. Kaitlyn pulled her skirt from Gracie's grasp and followed behind Matthew.

Matthew quickly climbed into the supply boat, but Kaitlyn stopped to stare at the twelve-inch gap between the two boats. She could feel her legs trembling beneath her as she tried to focus on getting to Amber and not on the terror that was pulsing through her. Just as she was about to leap across the gap into the supply boat, Rhonda let out a shrill scream. Kaitlyn's head instinctively jerked around to see what was wrong, but as she did, her foot caught on the rope that connected the two boats, and she lost her balance. In one terrifying moment, she could feel herself falling, and she was not sure if she would land in the supply boat or the water below. She let out a scream and then closed her eyes, too frightened to see what would come next.

Her upper body hit hard into the bow of the supply boat, but her legs splashed into the water. Kaitlyn scrambled desperately to grab hold of something to pull herself up. Everyone was screaming, but the worst expression of fear was on Matthew's face. He immediately bent over to help her, but his eyes were fixed on the water behind her. Kaitlyn wanted to look over her shoulder, but there was no need. The look on Matthew's face told her all she needed to know. She closed her eyes, unable to do anything else. Then with one heave, Matthew lifted her out of the water. They both crashed to the floor as a shark smashed into the bow of the boat where the two boats were connected. Kaitlyn's head shot around to where the shark had hit. The boat was still intact, but the shark's collision had caused a buckle in the metal, producing a sharp, three-inch protrusion just down from the bow.

Matthew lay on the floor of the boat gasping for air. He slowly propped himself up on his elbow and looked over at her, his chest heaving as he fought to catch his breath. Kaitlyn could see exasperation mixed with concern on his face.

"Do you have any idea how close that shark came?" he asked breathlessly. Then he closed his eyes as if to erase the image from his mind.

"I'm sorry," Kaitlyn whispered, "but I couldn't just leave Amber over here by herself."

Matthew looked over at Amber. She was still unresponsive, though her position had been jostled with all the movement.

"The rope's been cut," Pete shouted.

Matthew sat straight up and then sprang to his feet. Although the rope that had connected the two boats together was still attached to the supply boat that Kaitlyn and Matthew were in, the end that had been connected to the main boat was now trailing behind them in the water. The sharks had severed the half-inch-thick nylon rope as if it were a tiny shoestring. Kaitlyn felt sick. That could have been her.

"They're coming again," Rhonda screamed.

Gary immediately picked up an oar and began frantically digging into the ocean in an attempt to get away from the sharks.

"Stop!" Flip shouted to Gary. "You'll make it worse."

Gary just ignored him and continued to plunge the oar into the water, using all of his strength to manipulate the ten-foot oar. Sam reached for Gary's oar, but Gary shoved him back and continued digging in with all he had. He had no intention of giving up the oar without a fight. This time Donald got to his feet and both he and Sam jerked it from Gary's hands. By this time, the boats were almost a full boat-length apart. Matthew quickly picked up the excess rope that was left after tying the two boats together so he could toss it over to Flip. Only fifteen feet of length now remained of the twenty-foot rope.

Flip immediately set down his oar so that he could catch it. When Matthew tossed the rope, it landed in the water just to the left of the main boat. Matthew pulled the rope back, so that he could try again. Kaitlyn scanned the water, but from the screams coming from the main boat, she knew that the sharks had continued circling there.

Flip had to pick up the oar again, because the sharks were getting dangerously close. Kaitlyn and Matthew both watched in horror as

Flip and Sam stabbed their oars into the water. Kaitlyn could hear Gracie shrieking each time the boat tilted as the two men attempted to strike the attacking sharks. Kaitlyn could feel the burning in her stomach quickly turn to bile in the back of her throat.

Matthew began to wave his arms toward the main lifeboat.

"Somebody's got to catch this rope. We don't have any oars over here. We have nothing to defend ourselves with."

Kaitlyn's eyes shot over to the tent that they had made for Benton and Madison in the main boat. They'd made it from some of the blankets and both of the oars from the supply boat. She had completely forgotten.

"*Please* help us!" Kaitlyn screamed. "Don't leave us stranded out here without any oars."

Flip signaled for Matthew to toss it again. Matthew didn't hesitate for a minute. Kaitlyn watched anxiously as the rope hit the water just a few feet in front of the boat. Donald leaped toward the rope in an attempt to grab it, which sent their boat swaying. Gary sprang to his feet and grabbed Donald by the collar.

"What are you trying to do, *kill* us?" Gary growled. "I'm not going to die just so that you can save *them*," he shouted, gesturing over to Kaitlyn and Matthew.

"But . . ." Donald protested.

"I said sit back down and don't get up again," Gary hissed as he shoved Donald down hard. Donald's eyes were huge with a mixture of both fear and shock.

"The last thing we need is to start attacking each other," Sam shouted at Gary.

Gary instantly turned on Sam. Kaitlyn and Matthew could not see Gary's face or hear what he was saying, since his back was to them, but whatever he said sent Sam back a step.

"What did he say?" Matthew asked incredulously.

"I don't know. I couldn't hear him."

They both turned their attention to Flip, who was calling over to them.

"Matthew, forget about getting the boats back together right now. Get the flare gun and some flares so we can shoot the sharks."

Matthew scrambled over to the box that held the flares and threw it open. At first he stared down at the box in disbelief, then began frantically digging through it.

Kaitlyn could feel her stomach fall. Earlier that day she had seen Sam over in the main boat showing the empty flare gun to little Benton. She had forgotten all about it.

"It's over in the other boat," Kaitlyn said weakly.

Before Matthew could say anything, Flip held up the flare gun.

"Matthew, throw the flares. We've got the gun over here."

Matthew reached down and grabbed the three flares. With the combination of Gary's rowing and the choppiness of the water, the gap between the two boats had spread to about two full boat lengths. Matthew stood at the edge of the boat and held one flare up to signal that he was ready. After Flip waved his arms, Matthew threw the flare. Kaitlyn held her breath as the flare flipped end over end in the air. Though Matthew had played baseball in high school, the flare was considerably lighter than a baseball, proving to be a less accurate throw. Flip reached out to grab it, but the wind caught it and whisked it out of his grasp. It hit the water not five feet in front of the boat. One of the sharks came within inches of the flare as it slipped from view into the darkness of the ocean.

Matthew picked up another flare and again tossed it as hard as he could toward the boat. Although all the men aboard now had their hands stretched out to try to catch the flare, it again missed its mark and splashed into the ocean. Pete leaned forward to try and grab the flare before it sank. Donald had to reach out and grab Pete by the shirt to keep him from falling in.

"Try again," Flip yelled, his voice beginning to sound desperate.

Matthew picked up the third flare and threw it with all that he had. The aim was right on target, but the boats were just too far away. The flare slipped into the depths of the ocean, along with the last of their hope of shooting the sharks.

"I'm sorry," Matthew cried, his voice heavy with disappointment.

Flip did not even respond; he just turned and began searching the water for the sharks. The other men followed his lead, while the women and children sat huddled in the middle of the boat. Kaitlyn and Matthew both sat down and watched helplessly from the supply boat. Matthew buried his face in his hands in frustration. Kaitlyn was just about to reach out and touch his shoulder when Matthew sprang to his feet.

"Flip, the knife!" Matthew yelled. "Get the knife."

Flip looked across the water to Matthew.

"Are you *crazy?* You want me to try and stab the sharks?"

Matthew shook his head impatiently.

"No! I mean *yes!* But not with your hand. Get the medical tape out of the first-aid kit and tape the knife to one of the oars."

Flip smiled broadly. "Matthew, you're a genius."

Kaitlyn and Matthew watched as Flip hurried over to the wooden bench that opened up into a supply compartment and threw it open. Flip stared blankly down at the empty compartment.

"It's not here. It must be in your boat," Flip called back.

Matthew's eyes flew to the first-aid kit that had been placed on the bench next to Amber.

"You're going to have to try and throw it to us," Flip called out. "If we start rowing over to you, we'll only continue to draw the sharks to us."

"It'll never make it," Matthew mumbled under his breath as he scanned the distance between the two boats.

Kaitlyn reached out and grabbed ahold of his arm. "Matthew, you can do it." Then, without waiting for him to respond, Kaitlyn grabbed the first-aid kit and handed it to him. "You've got to try."

Just as Matthew reached out to grab the kit from Kaitlyn, the main lifeboat exploded in screams. Matthew whirled around to see its stern rise several inches above the water and then crash back down.

"They're all going to die," Kaitlyn cried as she clung to Matthew's arm.

"Nobody's going to die," Matthew said as he took the first-aid kit from Kaitlyn. Then he looked back to the other lifeboat. "Flip, get ready to catch this," he called.

Flip, who was holding onto the side of the boat to keep his balance, waved a hand toward Matthew.

"Throw it, Matthew. Throw it *now!*"

Matthew clutched the box tightly in his hand. He had seen how the wind caught the flares because of their shape and weight. This throw had to be good. With a look of determination, he tossed it as hard as he could toward the main lifeboat. Kaitlyn held her breath as it soared through the air toward Flip's outstretched arms. Then, not five feet from the boat, the box dropped into the water with a splash. Almost as quickly as the kit submerged below the water, it popped back up. They all stared helplessly at the plastic box that now floated in the water just out of arm's reach.

"Try and pull it to you with the oar," Matthew shouted.

Sam immediately grabbed an oar and stretched it out toward the floating box. The oar came down right on top of the box, submerging it below the surface again. When it popped back up, it was out of reach of the oar.

"You're pushing it away," Gary barked.

Sam threw the oar down and then leaned over the side of the boat, frantically searching the water around the boat. The sharks had temporarily disappeared from sight. Then his eyes went to the first-aid kit that bobbed gently in the water. Without giving it a second thought, Sam bent down and began pulling off his shoes.

"If anything happens to me you make sure that my family makes it out alive," Sam said to Flip. "Do you hear me?"

"Sam, what are you doing?" Morgan screamed.

Sam turned back toward his wife. "Making sure that *you* live." His voice caught when he said the last part. Then he turned back toward the water and jumped in.

"Wait!" Flip screamed.

But it was too late. Sam was already in the water. Little Benton lunged toward his father, but Donald grabbed the boy in midair.

"They're coming back!" Rhonda screamed as she pointed to a spot off in the water about fifty feet from them.

"Start rowing," Flip yelled.

Donald quickly set Benton down and grabbed an oar while Pete and Gary dug their oars into the water. Morgan screamed and then buried her face in Eleanor's arms. Kaitlyn and Matthew stood helplessly watching the whole scene across from them in terror.

"We're going to have to create a diversion," Matthew said.

Kaitlyn turned to look at Matthew. His jaw was flexed and his fists were clutched tight. "We're going to have to get the sharks to come over to us."

"*What?*" Kaitlyn asked breathlessly.

"Start screaming!" Matthew demanded. "Scream as loud as you can, splash in the water, bang on the side of the boat. Do whatever you have to."

"Matthew, this is crazy," Kaitlyn cried.

Matthew looked up at the sky. His blue eyes were deep and flashing. He closed them just for a second, and Kaitlyn could see his lips moving. When he opened them, he had a look of resolution on his face. Then, without another word, Matthew dove into the water.

Kaitlyn did scream, but it was not to get the sharks' attention. She watched as Matthew broke through the surface of the water several feet out from their boat. Then her eyes flashed out across the water to Sam. He had just retrieved the first-aid kit and was throwing it over to Flip. Flip caught the box in both arms just like a linebacker.

"I got it," Flip screamed. "Now swim, Sam, swim."

Everyone in the main boat was screaming hysterically as they watched the sharks approaching Sam.

"Stop screaming," Matthew called out.

Flip's eyes quickly shot to Matthew as he bobbed up and down with the movement of the water.

"What are you doing?" Flip yelled to Matthew. "You're going to get yourself killed."

Matthew ignored Flip and began screaming at the top of his lungs while thrashing his arms around. At the same time, Kaitlyn doubled up her fist and began beating the side of the metal boat. It only took a second for everyone in the main boat to realize what Kaitlyn and Matthew were doing.

"Everyone be quiet," Flip shouted. "They're trying to divert the sharks."

Everyone on the main boat became deathly silent as they watched Sam swimming for his life toward them. Donald had his arms stretched out as far as they would go toward Sam, while Flip held onto Donald's belt loop.

Kaitlyn watched as Sam crossed the last of the distance to the main lifeboat. It took Donald and Pete using all the strength that they could muster to yank Sam's large water-soaked body back into the boat.

"The sharks are turning toward Matthew," Pete breathed.

"Matthew, swim," Flip yelled. "The sharks are headed right for you."

Kaitlyn immediately stopped banging on the side of the boat. She could feel her body tingling with fear.

"*Please,* Matthew," she begged. "Swim faster."

He was digging his arms into the water with giant, frantic strokes, but he was still no match for the quickness and agility of the Great Whites. It reminded Kaitlyn of one of those awful nightmares where, no matter how fast you're trying to run, compared to the bad guy, you're moving in slow motion.

Kaitlyn's eyes were glued on Matthew. She was only vaguely aware of the screams and pounding that were coming from the main boat. Matthew was now only three strokes from her, but despite the noise coming from the other boat, the sharks remained right behind him. As Kaitlyn reached her arm out to grab Matthew's outstretched hand, she could see one of the shark's enormous jaws. Each of the triangular-shaped teeth was jagged, and sharp enough to bite clear through bone. Kaitlyn closed her eyes and pulled with all that she had, combining her body weight with Matthew's momentum to propel him into the boat. Almost simultaneously, the side of the boat lifted out of the water. For one chilling moment, Kaitlyn thought that the boat was going to tip over. She held her breath as it teetered in the air before crashing back down with her, Matthew, and Amber securely inside. Kaitlyn lay at the bottom of the boat, almost too petrified to move, while Matthew struggled to drag himself to his knees. Kaitlyn could see his limbs trembling from both fear and exhaustion. She watched as he looked back up at the sky.

"Thank you," he whispered. "Thank you!" His body was shaking, but his voice was sure.

"I've got it," Flip yelled from the main boat. He held up an oar that now had Benton's knife taped to the end of it.

Matthew slowly lifted his arm to signal that he had heard Flip. Then he turned back to Kaitlyn, still fighting to catch his breath.

"Are you okay?" he asked.

"Shouldn't I be asking *you* that question?"

Matthew looked over at Amber. She was still unconscious and lying on the floor of the boat in an awkward position. He started to make his way over to her, but as he did, his leg gave way. Kaitlyn's eyes shot down to Matthew's leg. His uniform was ripped and saturated in blood.

"Matthew, you're bleeding."

Kaitlyn immediately lifted Matthew's pant leg to reveal a large slash in his calf. The wound was deep and bleeding profusely. Matthew looked as shocked by her discovery as she was. The adrenaline that had been surging through his body had obviously numbed his senses.

"I guess the shark was closer than I thought," Matthew said breathlessly.

"That couldn't have been the shark," Kaitlyn insisted. "You still have a leg."

Kaitlyn reached over and grabbed a blanket that lay on the floor, then she began to wrap it around the gash to try to stop the bleeding. Once she was done, her eyes went to the jagged buckle in the metal that the shark had made with the first attack. Matthew must have brushed his leg right over it when she'd pulled him into the boat. She glanced back at Matthew. His face was quickly draining of all its color.

"Matthew, you're going into shock."

"I'm fine," Matthew said weakly.

Kaitlyn looked down at the blanket that she had just wrapped around his leg. It was already soaked and dripping with blood. Kaitlyn stood wringing her hands as her eyes raced around the boat in search of something, anything, that could help Matthew. Then she looked over at the main lifeboat. She could hear the smacking sound of the oars hitting the water in an attempt to strike the sharks, and the shrill screams from those aboard. Then, in desperation, Kaitlyn looked off into the distance, searching in every direction for any sign of a rescue ship, but there was nothing. Helpless and beaten, Kaitlyn sank to the floor of the boat.

"Matthew, I don't know what else to do," she cried.

Matthew reached out and touched a finger to her lips. Then slowly he closed his eyelids. For a minute Kaitlyn wanted to reach over and shake him. Then, in a voice that was nothing more than a hoarse whisper, Matthew began to pray. Kaitlyn sat gawking down at him in amazement as he turned their fate over to God. When he was done, he reached down and began unbuckling his belt.

"Apply a tourniquet," he said as he handed her the belt.

Kaitlyn's hands were trembling as she took the belt. She tried to push the situation out of her mind and focus, to remain calm. That was the one thing that her CPR instructors had repeated over and over again. Kaitlyn took a deep breath. She could do this. She had to. Kaitlyn could feel her breathing steady. She glanced at Matthew's face. He looked white and clammy, and his eyelids were drooping.

"Matthew! Stay with me," Kaitlyn shouted.

Kaitlyn reached down and removed the blood-soaked blanket. For a minute she just stared down at the open wound. The bleeding wasn't stopping. It was coming in spurts as if an artery had been cut. Kaitlyn glanced up at his face. She could tell he was on the verge of passing out.

"Matthew, you've got to stay awake."

Matthew opened his eyes, though it looked like it took all of his strength to do it. Kaitlyn quickly wrapped the belt just above the wound and cinched it as tight as she could. Then she grabbed a dry blanket, placed it directly over the gash, and applied pressure.

"You're going to be okay," Kaitlyn said firmly. Then she reached over and took his hand. "Don't give up."

# CHAPTER 18

Three years of training at the Miami Institute of Oceanography made Flip well aware of the deadly capability of his opponent. Sharks were natural eating machines. Three rows of razor-sharp teeth lined jaws that were strong enough to snap a man in two. Flip stared down into the water below him with his oar raised above his head, waiting as if to spear anything that leapt from its depths. Donald stood opposite him to offset his weight and watch for any sign of sharks on that side. Gary sat at the bow and Pete and Sam at the stern, while everyone else remained in the center.

Flip could feel the sun's heat sear through his thin cotton T-shirt. Sweat had poured off him yesterday, but that was not the case today. Though the heat had not abated, his body lacked the fluids necessary to perspire properly, which seemed to raise his body temperature.

"I don't see them," Flip whispered.

"Maybe they're gone," Donald suggested eagerly.

Flip shook his head. "I wouldn't count on it."

Donald swallowed hard. "Do you really think that you can stop them with that?" Donald's eyes were fixed on the knife that was taped to the end of Flip's oar.

Gary threw his head back and snorted sarcastically. "Yeah, right."

"If you've got a better idea, Gary," Flip snapped. "Let's hear it."

"We could always do what the old sailors used to do," Pete mumbled under his breath.

Gary shot Pete a glance that could have melted a glacier. Tempers were beginning to rise. Flip, who usually had a long fuse, was finding it increasingly difficult to overlook Gary's behavior.

"That's enough from all of you," Eleanor said sternly as she cradled Madison's sobbing form in her arms.

"She's right," Flip began. "Let's take care of one monster at a time."

Gary's eyes flashed with hate. He instantly threw his oar down and lunged at Flip, but Sam caught him by the arm.

"Are you *crazy?* You'll get us all killed," Sam shouted as he held Gary back.

"The sharks," Morgan screamed.

Flip whirled back around to face the water. "Where?"

Sam instantly let go of Gary and reached for his oar.

"There," Morgan shouted, pointing down into the water just to the left of the stern.

They all watched as the sharks brushed the surface just feet from their boat. Flip looked down at his patched-together harpoon. Though he was annoyed by Gary's remark, Flip wasn't entirely certain himself that his weapon would work. He tightened his grip and equalized his footing. Then he took a deep breath. If these sharks got within reaching distance, he would have to be ready. He knew that lives could depend on it.

They all took their positions as the first shark headed straight for them. The smaller shark was taking the lead, but the larger was only feet behind. Eleanor shielded Madison in her arms, and Morgan took a firm grip on Benton. Gracie and Rhonda huddled next to Karen, but Flip was only vaguely aware of any of them. His eyes remained fixed on the approaching sharks. In a matter of seconds the first would be within striking distance. Flip could feel his limbs trembling, though he fought to control them. The beating of his heart intensified with each passing second until it seemed to consume his whole body.

"Make it count," Sam urged.

Flip held his breath as the first shark slid beneath the boat behind him. He barely had time to raise his oar before the shark reemerged from under the boat. In one sweeping motion, his heart thundering against his chest, Flip thrust the oar down into the water.

* * *

Kaitlyn slightly loosened the belt that was cinched tight just inches above the gash on Matthew's leg. Now that the bleeding had lessened, Kaitlyn didn't want to risk overrestricting the supply of blood. The adrenaline that had stopped Matthew from feeling the initial effects of the wound had also worn off. Kaitlyn could feel him flinch as she readjusted the belt.

"I'm sorry," she said gently.

"How does it look?"

"It's deep, almost to the bone. But trust me, the bleeding has slowed down *a lot*. You had me really scared for a minute there."

"You and me both," Matthew admitted. "But it's not over yet."

Kaitlyn's eyes grew wide. "What do you mean?"

"Once the bleeding totally stops," Matthew continued as he gripped the bench next to him, "I need you to do something for me."

Kaitlyn followed Matthew's gaze to the box where they had placed Eleanor's little beaded purse with her traveling sewing kit. Although Matthew was not suggesting anything that she had not already thought about, Kaitlyn could feel her stomach turn. How was she going to be able to stitch Matthew's leg when she recoiled at the very sight of them stitching Amber's?

"There were still a few clean needles," Matthew offered.

Kaitlyn brushed back a few wet strands of hair that fell across Matthew's forehead.

"For now, just lie back and try to relax."

Matthew took her firmly by the arm and looked her straight in the eyes. Kaitlyn could feel his gaze penetrating right through her.

"Kaitlyn, I *need* you to do this for me."

Kaitlyn wanted to pull away, to run and hide from all of this, but there was nowhere to go. Right now she was the only one who could help him. Kaitlyn nodded.

Matthew squeezed her arm gratefully and then closed his eyes.

"I don't think I've ever been this tired in my whole life."

"You just did a twenty-five-meter freestyle against a couple of man-eating sharks."

Matthew smiled. "When I told my dad that I would come back with a few fish stories, this is not what I had in mind."

* * *

Once Kaitlyn had stitched and wrapped Matthew's leg, the two of them leaned against the side of the boat and looked out across the ocean. Though Matthew was trying to downplay it, Kaitlyn knew that he was in a lot of pain. With the boats still separated by a couple of boat lengths, and Flip adamant that they should not take the chance of rowing over yet for fear of attracting the sharks, the two of them started talking. Kaitlyn wanted to help keep Matthew's mind off the pain. They talked for at least an hour about everything from family to their hopes for the future. Kaitlyn even opened up and told him about her concerns over her parents' relationship since Leslie's death. Matthew listened intently and contributed where he could, but for the most part he just let her get it all out. When she was finally finished, she sat back and looked at Matthew curiously.

"I can't believe I just told you all that. I haven't even talked to Gracie and Amber about some of that stuff. I'm sorry."

"For what?"

"Talking your ear off."

Matthew shrugged. "I enjoyed it. Really."

"So, is your family close?"

"We're normal. We argue over whose turn it is to do the dishes or who has to ride in the back of the minivan with my little brother."

Kaitlyn tilted her head to the side with a questioning look.

"Let's just say that my brother has a weak stomach when it comes to long road trips."

Kaitlyn held up her hand. "No further explanation needed."

Matthew smiled. "But yeah, we're close. Family's what it's all about, isn't it?"

Kaitlyn looked at Matthew strangely. Here was this clearly masculine man professing that family was everything.

"What?" Matthew asked.

"It's nothing."

"No, tell me," Matthew persisted.

"It's just . . . well, I guess I don't hear that from a lot of guys."

Matthew smiled and then almost immediately winced with pain.

"Are you okay?"

Matthew shrugged it off with a wave of his hand. "This is nothing," he exaggerated, looking down at his leg. "I once caught a twenty-five-pound bass on the Green River just below Flaming Gorge Reservoir. She was a beauty, too. It took me almost thirty minutes to reel her in. Then, not three feet from the bank, I lost her on a snag." Matthew shook his head. "Now *that* was painful."

\* \* \*

Flip tossed Benton's knife over in his hand appraisingly, then he wiped the edge of the knife on his pant leg and pushed the blade securely back into the handle. He could still feel the residue from the medical tape on the hard, plastic handle. Incredibly, the tape had secured the knife to the oar enough to hold when Flip struck the shark. One clean, well-placed strike was all it had taken to discourage the shark. Matthew's plan had worked perfectly.

Flip looked down into the water. The glare of the sun made it sparkle like a million crystals. Flip shook his head. How could something so tranquil be so deadly at the same time?

"We're going to have to do something about all this water in the boat," Donald said.

Flip turned to Donald, but his gaze quickly fell on Karen. She was lying in a five-inch pool of water with her head resting in Gracie's lap. Gracie talked softly to her, but Karen seemed completely oblivious to anything but the excruciating pain that gripped her body. Flip quickly looked around the boat until his eyes fell on the empty five-gallon water jug.

"If we cut off the top we can use the jug to scoop out the water," Flip said as he tossed Donald the knife.

"Do you need any help?" Sam asked. He was sitting next to Morgan and Eleanor. Little Benton sat next to him while Madison snuggled in the security of her daddy's arms. Sam still looked spent from his recent showdown with the sharks.

"No, you just keep doing what you're doing," Flip assured him.

"What about me?" Rhonda spoke up.

"Why don't you go help Gracie?" Flip suggested.

Flip thought he heard Gracie sigh, but when he turned to face her, she coughed into her hand as if clearing her throat, then smiled. Flip looked over at Gary, who was sitting off by himself near the stern. He made no indication that he intended to help in any way, and after his behavior earlier, Flip had no intention of asking him. Then Flip looked across the water to Kaitlyn and Matthew. He knew that they would all be safer if their boats were closer together, but at this point he couldn't risk rowing over to them. The sharks were gone for now, at least, but the movement and the splashing of oars might attract them again. Flip slumped his shoulders and then slowly made his way over to Karen.

"How's she doing?" Flip asked Gracie.

Before Gracie could answer, Karen cried out and clutched at her stomach.

Flip bent down and took her by the hand. "You've got to hold on, Karen. You're going to make it."

Gracie lifted a questioning brow, but Flip ignored it.

"We're all going to make it," Flip continued. Then he glanced over at the blanket that Donald had stuffed into the hole in the boat. It was saturated, and water was seeping in at an increasingly rapid rate. "But right now, we need to get rid of all this water."

They all watched as Donald stabbed the knife into the water jug and began sawing back and forth. The plastic was thick, so it took several minutes before he pulled off the top and held up his handiwork.

"Looks great," Flip praised. "Now put it to work."

Donald scooped the jug down into the water, poured the salty contents over the side of the boat, and then plunged his jug back into the water. With a five-inch pool of water spanning a twenty-by-six-foot area, it took ten minutes to see any change in the level of the water. It took several more for the bottom of the boat to reemerge.

"We're all going to have to take turns with the bucket so the boat doesn't fill with water again," Flip said.

"I'll go next," Pete offered.

"I'd appreciate it, Pete," Flip said.

Then Flip sat down on the bench next to Gracie and Rhonda, his shoulders slumping wearily. Though he was trying to remain positive, the effects of the last few hours were weighing on him heavily. He felt thoroughly depleted.

"Are you okay?" Gracie asked gently.

"I'm fine," he said, trying to shrug it off.

"Well, you don't look fine," Rhonda said as she reached out and touched his arm.

Flip turned to look at Gracie as she gently lifted Karen's head and placed it on a dry life jacket.

"Since the two of you are both over here with Karen," Gracie began, "I think I'll see if Morgan needs any help with the kids."

"Thanks, Gracie. You've been a real life saver," Flip said.

"Since when is screaming hysterically helpful?" Gracie asked wearily.

Flip could see the frustration on Gracie's face. He had seen her struggle with her fear of the water. It was written all over her face every time the boat rocked. Flip wished there were something he could do to help. Instead, he sat in silence and watched as she carefully made her way back to her seat.

"How are you holding up, kid?" Gracie asked.

"I'm okay." Pete's dark eyes didn't do a very good job of hiding the truth. "My dad is probably getting pretty worried about me."

Gracie reached out and put her arm around his shoulders. "When we get back you're going to have an earload to tell him."

Pete relaxed his head against her shoulder and fell silent. Tempers had flared over the last few hours, but now everyone seemed to be lost in their own thoughts. A part of Gracie almost preferred the chaos. At least then she didn't have to think about what was happening, or even worse, what might happen in the days that followed.

Gracie glanced over at Benton. He was sitting on the floor of the boat under the shade of the tent, playing with his little car.

"Why don't you go get under the tent with Benton," Gracie urged. Though Pete's skin was naturally tanned, he too was starting to burn.

Gracie watched as Pete climbed into the tent, and then her eyes lifted. Flip had stood and was heading in her direction. Gracie quickly glanced over at Rhonda, who sat watching Flip go like she were a child who had just been taken from a candy store.

"Gracie, I don't want you to feel bad about being scared of the water," Flip said as he took the seat next to her.

Gracie smiled at him gratefully.

"So what made you decide to study oceanography?" Gracie asked. "Personally, I find composite volcanoes and their pyroclastic eruptions, magma chambers, and the eruption cycle of volcanoes like Mauna Loa in Hawaii to be the far more interesting science."

Flip looked at Gracie, visibly surprised.

"What?" Gracie asked. "Just because I joke around you think my brain is oatmeal?"

Flip shook his head. "I never said that. It's just that I'm . . ." Flip paused to choose his words.

"Surprised?" Gracie offered as she tilted her head and raised a brow in mock offense.

"No," Flip added quickly. "Impressed. I've never met a woman quite like you."

Gracie was completely taken off guard. She could feel her face redden, which only made Flip smile all the more.

"You have an incredible sense of humor," Flip continued. "You're obviously intelligent, and . . ." Now it was Flip's turn to blush. "Well, you get the point."

Gracie gaped at the man before her. Something was definitely wrong with this picture. There was absolutely nothing wrong with him. He was the Mary Poppins of smart surf dudes—practically perfect in every way. He was *not* the kind of guy she usually went for.

"I guess I'd better get back over to Karen," Flip said with a shrug.

Gracie only nodded. Her tongue was too numb to even attempt speech—not that anything sensible would have emerged even if she could have formed the words.

* * *

Kaitlyn pulled the bandages back from Amber's leg to expose her freshly stitched wounds. Her legs were badly bruised and swollen, but the stitches appeared to be holding. Kaitlyn looked up at Amber and smiled.

"So far, so good."

"How long was I out?" Amber asked, her voice noticeably dry and cracking.

"For a couple of hours," Kaitlyn admitted. "How do you feel?"

"Rough."

"Kind of like a ceiling caved in on you and an oceanographer stitched you up without painkillers?"

Amber grimaced. "That does sound pretty awful."

"That's not all. About an hour ago we were almost a T-bone steak for a couple of Great White sharks."

Amber cocked her head to the side. *"What?"*

Kaitlyn sat down next to Amber and told her all about the two sharks, the boats getting separated, and then finally about Matthew's leg.

"Where *is* Matthew?" Amber asked groggily.

Kaitlyn scooted to the side so that Amber could see him sitting behind her on a bench with his leg propped up on some blankets.

"Don't worry. I'm still around," Matthew joked halfheartedly. "Thanks to the handy work of Dr. Winters here."

Kaitlyn looked down at Matthew's leg. After she'd stitched him up, she had wrapped a clean strip of cloth around his leg.

"You might be calling me Dr. Jekyll after you see the stitches."

"What happened to the sharks?" Amber asked, her voice strained.

"They're gone for now," Matthew began. "But they'll be back when they're hungry enough."

Kaitlyn shot Matthew a sharp glance then turned back to Amber. "Flip jabbed one of them with a knife that he taped to the end of an oar. Since then we haven't seen them."

"I really don't mean to scare you," Matthew admitted gently, "but at the same time, it's better to know the truth so that we can be prepared."

*"Prepared!"* Kaitlyn exclaimed. "What can we do? We're just like a floating can of sardines to a shark."

Matthew shrugged. "Right now it's not the sharks I'm most concerned about." Matthew gestured over to the main boat that was still within shouting distance. "Gary isn't handling things very well, especially for a crew member. I can't believe I actually asked him to watch over you."

"Gary isn't really a member of the crew," Kaitlyn offered as she glanced from Matthew to Amber.

"*What?*" Matthew exclaimed. Amber looked equally confused.

Kaitlyn went on to tell Matthew and Amber everything. Matthew sat there shaking his head in silence, every once in a while stealing a glance across the water at Gary.

"I can't believe it," Matthew fumed. "And I'm stuck over here where there isn't a darn thing I can do."

Kaitlyn almost burst out laughing. "What exactly is a guy who uses the word *darn* going to do to a slimy worm like Gary?"

Matthew ran both his hands across his head, pulling his dark hair off his forehead. Kaitlyn examined him closely now that he was not aware that she was looking. His shirt was torn and dirty, and his hair was now as disobedient as she had thought his eyebrows to be. His once clean-shaven face now had the roughness of a two-day shadow. Kaitlyn grinned.

"What's so funny?" Matthew asked, eyeing her curiously.

"I was just thinking that you're going to make a great mountain man."

"Mountain man, huh?"

Kaitlyn laughed softly as Matthew reached up and rubbed at his scruffy face.

"Well, I'm not exactly Miss America myself," Kaitlyn admitted, looking down at the ragged green material that once resembled a grass skirt.

Matthew smiled and then blushed slightly.

"What?" Kaitlyn asked curiously.

"I think you look . . ." Matthew hesitated for just a moment as if he were debating whether or not to continue. Finally he shook his head and Kaitlyn knew that he would not be sharing whatever it was he had been thinking.

"Why don't you let me take a look at your head," Matthew offered in an attempt to change the subject.

Matthew leaned over and gently unwrapped the material, exposing a two-inch gash just below Kaitlyn's hairline. Although the cut appeared to have gone deep, it was not very wide.

"Well?"

"It's going to leave a scar, but it's right under your hairline, so I don't think it'll be that noticeable."

"Are you kidding? If we get out of this alive, I'm going to wear this scar proudly."

"How do you do it?" Amber broke in. "Joking around when we're stranded out here?"

"I don't know," Kaitlyn answered. "I guess I choose to get through it *by* joking around." Then Kaitlyn looked across the water to where Gary was sitting. "It's a better alternative than falling apart."

# CHAPTER 19

"A big juicy hamburger with lettuce and pickles and lots of ketchup and onions," Matthew said with a grin.

"Ohh, that sounds so good," Kaitlyn agreed. "How about a thick slice of German chocolate cake and three giant scoops of vanilla-bean ice cream to go with it?"

"How 'bout a whole half-gallon?" Matthew exclaimed. "Or even better, a full Thanksgiving dinner with all the trimmings. A big, juicy turkey, hot buttered rolls, and dressing. Lots of dressing."

"Cranberries, you can't forget the cranberries," Kaitlyn broke in.

"I don't really like cranberries," Matthew admitted, "but I'm so hungry, I could eat a whole plate of them."

"We've got to stop this," Kaitlyn began. "This is torture! Let's talk about something else or I'm going to go crazy."

Matthew quickly agreed. They had been on the lifeboat for just over forty hours. The hunger pains were now starting to live up to their name, and talking about food really wasn't helping matters any.

"All right. What do you want to talk about?" Matthew asked.

"Why do you only date girls from your church?"

Matthew lifted an eyebrow. For the last few hours they had talked about everything but religion. Matthew had wanted to bring it up since it was such a huge part of his life, but for some reason it was a lot harder than when he was on his mission.

"Well," Matthew began, thinking back to all the youth firesides, Sunday lessons, and family home evenings in his life that had been dedicated to that very subject, "there are actually several reasons, but only one major one. You marry who you date, and I want a temple marriage."

"I don't understand what that has to do with dating members of your church."

"To go to the temple, you have to be baptized into The Church of Jesus Christ of Latter-day Saints."

Kaitlyn wrinkled her forehead. "Okay, but what does it really matter what building or church you get married in, anyway?"

"The temple isn't just a building to us. We believe that it is a house of God. Marriage in the temple is performed by those with the proper authority to seal families together for time and all eternity and not just until death do us part."

"What do you mean, 'proper authority'?"

Matthew took a deep breath, praying that the right words would come. Then, almost immediately, he remembered an example from his mission.

"Kaitlyn, if you saw someone in a car speeding down the road, could you pull them over and give them a ticket?"

"No," Kaitlyn said, looking at Matthew oddly.

"Why?"

"Because I'm not a police officer."

"That's right," Matthew jumped in. "Because you don't have the proper authority. We believe that the authority to bind families together must be given by God and not man."

Kaitlyn nodded slowly.

Is there anything else you'd like to know?" Matthew asked, the missionary side of him kicking in.

"Aren't you the ones who believe in Joseph Smith?"

"Yes, we believe that Joseph Smith was a prophet just like prophets of old."

"Tell me more about the Book of Mormon," Amber interrupted, her voice strained and weak.

Both Matthew and Kaitlyn turned to look at her, surprised she had been following the conversation in her condition. Matthew reached out and took her hand in his with a tender smile.

"When did you two talk about that?" Kaitlyn asked, her face showing her confusion.

"Amber and I had a lot of time to talk when we were separated from all of you. God and religion have a habit of popping up in situations like that."

Then he looked back at Amber. She was looking at him expectantly. Matthew said a silent prayer and then began. He told them both that the Book of Mormon was a record of God's dealings with His children in the New World. He talked about Lehi and his family and how God had led them from Jerusalem to what would one day be called the Americas. Matthew then explained that God chose prophets for that area of the world to lead and guide His people, just as He had in other lands. Finally, he ended by sharing Joseph Smith's account of the First Vision. Matthew had recounted this event many times, but each time that he told it, a sense of wonder spread through him along with the same confirmation he had received when he had first gained his testimony. When he finished, he sat back against the side of the boat and waited for the two friends to respond.

Amber's eyes were wide, but she remained silent.

"And you *believe* that?" Kaitlyn asked incredulously.

"Yes, I do." His words were spoken with a quiet strength.

"How can you know something like that for sure?" Kaitlyn asked skeptically.

"The same way you or anyone else could know. I prayed about it."

"I've seen you pray," Kaitlyn began, her tone suddenly sharp. "Look around, Matthew. Where has prayer gotten you?"

"Just because we haven't been rescued doesn't mean that He doesn't hear us. Heavenly Father doesn't always answer our prayers immediately."

"Or at all," Kaitlyn snapped.

"He answers," Matthew began gently. "Just not always the way we want Him to."

"Look, it's getting late," Kaitlyn began. "Maybe it's time to see if they'll row over to us. It'll be dark soon, and it would be better if we were all together for the night." Without waiting for a reply, Kaitlyn stood and began waving her arms in the direction of the main boat.

Matthew recognized the nonverbal message Kaitlyn was sending him. On his mission he had learned to try not to let rejection get him down, but coming from her, the sting was so real that it was like a smack in the face. Amber tried to ease the sudden coolness of the situation as best she could.

"Thank you," she began hoarsely, "for sharing something so personal with us."

Matthew could tell that Amber really meant it. He smiled, but there was a heaviness in him that had not been there moments before.

\* \* \*

Though the sun had not completely gone down, the moon had climbed into the sky. It was full and round, promising to light the approaching nightfall like a beacon. Splashes of orange mixed with a shocking sprinkle of purple spread across the horizon. Though the sunset was beautiful, it paled in comparison to the clouds. They seemed to have woven a pattern to match the movement of the ocean waves below. Kaitlyn stared at it in wonder. It reminded her of countless sunsets she'd appreciated in the past. The world was going on regardless of everything that was happening to them, regardless of Amber's legs and Karen's battered ribs, despite the starvation and fatigue and all of the suffering they were enduring. Kaitlyn found this whole epiphany both enlightening and very, *very* depressing.

It had been about an hour since Kaitlyn had motioned for the main boat to row over to them. Once they were back together, Donald had immediately secured the two boats at the bow, while Flip took a look at Matthew's leg. The bleeding had completely stopped now. To Kaitlyn's surprise, Matthew was even able to stand, though she could see by the expression on his face that it was not without a great deal of pain. Matthew had also announced that he would spend the night in the main boat. He rattled off some lame excuse, but Kaitlyn was sure it was mostly because of her. Gracie had also decided to change boats and to come over with them.

Kaitlyn rolled a blanket up and propped it behind her head as a pillow. She tried to lie back, but her sunburn rubbing against the wool blanket beneath her made her skin feel on fire. Kaitlyn pulled the blanket from under her and then lay back on the floor of the boat. She closed her eyes and tried to force herself not to think about the pain, but every muscle in her body ached. Her stomach was knotted and cramped with hunger pains, which only added to the nausea caused by the constant rise and fall of the ocean. The adrenaline and movement of the day had distracted her from many of these feelings, but now they gnawed at her unmercifully. Kaitlyn could also hear little Madison and Benton whimpering with hunger. Adults going hungry was bad, but hearing these two children pleading for food was almost unbearable.

Kaitlyn glanced over at Amber. Her legs were swollen and oozing pus. Though she had somehow managed to keep her complaining to a minimum, she could not conceal the pain. With every jostle of the boat she moaned. Kaitlyn didn't know how she was able to bear it. Then Kaitlyn glanced over at Gracie. The blisters on her shoulders had combined into one solid, welted mass. Kaitlyn watched as she squirmed around trying to find a comfortable position, but there wasn't one to be found.

"Do you think the sharks will be back?" Kaitlyn asked apprehensively.

"I don't even want to talk about it," Gracie said as she shook off a shudder. "Just thinking about it makes me sick."

They were all silent now, allowing their minds to drift much like their lifeboat. The threat of the sharks was still very real, but it was the things that Matthew had said earlier that monopolized Kaitlyn's thoughts.

"Matthew's really something," Amber said, her voice no more than a hoarse whisper.

"He saved Sam's hide, that's for sure," Gracie added.

"I wonder what Greg's doing tonight," Kaitlyn began, trying to get her mind back where she thought it should be. "He was supposed to start a part-time job this week at his uncle's law firm. Right now he's just going to be helping out with errands around the office. But after law school he and his uncle have plans for him to become a full partner. Greg's uncle doesn't have any children, and when he retires he wants to keep the practice in the family."

"Brains, looks, and connections," Gracie said. "You sure know how to pick them. I, on the other hand, usually pass up all the good shiny apples for the rotten, stinky ones at the bottom of the barrel."

Kaitlyn couldn't help but smile. Gracie did have a knack for dating the oddest assortment of guys.

"Maybe you do it on purpose," Kaitlyn offered.

Gracie cocked her head to the side and wrinkled her forehead.

"Maybe you're afraid of getting into a serious relationship," Kaitlyn continued.

"And what do I owe you for this session, Doctor?" Gracie teased.

"I'm serious, Gracie. Maybe you're afraid that if you let yourself get involved in a good relationship, it could lead to marriage."

"Oh, yes, and that would be catastrophic," Gracie blurted sarcastically. "Who knows, maybe that would lead to a couple of sweet children, a good job, and a little white house on the upper side of town."

"Or . . . it could lead to a divorce like your parents'," Kaitlyn said gently.

Gracie's eyes grew wide and her jaw went slack. Kaitlyn immediately felt horrible.

"Gracie," Kaitlyn began regretfully, "I'm sorry. I wasn't trying to hurt you, *really*. I have no idea why you date who you date. Trust me, I get confused enough just dealing with my own—"

"You're right," Gracie interrupted, her voice soft and vulnerable. "I *am* afraid of marriage. I guess that's why I only date guys I would never even consider marrying. It's safe."

"Gracie, you don't have to explain yourself to me," Kaitlyn insisted.

"I always thought my parents were the perfect couple. When they got divorced, I started thinking that if it could happen to them, it could happen to anyone." Gracie's voice fell. "Maybe it could even happen to *me*."

"But that doesn't mean it will," Kaitlyn offered. "Realizing that it can happen might help ensure that it doesn't. Does that make any sense?"

Gracie smiled weakly. "I guess so. How did we get on this subject, anyway? I thought we were talking about *your* personal life. Besides," Gracie continued as she shot a quick glance over at the boat next to theirs, "I think my choice in men just might be improving."

Kaitlyn cocked her head to the side and then followed Gracie's eyes. "Flip?" She said it as a question, but something in her tone hinted that she was not terribly surprised.

"But we can talk about that later," Gracie said, trying to downplay the excitement in her voice. "It's your turn for the spotlight."

"All right, fair is fair," Kaitlyn said hesitantly. "Go ahead, ask away."

Gracie leaned back and appraised Kaitlyn for a second before she spoke. "Are you still sticking to your story? You know, the one where you insist that you're not attracted to Matthew? And before you even think about lying to me," Gracie continued, "remember that Amber and I are your best friends. Even if you *do* lie, we'll see right through it."

"Even if I *were* attracted to Matthew, we're just too different."

"Ah ha! So you admit it," Gracie said with a grin. "You *are* attracted to him."

Kaitlyn let out a long sigh. "Right now I'm so confused I don't know what I feel. Besides, we're stranded out here in the Caribbean. What are we talking about guys for? This is ridiculous."

"So," Gracie began soberly, "you would rather talk about starvation, dehydration, raw blistered skin, and possible death."

For a moment no one spoke. Their temporary diversion had been callously stolen from them, and they were instantly thrown back into the harsh sphere of reality.

"Do you really think that we'll all die?" Amber asked breathlessly.

Both girls turned to look at Amber. The fear in her eyes was real.

Gracie squirmed uncomfortably, but before she could speak, Kaitlyn spoke up. "I think I preferred the other conversation."

Gracie nodded. "Me too."

All three of them lay back and looked up into the sky, each one following her own thoughts. After a few minutes Amber broke the silence.

"So," Amber began, her voice shaking with the effort, "what did you think about what Matthew told us today?"

The look of disdain on Kaitlyn's face was easy to see, even with the moonlight beginning to wane.

"Let me see, what would the word be?" Kaitlyn said sarcastically. "Maybe *crazy?*"

Gracie propped herself up on one elbow, her curiosity at a peak. "What are you talking about?"

Kaitlyn knew that Gracie didn't have the foggiest idea what they were talking about because she had been in the other boat at the time, but she really didn't want to rehash the whole thing.

"It's one thing to only date people from your church," Kaitlyn began, "but believing all that other stuff. I mean, come on, that's just . . .'"

"Unbelievable," Matthew said calmly.

Kaitlyn's head jerked around to stare right into Matthew's face. For a second she just lay there staring at him. She had been so involved in conversation that she hadn't even heard him climb into their boat. The sound of the waves also aided his quiet approach.

"I didn't mean to eavesdrop," Matthew began as he reached down and picked up a blanket. "I was just getting a blanket for Karen."

"I'm sorry," Kaitlyn stammered as she sat up.

"It's okay," Matthew broke in. "You have a right to your opinion."

"Well," Kaitlyn began uncomfortably as she fought to regain control of her gaping mouth, "what I meant is that it just sounds a little too *miraculous* for me."

Gracie rubbed her hands together as if about to devour something delicious.

"I have a feeling that talking about my relationships is going to pale in comparison to this."

"Kaitlyn," Matthew began thoughtfully, "do you believe in the Bible? You were raised Christian, right?"

"Yes, of course, but what does that have to do with this?" she asked cautiously.

"Do you believe that Moses parted the Red Sea so the children of Israel could escape from the Egyptians?"

"Yes, but—"

"Do you believe that Noah and his family were saved on an ark while the rest of the world was drowned in a flood?"

Kaitlyn tried to respond, but Matthew appeared to be on a roll.

"Kaitlyn, God said in the Bible that He is the same yesterday, today, and forever. If He performed miracles for His children then, why wouldn't He perform them for His children now? Don't you think He loves *us* just as much as He loved *them?*"

"If He loves us all the same," Kaitlyn demanded, "then why did He ignore my prayers when I was in the hospital begging for my sister to live? Where was He then?" Kaitlyn could feel the anger growing inside her like a malignant tumor.

"Kaitlyn, I—"

"Who do you think you are, anyway? Moses?" she spat sarcastically. "Preaching to me about prayer and miracles. Where was my sister's miracle? Huh? Where was *her* miracle?"

Kaitlyn glared at Matthew, daring him to prove her wrong. Matthew's face softened, but his eyes only seemed to increase in their intensity.

"Kaitlyn, I'm just a guy from a small town in the mountains of Colorado. I don't pretend to know why bad things happen to good people. All I know is that life does have a purpose and that the things I told you are true. They really happened. If you want to know for yourself, ask God."

Then, without another word, Matthew turned and climbed back into the other boat. Kaitlyn sat there reeling, his words ringing in her ears. How could she have even *considered* having feelings for this guy? Kaitlyn turned her head and stared blindly off into the distance.

# CHAPTER 20

Kaitlyn willed her eyes to close and sleep to come, but all Matthew's talk of prayer had her thinking back to the day her sister died. Kaitlyn could feel the guilt and regret souring in her otherwise empty gut. Why did she suggest going to Greg's that day? Leslie hadn't wanted to go in the first place. Within seconds she could feel the guilt turning to anger. Why had God let her sister die? Why hadn't He answered her prayers? Now here was Matthew asking her to pray again. She let out a sigh of exasperation and then turned onto her side, trying to get her mind on something else. Amber and Gracie were asleep next to her and had been for at least half an hour now. Kaitlyn wished that she were asleep too, but her mind would not slow down enough to allow it.

The ocean breeze was cool. Kaitlyn breathed in deeply, filling her lungs with the moist salt air. The wind had picked up considerably in the last few minutes. She closed her eyes, temporarily lost in the moment as the cool breeze soothed her hot skin. When she opened her eyes again, a movement from the other boat caught her attention. Kaitlyn could see a large silhouette. She was almost certain it was one of the men, but with the clouds moving across the moon it was hard for her to make out exactly who it was. She watched as the figure slowly looked around the boat, took something from inside his life jacket, and lifted it toward his face. Even in the dim light, the motion was undeniable. Whoever it was, he was drinking something. Kaitlyn reached for the flashlight that rested not two feet from her. Then, as fast as she could, she aimed the flashlight toward the dark figure and turned it on. Startled by the light, Gary jerked the bottle down from his mouth, spilling part of its contents onto his shirt. As Kaitlyn began to shout, Gary immediately thrust the bottle back inside his jacket.

"What is it? What's the matter?" Sam shouted as he staggered to his feet. "Are the sharks back?"

Kaitlyn pointed her finger at Gary, who now stood glaring at her from the main boat.

"He drank something," she shouted, her voice full of anger.

"She must be delirious," Gary growled as he shielded his eyes from the flashlight.

"I saw you," Kaitlyn demanded. "I saw you drink something. Half of it spilled on your shirt."

Everyone was staring at Gary, who had a visible wet spot on his shirt.

"I washed my face in the ocean. Is that a crime?"

*"Liar!"* Kaitlyn exclaimed, her eyes burning through him. "I saw you take it out from under your life jacket."

"If she's lying, then just take the jacket off and show us," Flip said calmly.

"That's right," Sam agreed.

"Come to think of it, I've never seen him take it off. Not even in the heat of the day," Donald insisted.

"I'm not taking off anything," Gary said defiantly.

Sam was on his feet in an instant. Kaitlyn knew that he must be going on sheer adrenaline. Everyone was tired and suffering the effects of dehydration, but after Sam's bout with the sharks he had looked like he was driving on fumes. Now, as he stood glaring down at Gary, he looked refueled and ready to go. "If you know what's good for you, you best take off that jacket."

Sam grabbed Gary by the arms while Donald and Flip stood up to help him. The men were shouting and the women were screaming, which instantly woke little Benton and Madison from a deep sleep. The boat rocked violently as the men struggled to keep their grip on Gary. Kaitlyn, Gracie, and Amber watched the scene before them in panic. Kaitlyn could see by the expression on Gary's face that he had no intention of giving up without a fight. Matthew lumbered to his feet to help, with most of his weight on his good leg. He grabbed at

Gary, who yanked both arms free at the same time, smacking Matthew square in the face in the process. Matthew stumbled back a step, momentarily dazed. Kaitlyn thought for a second that he might fall, but somehow he managed to retain his balance. He wiped at the fresh blood on his lip.

"Take off your jacket!" Matthew demanded.

Gary looked him straight in the face and then spat at him. Disgusted, Matthew turned his head to the side and wiped his face on his shoulder.

"All right," Flip barked, "if you won't take it off, *we will.*"

Flip, Donald, and Sam seemed to hold Gary's arms with renewed strength, the anger inside them boiling. Matthew unsnapped the life jacket while Gary flung his arms around wildly, but this time the men held their ground.

"I saw something fall," Flip called out, and instantly bent down to feel around the bottom of the boat. His hands easily found the object, and he quickly stood to hold it up to the light. There was an audible gasp from everyone when they recognized a small flask. Flip unscrewed the lid and smelled the contents.

"It's water all right," he seethed.

Sam was livid. "You've been hiding water all this time when there are two babies aboard?" Sam pointed his trembling finger toward Benton and little Madison. "What else have you been hiding inside that jacket of yours?" he raged.

"He's probably got money stashed in there too," Pete broke in. "*Stolen* money!"

Everyone turned to look at Pete, confused as to how he fit into all of this. Kaitlyn turned to look also, although she had already suspected that it was Pete who had stolen her purse under threat from Gary.

"Shut up, boy!" Gary hissed.

Matthew thrust his arm back inside the jacket as the rest of them struggled to keep hold of Gary. When Matthew pulled back he held a large pouch in his hand.

"Give me that," Gary demanded.

The threatening tone in Gary's voice was undeniable, but Matthew just ignored him and unzipped the leather pouch. As he opened it, he took a quick intake of breath.

"There has to be thousands of dollars in here," he said, thumbing through the money.

"*You're* the thief, but you were going to let Pete take the fall for you. Weren't you?" Kaitlyn demanded as she looked with revulsion on this man she had once trusted.

Matthew, Donald, and Sam turned to look at Kaitlyn. As they did, Gary sprang forward. He grabbed for the flask of water that Flip had set on one of the benches. Sam reached out to grab him, but Gary squared off and punched him. Blood instantly dripped from Sam's nose. Morgan let out a scream, and Benton lunged toward the pile of people who were unsuccessfully attempting to get ahold of Gary.

"Stop it or you're going to tip your boat," Gracie yelled across to them.

Kaitlyn was trying to keep the flashlight on them, but with all the movement it was almost impossible. Then they heard a scream followed by a large splash.

"Someone fell in," Gracie screamed.

Kaitlyn shot the light toward the spot the splash had come from, but Morgan's piercing scream told her instantly who had fallen in.

"Benton!" Sam yelled as he searched the water for movement.

Kaitlyn frantically ran the light across the water and then stopped as a figure broke through the waves. She stared in confusion.

"Gary must have fallen in too," Kaitlyn said as she watched him struggle to swim.

"But where's Benton?" Gracie cried.

"Somebody *do* something," Morgan pleaded. "Benton can't swim."

Kaitlyn immediately handed the flashlight to Gracie.

"Kaitlyn, what are you doing?" Gracie asked anxiously.

Without answering, Kaitlyn took one more look down into the water, took a deep breath, and dove in.

The screams from all those aboard were now only muffled sounds as Kaitlyn's body penetrated the cool water. She could feel her blood turn cold, not from the water, but from the fear that seemed to instantly grip and paralyze her as Matthew's words—that the sharks would return when they were hungry enough—flooded her thoughts.

She wanted to turn back, to get out of the water and protect herself, but the image of the boy and the sound of terror in his mother's voice propelled her forward. Kaitlyn began swimming as fast as she could in the direction the splash had come from. She tried to push the weariness of her limbs and the dull pounding ache from the cut on her head to the back of her mind. She reached her arms out, grasping in all directions, frantically searching for Benton. Her eyes were open, but except for the faintest light coming from the moon, it was almost pitch black. When she could not feel anything around her, she forced herself to descend deeper into the ocean, trying not to think about what she might find instead of Benton.

Kaitlyn could feel her lungs burning for oxygen. She knew that she would have to surface for air soon. She was desperate now, straining her stinging eyes to see anything through the inky water. Then, just in front of her, she saw it, something darker than everything else. Kaitlyn closed her eyes, momentarily too terrified to move. A part of her wanted to swim as fast as she could back to the boat, but if it was a shark, it was already too late. It would reach her in a matter of seconds and then it would all be over. *Stay in control,* her mind screamed. *It's Benton. It's got to be Benton.* Kaitlyn swam toward the object, then slowly she reached out. It *was* Benton! Her mind flooded with relief. Quickly Kaitlyn grabbed the boy, pulled him to her, and, placing one arm around his waist, started for the surface.

She could feel her lungs burning and her head spinning as she made her way to the top. After what seemed like forever, but was actually only seconds, Kaitlyn broke through the surface. It took every ounce of strength she had just to hold her head above water. She gasped for air and then tried to raise Benton's head out of the water. His small, unresponsive body felt like a ton of bricks in her trembling arms. She tried to kick her legs to keep them both above water, but her legs felt like they were trapped in cement. Little white lights flashed through her eyes as she gasped for oxygen. Somewhere off in the distance she could hear screaming and shouting followed by a splash, but all sound seemed to be fading as the lights in her head intensified. Within seconds, Kaitlyn could feel Benton being taken from her arms. Now, with the use of both arms, she fought to keep her head above water, but no matter how she struggled to prevent it, she could feel her strength waning. Slowly she could feel herself slipping back into the depths of the ocean.

* * *

Gracie could feel the force of the wind and the cool mist of salt water across her body. Her hand trembled as she tried to hold the flashlight steady on Sam as he cut through the rising waves. Sam fought to keep Benton's head above water, but despite his efforts, Benton's head bobbed lifelessly. Sam crossed the last of the distance back to the boat, and as soon as they were within arm's reach, Flip scooped Benton's small body from the water, laid him on the bottom of the boat, and checked for vital signs. Donald knelt down opposite him and assisted with chest compressions as Flip started mouth-to-mouth resuscitation. Morgan knelt at her son's feet, begging him to breathe. Gracie turned away; she felt like her heart was being wrenched in two. She could not bear to watch the life slipping from this little boy.

"Gracie, where's Kaitlyn?" Amber asked slowly.

Gracie's head shot around to the spot where Kaitlyn had been only seconds ago, but she saw nothing but rolling waves. She turned back to face Amber, her expression panicked.

"Where did she go?" Gracie asked, her voice giving way to the fear that was raging inside her. "I thought she was right behind Sam."

Gracie turned back to the main boat. Flip and Donald were still performing CPR on Benton while Sam struggled to pull himself back into the boat.

"Where's Matthew?" Gracie cried.

Amber pointed to a spot farther off in the water. "He dove in to help Gary."

"*Gary?*" Gracie shouted in disbelief. "This can't be happening. Somebody has got to go get Kaitlyn. She's drowning."

Gracie looked back to the spot where she had last seen her friend. She could feel her heart thundering against her chest. Somewhere off in the distance lightning flashed across the sky. Gracie felt numb. Her mind whirled back to another time and place. She could see rescue workers gathered around a cold, limp body. The sound of sirens blared in the background as they fought desperately to save the man, then the paramedics stepped back, shaking their heads. It was too late. There was nothing more they could do. Gracie's mind zoomed in on the dead man's face, but this time it was not the man's face at all. It was Kaitlyn's.

"No," Gracie screamed as a cold shiver shot up her spine. "I can't let this happen." In one motion, she ripped off her life jacket and dove into the darkness.

* * *

Kaitlyn choked on the pungent water that had filled her lungs as she gasped for air.

"She's breathing!"

Kaitlyn could hear someone speaking, but they sounded muffled. A light shone into her face, causing her to squint. Instantly the light veered off, allowing her to attempt to focus on the images before her.

"Kaitlyn! Are you all right?"

The words finally registered about the same time that the image materialized. It was Gracie. Her hair was dripping and her face was filled with emotion.

"She's alive!" someone was shouting.

Kaitlyn's eyes went to the other figure standing over her. It was Flip. She tried to lift her head, but he held her down.

"Just lie back."

"Benton . . . ?" Kaitlyn moaned.

"He's alive," Flip began. "You saved his life."

Kaitlyn could feel her stomach contracting. She turned her head to the side to expel what was left of the foul water in her stomach. When she was done, Flip slowly helped her up to a sitting position against the side of the boat. Every inch of her body ached.

"Are you okay?" Amber asked weakly.

"My lungs feel like they're on fire."

Kaitlyn turned to look toward the bow as Sam climbed into their boat. When he reached her, he scooped her up and wrapped her in a crushing embrace.

"Thank you!" he said, his voice low and shaking.

It was all he could manage. The dehydration had snatched from all of them any tears at this point, but his eyes were filled with an immeasurable joy and gratitude that Kaitlyn had never before seen. She nodded, not trusting her own voice. Then he gently set her back down. Kaitlyn watched silently, with her heart in her throat, as Sam climbed back into the main boat and took his small son into his arms.

"How did I get back to the boat?" Kaitlyn asked, turning to Amber. "All I remember is Benton being taken from my arms and then sinking back into the water."

Amber didn't say a word, just turned her eyes to Gracie sitting alone at the bow of the supply boat. In the moonlight Kaitlyn could see long strands of damp, black hair across her back, stretching her curls out so that they appeared much longer than usual.

"*Gracie?*" Kaitlyn whispered in complete astonishment. Amber nodded.

"Gracie went into the . . ." Kaitlyn's voice caught. "Into the *water?*" Her feelings were already at the surface, but now they threatened to overflow.

Kaitlyn struggled to her feet. Her limbs reminded her of the wobbly legs of a newborn colt as she made her way to Gracie. When she sat down, Gracie turned to face her. At first both girls just stared at each other, exchanging emotions and feelings that words could not possibly express, then they embraced and cried in each other's arms.

"You did it, Gracie," Kaitlyn exclaimed, her voice choked with emotion. "You went back into the water. You saved my life."

"I had to," Gracie said softly. "I couldn't just do nothing and let you die."

"Someone throw me a rope," Matthew cried.

Kaitlyn pulled back from Gracie and looked over into the main boat while Gracie reached for the flashlight. Matthew had Gary propped up against the side of the boat. Gary was out cold.

"What happened?" Kaitlyn asked as she watched Flip and Matthew tie Gary securely to one of the bench seats.

"After you dove in to find Benton," Amber explained, "Matthew swam out to help Gary."

Kaitlyn's eyes widened.

"Everyone else was busy with Benton."

Kaitlyn nodded and then glanced over at Matthew.

"I didn't see it all happen because I dove in to help you, but the others said that when Matthew got out to Gary, he began to pull Matthew under the water to keep himself up. Matthew was having a hard time as it was because of his leg."

"So what happened?"

"Matthew finally had to punch him in the face to get him to stop."

Kaitlyn's eyes fell on Matthew. "I can't believe Matthew risked his own life to save *him.*"

Kaitlyn shook her head in wonder. Amber was right. Matthew *was* something. Her gaze then fell on the small boy in Sam's arms. Every ounce of strength that Kaitlyn had reserved in the last few days was now spent. The reality of that was sure to have consequences and Kaitlyn knew it, but somehow, as she looked over at Benton in his father's arms, she had no regrets.

# CHAPTER 21

Kaitlyn pulled the cotton sheets up around her face as she snuggled her head against her soft feather pillow. The bedding smelled fresh. Not like the flowery detergent that Mom usually used. This smelled more like . . . What was it? Was it pine? No, no it wasn't pine. It smelled more like a fresh ocean breeze. Oh well, it didn't matter. She was so tired, nothing mattered.

"Wake up, Kaitlyn."

Kaitlyn opened her eyes to look at the person above her.

"Mom?" she said groggily.

Her mother smiled down at her—that big smile that was always so infectious.

"Is it time to eat?"

"Kaitlyn, wake up!"

"Just a few more minutes, Mom. I'm so tired."

"Kaitlyn, it's me, Gracie. Snap out of it. You're hallucinating."

Kaitlyn stared up at the person above her. She squinted her eyes in the morning sun as the image before her transformed into the face of her friend.

"Gracie?" Kaitlyn said, the confusion heavy in her voice.

Kaitlyn felt as though she were fighting to pull her mind out of a pool of quicksand. Every thought was strained, and her perception was muddled.

"Kaitlyn!" This time Gracie shouted it.

Something in Kaitlyn's mind snapped and she was instantly pulled from the muddy pit of sand that held her mind prisoner. A chill shot through her as she looked up at Gracie. Her friend's face was so burned it was swollen, her eyes were dull and lined with large dark circles, and her full lips were now shriveled and cracked, with dried blood along some of the deeper cuts.

"Kaitlyn, are you okay?" Gracie's brow was furrowed with concern.

Kaitlyn's heart was racing. If Gracie was in this kind of condition, what about Amber? Was she even alive?

"Amber?" Kaitlyn whispered.

Gracie glanced over at Amber and then back down at Kaitlyn.

"She's still alive."

Kaitlyn's body began to relax, but then almost immediately stiffened. She sat up and her eyes swept the main boat until finally they rested on Karen.

"She's still sleeping," Gracie offered. "I know. They were the two I was worried about too. Well, them and you."

"Me? I'm fine," Kaitlyn said as she attempted to sit up. Gracie reached out to help, but her own hands were shaking.

Once she was sitting, Kaitlyn had to grab ahold of her head with both hands because of the sharp, shooting pains that were ricocheting inside her skull.

"I know," Gracie began. "My head feels like an orange crammed into one of those super turbo juicers you see in infomercials."

"I can't believe we haven't been found yet." Kaitlyn looked up at the sky. "It's been three days."

Her tongue was swollen and kept sticking to the roof of her mouth, so it was difficult to speak. She tried to moisten it, but the saliva in her mouth was much thicker than normal and almost made her gag.

Kaitlyn looked over into the main lifeboat, allowing her eyes to roam from face to face. Even after seeing Gracie, Kaitlyn was still shocked by their appearances. All the faces looked drawn and haunted. Each movement they made was slow and deliberate, as if the smallest amount of exertion took every ounce of strength. Kaitlyn understood, because that was exactly how she felt.

Kaitlyn glanced over at Matthew. He was sitting next to Karen, holding a damp rag on her forehead. The curves along his cheekbones looked more prominent than when she had first met him, and his white shirt seemed to fit loosely around his broad shoulders. Kaitlyn could feel a lump forming in her throat.

"Is this ever going to end?" she croaked.

"It will end," Gracie said slowly. "I just don't know how."

Kaitlyn massaged her temples with her fingertips.

"Amber's running a fever," Gracie said hesitantly.

Kaitlyn's body stiffened. "How high is it?"

"She's warm. I've been putting wet rags on her head for the past twenty minutes or so."

Kaitlyn struggled to her feet. Her legs were trembling so severely that for a second she thought she might fall. She stood motionless for a moment as she fought to regain control of her legs, but even that small amount of motion intensified the pounding in her head to the point that she began to retch. Gracie grabbed her arm to steady her as she leaned over the edge of the boat.

"Just sit back down. I'll handle it," Gracie said, though her own body was only slightly more stable.

"If I sit back down," Kaitlyn said weakly, "I'll never get back up."

Kaitlyn staggered over to Amber. Her entire equilibrium was off, and her legs felt like heavy logs; each step was labored and deliberate. Once she sat down, she reached out and took Amber's hand. It was warm just like the rest of her fevered body. Amber was shivering and squirming. Kaitlyn glanced down at the bandages wrapped around her legs. They were heavily soiled with drainage. Her eyes were closed, but she was very much awake. Her face was flushed and drawn with pain.

"Amber, it's me," Kaitlyn said softly.

Amber opened her eyes and slowly turned her head to look at Kaitlyn.

"My legs," Amber moaned. "They hurt so bad. I don't know how much longer I can take this."

Kaitlyn bit down on her lip. "I know, Amber. I know."

Kaitlyn wanted to cry. She felt helpless. When Leslie died, it was over in seconds. Her heart still ached every time she thought about it, but she wasn't conscious when Leslie took her last breath. She didn't have to watch life slowly being drained from someone she loved.

"You can't give up, Amber," Kaitlyn said as she squeezed her hand. "I won't let you. Do you hear me? I won't lose another person I love. I won't."

Kaitlyn held Amber's hand until she finally fell into a fitful sleep. Then Kaitlyn glanced over at Matthew sitting next to Karen. Kaitlyn could see the strain in his face from his own injuries, but incredibly, he was still using his energy to help others. Kaitlyn's throat constricted. Why had she gotten so angry with him? Kaitlyn looked away from Matthew to the ocean beyond. She couldn't answer that question now any more than she could last night. One thing she did know for certain—no matter how hard she tried to deny it or fight it, she was beginning to have feelings for him.

"Tell me this is almost over."

Kaitlyn looked up as Gracie sat down on the bench next to her.

"Tell me I'll see my parents again," Gracie continued, her voice strained with desperation.

Kaitlyn reached over and grabbed Gracie's hand. The two of them sat in silence as Gracie's plea hung in the air.

# CHAPTER 22

After the incident with the sharks, no one wanted to get back into the water. The empty water bucket was now being used as a toilet, with blankets held up for privacy. It was primitive, but it was better than sitting in their own filth or taking their chances in the water, although after being stranded for three days with very little food and water, there was little need for the bucket. For the most part it was used to bail water from the floor of the main boat. In the condition that they were in, this task became extremely arduous. Matthew made a rotating schedule for that, as well as for keeping a lookout for any rescue ships or planes.

Kaitlyn sat in the main lifeboat and scanned the cloudy sky above them. It was her turn to serve as lookout, but so far she hadn't seen any sign of a rescue plane. Kaitlyn's face fell. It had been three days since they'd evacuated the ship. At least the weather had given them a small reprieve from the sun. The shade from the clouds and the cool ocean breeze were a nice change from the sting of the sun's undeterred assault. The last few hours they had been subjected to a slew of threats from Gary, but now he sat silent, brooding. Everyone avoided making eye contact with him.

Kaitlyn glanced around the lifeboat. Benton was sound asleep under the shade of one of the tents. He had not moved around at all today, but at least color had returned to his freckled checks. Kaitlyn's gaze fell on little Madison, curled up and whimpering on her grandma's lap. The lack of food and water was taking its toll on Madison's small frame. Eleanor was attempting to sing a lullaby to Madison, but her own throat was so dry that every note seemed to crack. Eleanor's morale seemed to be holding up better than her frail body. Her wrinkles had deepened overnight, and she had lost weight so quickly that her skin seemed to hang on her. Eleanor gently stroked her granddaughter's hair and then kissed her softly on the forehead. Kaitlyn quickly turned away, not wanting to intrude on such a private moment. She could feel the stinging in her own eyes, but the tears would not come.

"She'll be three next Thursday," Eleanor said softly.

Kaitlyn slowly turned back to face Eleanor, but the older woman was still looking down at her little granddaughter. Kaitlyn thought for a minute that Eleanor had not been speaking to her, but as she began to look away, Eleanor lifted her eyes.

"She *will* see Thursday, Kaitlyn, and so will you!"

Kaitlyn wanted to cry, but instead lowered her eyes and nodded. She wished she could share Eleanor's optimism, but she was just so weak and tired.

"My husband passed away ten years ago."

"I'm sorry," Kaitlyn offered, not sure where Eleanor was going with this.

"Don't be. We had forty-two wonderful years together—some more wonderful than others," she admitted with a gentle smile. "Most couples nowadays don't even last two or three years together, and it's not death that separates them. It's giving up when things get tough. Believe me, in marriage, just as in life, there will come those difficult times. But if my husband and I had given up, if we had turned our backs on the future just because the here and now was a little bumpy, we would have missed the strength that comes from weathering a storm." Eleanor reached over and squeezed Kaitlyn's hand. "Don't give up! Weather this storm."

Kaitlyn gulped hard. She knew Eleanor was right. She had to find the strength and courage to keep fighting. She glanced over at Matthew, Flip, and Pete. They were making another attempt at fishing. Kaitlyn watched as Matthew patted Pete's shoulder and then smiled at something the boy said. Her mind wandered to what kind of a father Matthew would be. He was so good with Pete, Benton, and little Madison. Greg had said that he would not be ready for children until he was established in his career, rattling off something about how much it actually cost to raise a child and that he needed to sink every spare dime into building up and expanding his practice. Kaitlyn wondered if the practice would ever feel big enough for Greg.

"How did you know when you were in love?" Kaitlyn asked softly, turning to Eleanor. Then she glanced back over at Matthew. "I have a great guy back home who loves me, and I'm pretty sure he wants to marry me. He's starting an incredible career and my family just adores him—in fact, in my father's case, that would be an understatement. He's smart, ambitious, and handsome. Then there's this other guy—"

"I had a wonderful man just like that," Eleanor broke in.

"Your husband?"

"No, but he was wonderful. I even loved him. But when I met my husband, I just knew."

"*How* did you know?"

"Trust me, you just do," Eleanor said with a gentle smile.

Kaitlyn sighed heavily. The man she *knew* she could have, she'd thought very little about since leaving Minnesota. The man that she could not get her mind off . . . Kaitlyn stopped herself. No matter what she was beginning to feel for Matthew, it would never work. Their religious views were just too different.

"Why don't you talk to him?" Eleanor suggested as she motioned with her head toward the figure that was approaching. Kaitlyn turned to see Matthew slowly making his way toward them. She quickly looked back to Eleanor to ask her how she knew, but Eleanor only smiled and patted her knee.

"Tell him how you feel," she whispered.

Matthew smiled warmly at Eleanor as he hobbled over, then looked hesitantly down at Kaitlyn.

"I checked on Amber about a half hour ago and thought you might like a report," Matthew began apprehensively. "Her fever seems to be holding steady."

"I need to get back over there."

"Actually, she's sleeping now," he said.

"That's not such a bad idea," Eleanor began as she exaggerated a yawn. "Why don't you two go back to the other boat and talk and let this old granny get a little shut-eye?" She stole a knowing wink at Kaitlyn.

* * *

Kaitlyn reached down to feel Amber's forehead. She would have rechecked her wounds to prolong sitting down next to Matthew, but Amber was asleep and Kaitlyn didn't want to take the chance of waking her. She glanced over at Matthew. He was sitting on a bench watching her quietly. He smiled, but it was more of a polite smile rather than one of his usual full-face grins. Then Kaitlyn glanced over at the other boat, which held everyone else. If she wanted to talk to Matthew alone, she knew she had better do it now. Kaitlyn did one last adjustment on the makeshift tent they had made to shield Amber from the sun, then sat down in the seat next to Matthew. At first neither of them spoke. Kaitlyn watched as the waves peaked and sprayed, while Matthew stared blankly down at his hands.

"How's your leg?" she finally asked.

"It's okay."

Kaitlyn didn't know who he was trying to fool; she had seen how he grimaced when he walked. Jumping in to save Gary had only made it worse.

"Maybe I should take a look," Kaitlyn offered.

"Don't worry about it. I'm fine."

"Hey, I was there. Don't forget, that's my stitching under that wrap."

"I haven't forgotten," Matthew said, his voice suddenly serious.

Kaitlyn looked up, and for a second their eyes met. Kaitlyn could feel her heart thundering. Her head was dizzy with exhaustion, her entire body ached, and yet somehow she could still feel her stomach flip-flop as she looked up at Matthew. Then she looked out across the water while Matthew stared back down at his hands. The silence between them seemed to stretch on, each of them waiting for the other to begin. Finally Kaitlyn couldn't stand it anymore.

"Matthew, do you have feelings for me?"

Matthew didn't even look up; he just stared more intently at his hands. Kaitlyn could feel her face flush under her sunburn. Why had she asked him that question? Hadn't he already made himself clear on the subject? Kaitlyn needed to go somewhere—anywhere away from him.

"Yes," he said reluctantly. "I do."

His head came up, and for a moment they just looked at each other. A thrill shot through Kaitlyn like a surge of adrenaline. She wanted to throw her arms around him and tell him everything she had been feeling, but something in his eyes stopped her.

"But?" she whispered, not really wanting to know.

"A couple of years ago a friend of mine got married. It was a beautiful chapel wedding. But when the minister said those words, 'until death do you part . . .'" Matthew shook his head. "Kaitlyn, I don't want my marriage to end at death."

"Who said anything about marriage?"

"I didn't mean—"

"Attraction and having feelings for someone is a long way from marriage and commitment."

"True," Matthew said hesitantly. "But I can't take that chance. I already know how I'm starting to feel about you."

Kaitlyn looked away in frustration.

"Do you have any desire at all to read and pray about the Book of Mormon?" he asked.

"No," Kaitlyn said sharply. "So, ultimately your feelings for me do depend upon my believing . . ." she paused to search for the right words, "your story?"

Kaitlyn could see the anguish in Matthew's eyes. She quickly looked away. She had her answer—or at least, all the answer she needed.

"Your not believing doesn't change how I feel about you, but if I stopped living what I believe, it would change how I feel about myself."

Kaitlyn's heart was pumping and her mind racing with a mixture of embarrassment, anger, and pain. She wanted to lash out and hurt him the way that he was hurting her.

"The reason I asked you if you were attracted to me was because I wanted to let you know right up front that I'm engaged. Or at least I will be when I get back home. I think you're a nice guy, but that's all," she lied. She could feel her lower lip quivering as she spoke. "Anyway, I just wanted to get that cleared up between us."

Matthew's eyes seemed to go right through her. He opened his mouth to say something but then quickly shut it and looked back down. Kaitlyn looked at him in disbelief. How could he not at least try to make things work? She immediately got up and climbed back into the other boat before her emotions gave her away.

# CHAPTER 23

Flip tested the tension of the line on his handmade pole and then looked over at Benton. The boy's face was severely sunburned, and his nose and forehead were blistered. The exuberance that had been in him a couple days before was gone. Flip wanted to smile, to reassure him that everything was going to be fine, but how could he when he was not sure of that himself?

Flip covered his face with his hands. He had never been one to shed tears, but today he wanted to cry like a baby. He wanted to cry for this little boy who might never be a man; he wanted to cry for himself and all the things he would never get to do. He only had a few years left before he would graduate from college and start his career, a career he had dreamed about his whole life. He looked out across the ocean and laughed bitterly. It was ironic that his career would have been studying the massive ocean that now held him prisoner. Flip was pulled from his dark thoughts by a small hand on his shoulder.

"Don't be sad, Flip," Benton urged.

Then the small boy reached into his pocket and pulled out the shiny, red car that had occupied him for so many of the hours they had spent floating around aimlessly on the ocean. He looked thoughtfully down at it and then extended it to Flip.

"Here," Benton said and placed the car in Flip's hand. "Now you won't be sad."

Flip stared in amazement at this child who was trying to comfort him when only last night he had barely cheated death. Flip closed his fingers around the little car. Then he watched as Gracie, who was sitting between them observing the whole exchange, patted her lap for Benton to sit down. Benton climbed weakly up onto her lap and then laid his head against her chest. As Flip looked back down at the car, Gracie reached out and touched his arm. He smiled at her weakly, pushed the car deep into his pocket, and put his hand on top of hers. For several seconds they just sat there, each one drawing on the other for strength.

It didn't take long before Flip could see Benton's breathing deepen. Gracie slowly began to stand so that she could carry him over to the small tent that they had fashioned. It didn't allow for a lot of space, but in the heat of the day at least five adults could huddle under the shade.

Flip quickly leaned his makeshift fishing pole against the side of the boat and stood to take Benton from her. She gratefully handed the child over, and Flip noted the exhausted shaking of her limbs.

As soon as Flip took Benton from Gracie, he saw the pole jerk. At first he wasn't sure if he had actually seen it or if he had just imagined it. The dehydration had made him nauseated and light-headed, so if he turned his head too quickly everything would begin to spin. As he slowly turned to look more closely at the pole, the line tightened again. Flip quickly gave Benton back to Gracie and grabbed the pole. Just as he got a good hold on it, the line went taut. Flip grabbed the string and gave it a quick jerk to ensure that Rhonda's earring was firmly into the mouth of whatever was on the other end of the line.

"Did you hook it?" Gracie cried.

"I got it," Flip said, trying not to give way to the excitement that was surging through him. "Now if I can just keep it."

For the next couple of minutes, everyone watched anxiously as Flip carefully pulled the string in. It didn't take long for the water at the surface to ripple and for the brightly colored fish to make its first appearance. Pete was on his feet cheering while the rest of them watched nervously. Once the fish was within arm's reach of the boat, Flip bent down and lifted it out of the water and onto the floor of the boat. The fish only weighed a couple of pounds, but Flip was beaming as if he had caught a giant sea bass. He instantly turned around to face Benton, who was now sitting on Gracie's lap, rubbing his eyes sleepily. He'd been awakened prematurely from his nap by the cheers that erupted when the fish was pulled in. He hadn't quite grasped what had just happened. Flip picked up the fish, still flailing around and dripping water, and held it up for the boy to see.

"We did it, Benton! We caught your fish!"

* * *

Flip gutted and cleaned the fish and cut it into sections while Benton watched proudly.

"I told you I could catch big fish," Benton beamed.

Flip looked down at the fish with a smile. It was no longer than the length of his arm from elbow to fingertip.

"You sure did," Sam said as he reached over and gripped his son's shoulder.

"Anyone for sushi?" Flip asked as he held up the first slice.

The sight of the uncooked meat would have usually turned Kaitlyn's stomach, but now she eyed the raw flesh as if it were a sirloin steak. Flip looked around the group until his eyes finally rested on the little boy next to him.

"Well, little man, I think it's only fair that you go first."

Benton's eyes devoured the meat hungrily as he reached out his little hands. Once he had it in his grasp, he bit a mouthful of the fish and began to chew. They all watched in anticipation as Flip cut each of them a piece. Then, one by one, Matthew began to pass them out.

"Try not to eat it too fast," Flip urged as he continued slicing the meat.

His words seemed to fall on deaf ears. Several of them stuffed the meat into their mouths greedily, eating whole pieces without even chewing. Kaitlyn watched as Matthew took a piece over to Karen.

"What are you wasting food on her for?" Gary grumbled.

They all turned in disbelief to the man tied up at the stern of the boat.

"She'll be dead in a couple of hours, if that long. Look at her—she's a walking corpse now," Gary added callously.

Kaitlyn wanted to leap across the boat at Gary, but instead her eyes instantly went to Karen, who was still conscious and, from the look on her face, very much aware of what Gary had just said.

"He's right," Karen admitted softly. "Give my share to the children."

"Why them?" Gary barked. "Give it to someone who's got a chance of making it out of here alive."

They all gawked at Gary as if he were a mad dog frothing at the mouth.

"Listen, you . . ." Flip struggled to even find the words, he was so angry.

"No, *you* listen. This is a fight for survival now. Either the strong rise to the top or they get trampled down with the weak. And I'm not about to be dragged down with *them.*"

"We're not animals," Matthew said, struggling to keep control of his voice. "We're human beings."

"Look at her," Gary demanded. "You can't honestly tell me she's going to make it."

Eleanor stood up and faced Gary. "Listen, mister, we've heard just about enough from you."

Gary rolled his eyes. "All right. *Fine!* Waste it on her if you want, but in the end you'll wish you had listened to me." Then he turned and took a bite of his own fish.

Kaitlyn glared at Gary. How could anyone be so cold? She was still stewing when the boat began to rock. Kaitlyn quickly looked over at Gracie, who was climbing into the supply boat to give a piece of fish to Amber. Kaitlyn looked down at the slice of fish she still held in her own trembling hands. Even though the pain in her stomach tore at her unmercifully, she knew she would have to eat the meat slowly; she couldn't risk her stomach cramping again and losing the only real sustenance she had received since evacuating the ship.

She was about to take a bite of her fillet when she noticed Matthew off by himself holding his own uneaten piece of fish with his eyes closed and his head lowered. Though he was not saying anything out loud, Kaitlyn knew he was praying.

"Hey, if you don't want yours," Flip teased as he looked over at Kaitlyn. "I'll be more than happy to eat your share."

"Obviously she's not accustomed to such a delicacy," Rhonda said, her voice dripping with superiority.

Gracie, who was over in the supply boat, must have overheard Rhonda's comment, because she immediately came to Kaitlyn's defense.

"See, it's not that Kaitlyn doesn't *like* sushi," Gracie began. "It's just that she doesn't know how to eat it." Gracie turned to Kaitlyn. "When you eat it, you have to pretend that you're a pretentious snob. Then that slimy slab of raw meat will melt in your mouth like chocolate. Here, watch me."

Gracie put her hand on her hip, stuck her nose straight up into the air, and took a bite of her fish. After she was finished, she kissed her fingers in imitation of a stereotypical French chef.

"Voilà! Not bad. Not bad at all." Then she corrected her lapse in affected dignity. "It is quite palatable," she solemnly declared.

"Kind of tasted like tuna to me," Donald said with a shrug.

Rhonda glared at Gracie, her head cocked and lips pinched together.

"Very funny," she snapped sarcastically.

Kaitlyn glanced over at Matthew to see his reaction, but he had moved to the far end of the boat and was gazing off into the distance.

# CHAPTER 24

Kaitlyn looked up as the corner of the tent lifted. Rhonda looked down on Kaitlyn, Gracie, Flip, Donald, and Matthew. The five of them were huddled tightly together to escape the assault of the afternoon sun. Rhonda didn't say a word; she just started to move in next to Kaitlyn.

"What are you doing?" Flip began as he glanced down at his watch. "It's just barely after four. Isn't it your turn to stand watch?"

"My shoulders are too burned. I couldn't stand another minute out there in the sun, so I asked Sam to take my turn."

Flip shook his head, not even trying to hide his irritation.

Kaitlyn was a little surprised that Sam had agreed. He didn't take guff from anyone, but she also knew that Sam's first priority was his family, and he probably didn't want to take the chance that Rhonda would curl up under the shade of one of the other tents and miss spotting a ship.

"We're all burned," Gracie said sharply as she looked down at her own blistered skin.

"Look," Rhonda began sarcastically. "I know you don't like me. My family's wealthy and I'm—"

"Spoiled and lazy," Gracie finished.

Rhonda stared down at Gracie, her eyes wide and her mouth open.

Kaitlyn watched as Gracie attempted to swallow but apparently couldn't because her mouth was too dry. "Look around, Rhonda. This isn't your local country club."

"I don't have to listen to this," Rhonda grumbled.

"Oh, yes you do," Gracie shot back. "For the past few days we've listened to your whining and your pouting and we've put up with your snotty I'm-better-than-you attitude—but no more. This is serious. We might just be the people you die with."

Everyone sat in silence, Gracie's words sweeping over them like a cold breeze. Death had been the unspoken thing on everyone's mind the last few hours, but now the inevitable was out in the open. Kaitlyn looked up as Rhonda's expression changed from one of anger to defeat right before their eyes. Rhonda quickly turned to leave, but Kaitlyn reached up and grabbed her hand. Rhonda stood motionless with her back to them.

"You're right," she admitted, her voice beginning to crack.

Kaitlyn's eyes opened wide. It was the first honest emotion she had seen from Rhonda.

Rhonda slowly turned to face them.

"I'm just so scared," she admitted, her voice trembling.

"We all are," Flip admitted.

"Look, Rhonda," Gracie began, only this time her tone was more gentle. "We need your help. If we're going to make it, we're going to have to work together."

"Come on, you might as well get out of the sun," Kaitlyn said as she gently pulled Rhonda down to sit next to them in the shade.

The scowl that had been on Rhonda's face for the majority of the past few days softened into a genuine smile. "Thank you."

"I'm next to stand watch," Donald quickly added, "but I'm pretty sure that Sam was scheduled after me. Maybe you could pay him back by taking his turn."

Rhonda looked over at Donald, and then one by one at the rest of them. Kaitlyn could tell by the expression on her face that for the first time in a long time she felt a part of something bigger than herself. She felt a part of them.

"All right."

Kaitlyn smiled. "First step, standing watch, next step, humanitarian relief in Afghanistan."

"Let's take one step at a time," Rhonda said.

"You never know," Donald offered. "I spent the year before I started college working in the Peace Corps in Africa."

Kaitlyn lifted one of her eyebrows appraisingly. "Really?"

Donald nodded. "It was the best thing I could have done. It's amazing how ungrateful you can become until you see people struggling just to find clean drinking water. Anyway, the following few years, I think it helped me to be a better student and hopefully, ultimately, a better person."

"Where did you go to college?" Gracie asked curiously.

"Harvard."

Rhonda openly gaped at Donald in complete amazement. "You attended Harvard University? *The* Harvard?"

Donald looked a little embarrassed. "I lucked out with my SATs."

"No one just lucks out and ends up at Harvard," Flip said with a shake of his head.

"You told us that first day that you work with computers," Kaitlyn began appraisingly. "What exactly do you do?"

"Have you ever heard of Boydes Micro Intelligence?"

"Who hasn't?" Rhonda began. "It's been in the top one hundred companies for the past two years. Their president is some young hotshot computer genius . . ." Rhonda's mouth fell open. "No way!" She shook her head and then stared at Donald as if she were meeting a rock star. "*You're* Don Boydes? *The* Don Boydes? You can't be. I saw a picture of him in one of my father's business journals."

"It's amazing what a haircut, a shave, and a thousand-dollar suit can do to your appearance," Donald said, his voice holding no conceit.

"Not bad for unemployed," Gracie said, echoing Rhonda's comment from that first day.

"Why didn't you mention that you just happen to be one of the youngest financial moguls in the country?" Rhonda asked incredulously.

"Because running Boydes Micro Intelligence is just what I do," Donald began sincerely. "It's not who I am."

Kaitlyn smiled as she looked across at the man before her. He was about as unassuming as they come in a pair of faded blue jeans and a simple cotton T-shirt, when in actuality the guy could probably afford to own a chunk of Rhode Island.

For the next ten minutes they all sat back and listened as Rhonda fired question after question at Donald. Up to this point Rhonda had avoided him as if he were a mongrel dog with fleas, but now she was treating him more like royalty. Finally, when there was a lull in the conversation, Matthew looked over at Donald.

"How long were you in Africa?"

"Only a year, but I learned a lot in those twelve months."

Matthew nodded his head knowingly. "I spent two years down in Mexico."

Kaitlyn glanced at Matthew in surprise.

"What part?" Donald asked. "I have some financial entities in Mexico City."

"I moved around a lot, but most of my time was spent in Veracruz. I met people there I'll never forget." Matthew's face broadened into a thoughtful grin. "There was one family in particular. Their daughter was amazing. She had beautiful brown eyes that could melt your heart in an instant."

Donald smiled. "And you came home because . . . ?"

Suddenly Kaitlyn was very jealous, and that irritated her.

"Did you use your *Mr. Right* pickup line on her too?" she asked sharply.

Matthew turned to look at Kaitlyn as everyone else fell into an uncomfortable silence.

"I don't think her mama would have appreciated that. Tia was only eight."

If Kaitlyn felt bad because of her sarcastic jab, Matthew's next statement made her want to slither right under one of the benches.

"Tia was born without legs," Matthew continued. "Her family was very poor, so prosthetics were out of the question." Matthew shook his head. "But I'll tell you what, I've never seen such a happy, upbeat kid in my life. Not once did I see her sitting around feeling sorry for herself or limiting her potential. If there was any way possible to do something, she found it. She inspired everyone around her. Including me," Matthew admitted reluctantly. "Before I found her family, I was starting to question whether I should even be in Mexico. My family's business was struggling at the time, and I was afraid that the girl I was dating back home might get distracted by a few of my not-so-loyal friends. But when I met Tia, it changed my whole outlook. I ended up staying in Mexico a full two years and had experiences that will stay with me a lifetime."

They all sat there for several seconds without saying anything. Finally, Rhonda worked up enough nerve to asked Donald a few more questions about his business. Kaitlyn glanced back at Matthew. He was sitting shoulder to shoulder with Flip in an awkward slouched-over position so that his head would not brush against the top of the tent. A bluish-purple bruise ran along his cheekbone where Gary had smacked him and, from the expression on his face, the gash on his leg was really bothering him. Matthew looked up and met Kaitlyn's gaze. Physically he looked miserable, but something in his eyes still seemed very much alive.

* * *

Kaitlyn held onto Karen's hand as another surge of spasms shook the woman's body and twisted her face in agony. Karen's fever had steadily increased over the past hour, causing her to slip in and out of consciousness. Everyone aboard seemed painfully aware of the battle she was waging. Every second counted, every minute was earned and fought for.

"Take deep breaths," Kaitlyn urged as she gripped her burning hand.

Once the pain ebbed, Karen groped for air.

"I can't breathe," she wheezed.

"You've got to relax," Kaitlyn pleaded.

"Water. I need water."

They were all in desperate need of water. Kaitlyn had never longed for anything in her life as much as she did for water now. Karen's fever had only intensified the speed at which she was dehydrating. The transformation over the last few hours was frightening.

"Soon," Kaitlyn whispered. "We'll get some water soon."

Kaitlyn dipped the rag she was using to cool Karen's fever into the ocean, then wrung it out. She placed it on Karen's head, but it was only minutes before the rag was warm. She immersed the cloth in the ocean again and pulled it out, licking her lips as she watched the water fall from it in a stream. Her mouth was so dry it felt like sand. For a moment Kaitlyn had the strongest urge just to plunge her head into the clear, cool water and drink until her stomach was full. Flip had already warned them about drinking salt water, but several times that day Kaitlyn had found herself staring at it thirstily.

"I need you to do something."

Kaitlyn turned back to Karen.

"What is it?" Kaitlyn asked as she reached for Karen's quivering hand. "What do you want me to do?"

"Trevor—" Karen had to stop as the pain intensified.

"It's okay," Kaitlyn reassured her as she bent in closer. "Take your time."

Karen had her eyes closed tightly as she struggled to endure the constant, grueling pain, but she slowly opened them and looked straight up at Kaitlyn.

"My son, Trevor," Karen began again, her voice low and raspy. "Take him home."

"What do you mean?"

"Take him back to Iowa."

Kaitlyn shook her head. "You can take him there yourself."

Karen continued on as if Kaitlyn had not even spoken. "Tell my mom that I'm sorry. Tell her . . ." Karen paused as she tried to control her emotions, "that I love her and I've missed her so much."

"Karen," Kaitlyn pleaded. "You can't give up."

"*Please,*" she begged as she reached out and squeezed Kaitlyn's hand. "I never should have left, but I can't undo that now. Please, Kaitlyn, help me reunite my family. I want my mom and dad to see their grandson."

Karen's face was drawn and her voice filled with desperation.

Kaitlyn bobbed her head. "I promise, Karen. I'll take him home."

# CHAPTER 25

It was day four with still no sign of rescue. Everyone seemed to be slowing down to conserve their strength, limiting movement to absolute necessity. Though they had each eaten a slice of fish yesterday, the effects of going without water were proving to be far more debilitating than hunger. The motion of the waves was also increasing. The waves were not intense, but the resulting nausea was. Gary had also become vocal the last couple of hours, pestering Matthew and Flip repeatedly to untie him. The very idea sent a shiver up Kaitlyn's spine.

Kaitlyn glanced over at Rhonda. To her credit, last night she had taken Sam's turn to stand watch, and then this morning she had gotten up without complaint and taken her own. Kaitlyn's eyes then fell on Eleanor sitting next to Karen in the main boat. She had a wet rag on Karen's head, trying to cool the fever that was ravaging her weak body. Despite her effort, Karen seemed to be growing more delirious. Any hope that she would survive was quickly fading. In fact, they were all amazed that she had held on this long.

Kaitlyn looked around her own boat at Gracie, Amber, and Pete. The four of them were in the boat with all the supplies, while everyone else sat resting in the main boat. It was the first time since the evacuation the four of them had been alone together. Kaitlyn's eyes lingered on Amber. Her fever had begun to escalate dangerously over the past thirty minutes. Also, when Kaitlyn had last changed her bandages, her legs underneath were warm and inflamed, and a red streak led up her leg. The infection was getting into her bloodstream.

"You don't think we're going to make it, do you?"

Kaitlyn glanced up from her thoughts to face Gracie. Almost instantly, she looked away. There was no sense in lying. Even if she had tried, Gracie would have seen right through her.

"I don't know, Gracie. I just don't know."

"If we don't make it out of this," Amber choked out, her voice strained with the effort. "I want you guys to know how much I love you."

Gracie and Kaitlyn both turned to look at Amber. Her appearance had changed much more drastically in the past few hours than their own. The fever seemed to be sucking every drop of moisture out of her frail body; the dark circles around her eyes now fell halfway down her face, giving a raccoon appearance to her already sunken cheeks.

"Don't even talk like that, Amber," Gracie said with a scowl.

"When would you like me to start talking like that? We've been out here four days." Amber's voice sounded hoarse and dry. "I don't want to die without saying good-bye."

Kaitlyn nodded her head because she was too choked up to speak. She knew exactly how Amber felt. Kaitlyn bent over to hug Amber. She could feel the heat from Amber's fever almost before she touched her, and she was shivering uncontrollably. Kaitlyn held onto her friend, both of them crying though the tears could not fall. When Kaitlyn finally looked up, Pete was looking right at her.

"Kaitlyn, are you afraid to die?"

"Pete, we're not going to die," Kaitlyn said tenderly.

"I'm not afraid anymore," Pete said boldly.

Kaitlyn's eyes were wide.

"I've felt real close to my mom today. Almost like she's with me. Helping me. Telling me it's okay."

Kaitlyn pulled him into her arms. When Pete pulled back, his eyes were lowered.

"I need to tell you something."

"What is it, Pete?" Kaitlyn asked softly.

He hesitated for only a second, but then like a faucet that had just sprung a leak, it all came gushing out. "The reason that I knew Gary had all that money was because I helped him steal it. Gary threatened me, but it was still me that snuck into your room. *I* stole your money. *I'm* the thief!" Then he paused to catch his breath, as though his confession had taken all of his strength.

Kaitlyn surveyed the boy before her. He had his eyes lowered so that his lashes showed long against his bronzed cheeks. The big brown eyes that had danced with pleasure a few days ago when Flip had joked with him were now filled with guilt and shame.

"Pete, it's all right," Kaitlyn soothed as she reached out and took the boy into her arms.

"I'm sorry," he whispered.

"I know you are."

Kaitlyn could feel his whole body relax, as if an incredible load had just been lifted from his shoulders. When he sat back down, Gracie put her arm around his shoulder and squeezed.

"This was definitely *not* the vacation I had planned," Gracie admitted as she licked her cracked lips. "I was supposed to be on a warm beach with two muscular natives fighting over me."

"You did catch Flip's attention," Kaitlyn said.

Gracie smiled weakly and then brushed back her hair with her hand. Her curls were stiff from the salt water. "Not bad for someone who hasn't had a bath in four days," she bragged.

"Don't remind us," Pete said.

Kaitlyn would have laughed, but that would have taken more energy than she had left.

"So much has happened," Gracie began weakly. "I don't even feel like the same person." She tried to swallow, but there was no moisture left in her mouth. "A few days ago my biggest worry was whether or not to super-size my fries. Now I wonder if I'll ever make it off this boat alive."

They all turned as Amber moaned in pain.

"She needs help," Kaitlyn cried as she looked helplessly over at Gracie.

Both Kaitlyn and Gracie turned as the boat began to rock. Matthew had climbed into their boat and was slowly hobbling over next to them. He gingerly knelt down next to Amber and took her hand. Amber's face was flushed and distorted with pain, but her eyes opened as soon as Matthew touched her.

"I'm so scared," she whispered, her voice barely audible. "I don't want to die."

"I know," Matthew soothed as he reached down and stroked her hair.

"Will you pray for me?"

Matthew nodded and released her hand to place both of his on her head, then he bowed his own. Kaitlyn strained to hear the words that he spoke, but his voice was too soft. As Kaitlyn watched the scene before her, she began to feel a warmth spreading through her entire body, as though someone had just placed a warm blanket around her. It felt calming, almost peaceful. Like a warm August day. After several minutes, Matthew lifted his head. Amber's eyes were shining.

"Thank you," she whispered.

Kaitlyn stared at them in wonder.

"Someone help me," Eleanor cried. "She's stopped breathing!"

Kaitlyn jerked around to look at Eleanor, sending her own head spinning. Eleanor was in the main lifeboat sitting next to Karen, but as Flip rushed over to her, she moved out of the way, letting Karen's hand fall limply to the floor. All of a sudden, Kaitlyn could not breathe. It was as though a thousand pounds had just been placed right on top of her lungs. Her muscles were constricted so tightly that they seemed to be forcing all the oxygen right out of her, emerging from her larynx in the form of a shrilling scream.

"No! Karen, please. You can't die!"

Kaitlyn got to her feet, stumbling toward the bow of the supply boat. Her head was swirling in one direction, while everything else around her seemed to be spinning in the opposite. She tried to focus her eyes long enough to appraise the six-inch gap between the two boats, but in her weakened state, the distance looked as immense as the Grand Canyon. Kaitlyn tried to look back across at Karen, but the churning in her head only seemed to be intensifying. It reminded her of when she was a little kid and her dad would spin her around and around in his arms in the backyard and then set her down. She would stumble around in a whirlwind of motion for several seconds and then collapse into the fragrant grass to stare up at the twisting sky. Only this time there seemed to be an obnoxious buzzing sound that accompanied the spinning. Kaitlyn reached out to steady herself with the side of the boat. That seemed to help the spinning somewhat, but the buzzing persisted. In fact, it seemed to be growing. Kaitlyn grasped her head with both hands to try to stop it.

"Kaitlyn, sit down," Gracie cried. "There's nothing more you can do for her now."

"Shh," Kaitlyn demanded, as she cocked her head to the side.

*"What?"* Gracie asked. "What is it?"

"Listen!" Kaitlyn exclaimed, her eyes suddenly wide.

Then they heard it. At first it sounded like the gentle humming of a bumblebee, but as it neared, the sound intensified to the undeniable roar of a jet.

"A plane," Kaitlyn began, her voice no more than a whisper.

Gracie staggered to her feet while everyone squinted up in amazement as the plane came into view. Within seconds it was directly overhead. Rays of light reflected off the metal as it circled above them. Kaitlyn's mind could barely grasp what was happening. She had just surrendered to the fact that this might be the end. Then, out of nowhere, streaking across the sky with a rumble like thunder booming from its engines, emerged their rescuers. Everyone was hugging and crying and waving up into the sky.

"It's over," Gracie sobbed. "I can't believe it."

Kaitlyn could feel her whole body tingling with unfathomable joy. Then almost instantly the feeling was darkened, as if a black cloud had just shadowed all the rays of the sun. Kaitlyn turned back to the lifeless body lying in the other boat. Flip and Donald were still bent over, working feverishly on Karen despite the plane—or maybe because of it. Karen could not die seconds before they were rescued. That was just too much to take. With renewed determination, Kaitlyn carefully crossed from the supply boat and made her way to Karen. Before she could even kneel down, Donald's head shot up.

"I've got a heartbeat!" he exclaimed. "It's weak," he admitted cautiously, "but she's alive."

Flip cocked his head around to look at the plane that was now circling back toward them.

"She needs help *now!*" Flip began. "I don't know how much longer she's going to last."

Matthew, who had also climbed into the main boat, stepped between Kaitlyn and Flip. Without a word he placed his hands on Karen's head. Again, as soon as Matthew began his prayer, the same warm, comforting feelings filled Kaitlyn's mind. When Matthew finished, Kaitlyn felt a sense of peace. She reached out and took Karen's hand in her own, then bent and whispered in her ear.

"It's going to be okay, Karen. They've found us."

# CHAPTER 26

The plane did a large circle in the sky above them, rocking its wings back and forth, then left. For the next twenty minutes, everyone was beginning to fear that the plane had not actually spotted them when a Coast Guard helicopter finally arrived, its giant blades slicing through the air and sending ripples across the water around the boat. Two men dressed in black wetsuits plunged from the helicopter down into the clear water. After they broke through the surface, a small bundle was also tossed down from the hovering chopper. One of the men swam over to retrieve the bundle, while the other swam toward the lifeboats. Flip, Donald, and Matthew reached out their hands to help the first man into the boat. Everyone else watched anxiously as the man removed his dripping mask.

"How y'all holdin' up?" he asked, his gentle eyes going from face to face.

"Let's just say you got here in the nick of time," Matthew acknowledged gratefully.

"Sorry it took us so long to find y'all," the man continued. "That storm scattered those lifeboats from here to Timbuktu. I haven't had such a challenge findin' somethin' since my two-year-old swallowed my wife's diamond ring. We found it all right, but . . ." He wrinkled up his nose. "You can bet the pig farm it was one of the messiest Search and Rescue operations I've ever had to do. By the way, my name's Dillon."

Kaitlyn smiled. This man was not particularly handsome, but his smile was warm and his endearing southern accent so reassuring that, as far as Kaitlyn was concerned, he could have passed as an angel.

They all turned as the second rescuer reached the boat. Dillon extended his hand and pulled the man from the water with one large pull. It had taken Matthew, Flip, and Donald using all of their strength to hoist Dillon from the water. Kaitlyn looked over at Matthew. He looked completely drained from the effort. Kaitlyn had seen him fussing with his leg a lot the past few hours. Though he was not about to admit it, Kaitlyn was afraid that his leg was not doing as well as he had led them to believe. Kaitlyn could feel a swirl of emotion rush through her. Since she had asked Matthew if he had feelings for her, she had purposely avoided him. It was not that her feelings for him had changed; the problem was that her feelings for him had *not* changed. Matthew's prayer and the feelings it invoked in her only seemed to add to her confusion.

Kaitlyn diverted her eyes over to the man that had just been pulled from the ocean. He was a little younger than Dillon, with a long face and small blue eyes. Strands of damp, sandy blond hair fell down from underneath his wetsuit cap. Kaitlyn watched as he opened the box next to him and withdrew a bottle of water. In that second she would have thought she had just discovered the Seven Cities of Cíbola with all their fabled treasure. Every eye was wide and glued to the water. Before anyone could move, Benton slowly got to his feet and staggered forward. His little legs could barely hold his slim form. Kaitlyn wanted to cry. The rescuer eagerly handed the little boy the bottle, but once Benton had it in his hands, he just stood there motionless. He eyed the water longingly for several seconds, then he turned and walked over to stand in front of Madison. She was sitting on her mother's lap, too drained to even move. Without a second's hesitation, Benton handed the water to his sister. Kaitlyn shook her head in wonder, although she wasn't surprised.

Morgan immediately unscrewed the lid and held the water up to her daughter's parched lips. Sam bent down and pulled his son into his arms. The little boy almost disappeared in the hug. Kaitlyn smiled, though her cracked lips began to bleed with the effort. Over the past four days, Kaitlyn had seen Sam growl like a grizzly protecting his young cubs and then, in moments like this, soften like a big overstuffed teddy bear. Apparently the apple was not going to be falling too far from the tree. This freckle-faced boy was following right along in his protective father's footsteps.

"Don't worry," the rescue worker began as he held up several more bottles. "There's plenty for everyone."

After he had passed out the water bottles, he made his way over to Karen. Dillon was already at her side. Though she was breathing on her own, it was shallow and she was completely unresponsive. Dillon pulled a walkie-talkie from a pouch connected to his wetsuit.

"Female, 30 to 35. Possible internal damage. Pulse rate weak and sporadic. Extensive abdominal injures."

Kaitlyn could hear Dillon still communicating Karen's condition to a voice on the other end of the static as she made her way over to the supply boat with three bottles of water. Gracie met her at the bow and eagerly accepted her bottle. Kaitlyn unscrewed the lid on the second bottle and then walked over to Amber, whose teeth were chattering now, she was so chilled with fever. Kaitlyn held the bottle up to Amber's mouth with one hand while she attempted to hold her head up with the other. The result was that almost as much water trickled down her chin as went into her mouth. Kaitlyn licked her lips longingly. Her own tongue was swollen and felt as dry as sandpaper.

"Don't give her any more water."

Kaitlyn turned around to face the second rescuer, whom she had overheard Dillon calling Jackson. He was just climbing into their boat.

"What do you mean?" Gracie spoke up.

"Until we assess their physical state," Jackson continued, "and make sure it's safe, those with severe injuries need to wait just a little longer."

Jackson reached out and took Amber's hand. "I'm sorry. We just don't want to make things any worse for you."

Amber nodded reluctantly.

"I promise, after the doctor checks you out and everything is okay, I'll personally see to it that you get all the water you can hold."

As Kaitlyn listened to the two of them, she began drinking her own bottle of water greedily. Water had never tasted so good. When she was done, she could feel it sloshing around in her otherwise empty stomach. They all looked up as a clap of thunder echoed off in the distance. Overhead the sun was still shining down in force, but off to the right the sky was black as night. A strike of lightning illuminated the dark clouds.

"The storm isn't too far behind us," Jackson admitted. "We were just about to call it a day when we spotted you."

He was doing a good job at keeping his voice passive, but something in his eyes bothered Kaitlyn. She looked back at the clouds off in the distance. Though the sun was still beating down on her raw skin, the smell of rain was clearly evident in the warm ocean breeze.

* * *

"Okay, folks, this is how it's gonna work," Dillon began as he looked around at everyone in the main boat. "We'll load the two critical passengers first and take them to a waiting rescue ship. Then, as soon as we get a second chopper, we'll start with the—" A loud crack of thunder stopped him in midsentence. Dillon looked up at the sky. It had been about five minutes since they had spotted the storm off in the horizon. Now it was threatening to overtake them. "Then," he continued, trying hard not to look concerned, "when the second chopper arrives, we'll start with the women and children."

"By then we'll be dead," Gary growled.

Dillon looked over at the man who sat tied up on the floor of the boat in about four inches of water. He didn't look surprised, since he had already been apprised of the whole situation with Gary.

"Just relax," Dillon warned. "That second chopper is already on its way. In fact, there's a good chance it'll get here before this one even leaves. So what do you say we stop all this jawin' and get to work?"

It wasn't hard to see why Dillon was in this line of work. He had a calming influence about him combined with a no-nonsense, take-charge attitude, which made him exceptionally well suited to Search and Rescue. Kaitlyn could feel the tenseness in her muscles begin to relax—until she made the mistake of turning to look at the storm. Off in the distance she could see sheets of rain pouring from a charcoal sky, while lightning flashed life into the approaching monster. Kaitlyn could feel the blood inside her veins turn cold. No amount of comforting could blot out the obvious. The last time that she had seen a storm this ferocious they had evacuated right into the heart of it.

"I don't want to leave without you," Amber said as she grabbed both Kaitlyn and Gracie's hands.

Gracie looked from Amber back to the storm. "I never thought I'd be jealous of someone whose legs had been crushed."

Gracie was joking, or at least Kaitlyn thought she was, but the fear in her eyes was real.

"You heard what Dillon said," Kaitlyn reassured her. "That second helicopter could be here any minute."

They all looked up as a stretcher was lowered to the lifeboats. Jackson, who had gone back to the main boat to help Dillon, stretched his arm out to grab ahold of it, and Dillon reached out to help. Once they had it secured, the two men hoisted it over to Karen.

"I'll be right back," Kaitlyn said to her friends in the supply boat.

The waves were starting to pick up now, making movement within the boats much more difficult. Kaitlyn cautiously made her way over to the main boat. She was still sluggish and weak, but having the rescuers with them somehow gave her added strength. Dillon and Jackson struggled to lift Karen onto the stretcher. Once that was done, Jackson began strapping Karen in while Dillon reattached the cable so that she could be pulled up to the waiting helicopter. Kaitlyn quickly knelt and took Karen's hand in her own.

"You made it, Karen," she whispered as she squeezed her hand. "You're going home."

"Ma'am, we've got to send her up," Dillon urged as another fierce rumble echoed across the waves.

Kaitlyn nodded her head. She squeezed Karen's hand one more time, even though Karen was unconscious, then she moved back and watched as the stretcher was lifted up into the sky. The first sprinkles of rain were just starting to fall. Kaitlyn reluctantly turned and made her way back to the supply boat. Now that Karen was secured, Kaitlyn knew that Amber would be next. Dillon and Jackson followed right behind her.

"All right, little lady," Dillon said with a wink as he approached Amber. "It looks like it's your turn."

Amber stared up as the second stretcher was lowered. Her eyes were wide.

"I know it looks kinda scary," Dillon admitted. "But just think of it as a ride at the county fair."

"A ride with razor-sharp blades that could slice you in two," Amber added, her voice shaking.

"That's for sure," Pete said as he stared up at the enormous machine hovering above them.

Kaitlyn turned to look at Pete. He had sat so quietly the last few minutes that Kaitlyn had almost forgotten he was there.

"Is there any room for children on this run?" Kaitlyn asked softly.

Jackson glanced up at Kaitlyn then turned to look at Dillon. Both men seemed to be communicating, even though nothing verbal was said.

"Actually, I think we *will* send the kids in this load," Jackson admitted.

Kaitlyn was not the only one with serious concerns about this storm. If there was any possible way to evacuate the children, they were going to have to do it now.

"Hey, somebody untie me. My wrists are raw."

Kaitlyn turned to look at Gary. He had his tied hands raised toward Flip.

"If that storm is as bad as the last one," Gary continued, "I'm going to need both my hands free just so I can hold on."

Sam shook his head adamantly. "No!"

"Sam, you've got to think rationally," Morgan urged her husband. "We can't leave him like that."

"Maybe if he gets swallowed up in the ocean, then he'll know how our son felt."

"*Sam,*" Eleanor scolded.

A hint of shame crossed Sam's face.

"As much as I hate to admit it," Flip began, "Gary's got a point. If that storm reaches us before the helicopter, he's going to need to be untied."

Flip looked over at Matthew for his opinion. Matthew sat there for a moment, then nodded his head. They didn't have a choice. Flip pulled the knife from his pocket.

"One false move and I'll put the ropes back on," Flip said firmly. "Do you understand?"

Gary nodded but kept his jaw tight.

Kaitlyn's focus went back to Amber, as the last of the belts were fastened.

"Okay, she's ready," Jackson said as he signaled up to the helicopter.

Kaitlyn reached out and took Amber's hand. She was still hot with fever.

"You're going to be okay, Amber," Kaitlyn said as she forced a smile.

"It's not me I'm worried about," Amber said, gesturing to the approaching storm.

Kaitlyn and Gracie stood back as the stretcher began to lift. Kaitlyn could feel the effect of Amber's foreboding words knotting in the pit of her stomach. She tried to shrug it off, but with each rumble of thunder the feeling deepened. Kaitlyn glanced over at Gary. The ropes were already off his hands, and he was massaging his wrists. Kaitlyn could feel acid burning in the back of her throat.

She quickly shielded her eyes from the rain and stared back up into the sky. Amber was just being lifted into the safety of the chopper. The rain was still relatively light, but the wind was building velocity with each passing minute. Kaitlyn was grateful that Amber was lifted when she was. The harness that was lowered next was tossed around effortlessly by the growing gusts.

"Everybody get down," Jackson demanded.

Dillon reached out and grabbed the harness.

"We're going to have to do this quick," Dillon called over to Sam. "We'll take the little girl first."

Sam reached over to take Madison from his wife. Morgan's face was twisted with emotion.

"Morgan, she's got to go," Sam pleaded.

"I know," Morgan cried.

She hugged and kissed her daughter one more time before handing her over to Sam. Sam kissed Madison tenderly on the forehead. Several days ago, Madison would have probably gone into the harness kicking and screaming, but four days of starvation had left the child drained and listless.

Kaitlyn looked back at the approaching storm. The front of it was just starting to reach them. Within minutes, an airlift evacuation would be impossible.

"Take it up. Take it up," Dillon demanded as he waved his signal.

They all watched in fear as Madison was lifted up into the twisting sky.

Dillon turned back to Sam. "Okay, the boy's next. Get him ready. We don't have a second to spare."

Sam went over and knelt beside his son. The wind had picked up so much that Sam almost had to shout at the boy.

"All right, little man . . ." Sam stopped and began shaking his head, as he fought to regain control. "You take care of your sister. Do you hear me?"

Benton's head bobbed up and down and then he threw his arms around his dad's neck.

"What about the rest of us?" Gary turned to Dillon and demanded. "Where's the other chopper you promised?"

"We're just gonna have to hold on until they get here," Dillon hollered over the howl of the wind.

"Who do you think you're kidding?" Gary shouted. "Even if the other chopper gets here, it's not going to be able to hold us all! Then we're going to be left to the mercy of *that!*"

They all stopped to look at the storm. The clouds were like an enormous black cloak draped across an angry ocean. Gigantic waves sprang out from the ocean's depths, threatening to reach up and blend into one solid mass of coal-black darkness. Kaitlyn could feel an eerie tingle sweep through her entire body. One look at the storm could terrify even the most experienced sailor, but this time it was not just the storm that had Kaitlyn's flesh crawling. It was the tone in Gary's voice; he was getting desperate.

They all looked up at the helicopter as the last harness was lowered. Just before it reached the main boat, a huge gust of wind rocked the chopper. Everyone began to scream as the massive machine twisted around in the air above them, its huge blades tilting toward them. The lethal blades were so close that Kaitlyn could feel the air beat from their rotations. She was sure that in seconds it was going to crash down on top of them, slicing them to bits. Then, at the last possible minute, the pilot somehow regained control and pulled the chopper up. The lowered harness now soared through the air over the main boat like a pendulum.

"You can all wait around if you want," Gary screamed. "But I'm getting out of here."

Flip reached out to grab him, but it was too late. Gary dove at the harness, causing it to swing out across the water.

"Grab him," Sam demanded as Gary swung back toward the boat.

In a clash of arms and legs Gary slammed right into Flip. For a minute Kaitlyn thought that someone would end up in the ocean, but Gary managed to keep his grip, and Flip crashed into the side of the boat. Though he hit hard, with adrenaline pumping through him, Flip found the strength to drag himself back up and try to grab Gary's legs. This time, Gary was just too far out of reach. Even Sam, standing on top of a bench seat, couldn't reach him. The helicopter pilot had no choice. Time was running out. He had to pull Gary up instead of little Benton. With Sam shouting wildly up at the sky, Gary disappeared into the belly of the rescue chopper. The rest of them stared in shock as the helicopter turned and left them to the fury of the ocean. Kaitlyn buried her face in her hands. She could hear Sam screaming at the top of his lungs until he was hoarse and the sound of the blades had melted into the howl of the wind.

"The second chopper isn't coming, is it?" Donald called out.

Dillon stood there for several seconds and then slowly shook his head.

"Even if they wanted to, the storm is just too strong now. They can't risk any more lives."

"You mean we're on our own?" Rhonda cried.

Dillon lowered his gaze. There was nothing more he could say.

Kaitlyn turned back to look into the fury of the gale. There didn't seem to be any way out of this one. Within minutes, the storm would be crashing down on top of them. If the last storm had shown any mercy at all, this one threatened to make up for it.

"Everyone into the other boat," Dillon said as he pointed at the leak in the main boat.

The waves were thrashing furiously now, causing the two boats to ram each other. If they remained tied together, it would be just a matter of time before they were both torn to pieces. Dillon and Jackson climbed into the supply boat and then stood at the bow to help the others across the gap. Once they were safely aboard, Flip and Matthew began throwing the wooden boxes overboard so that the boat wouldn't sink. Then Flip quickly sat down next to Gracie. He reached out and took Gracie's hand and pulled her in close to him, while Pete took a seat next to him. Matthew hobbled over and sat down next to Kaitlyn.

"We're going to have to separate the two boats," Dillon called out as he pointed to the main boat.

Jackson immediately pulled out his knife and began sawing at the rope. Twice he had to yank his arm out of the way as the two boats slammed into each other. Once the rope finally snapped, Jackson dove for the bottom of the boat as a giant wave nearly buried them.

"Turn on the rescue beeper," Jackson cried as he groped for something to hold onto. "They'll need to know where we went down."

Kaitlyn could feel all the blood drain from her face. "What do you mean, where we went down?" she screamed.

"Hold onto something," Dillon yelled, "Then don't let go no matter what happens."

Kaitlyn could hear his words, but her brain was too numb to process the information. She just sat there gaping at the growing waves. She had the same helpless feeling of terror she had experienced when she watched the truck plow into her and Leslie. Matthew reached out and wrapped his arms around her. Kaitlyn immediately buried her face in his chest and clung to his tattered shirt.

"I don't want to die," she sobbed.

Matthew pulled her in closer. "Whatever happens, I want you to know—"

A loud blast from somewhere behind them stopped Matthew in midsentence, and they all turned and strained their eyes in its direction. At first there was nothing but the wailing of the wind and the thrashing of waves. Then the sound came again, only louder.

"It's the rescue ship," Dillon yelled.

"Where?" Rhonda shouted.

Dillon pointed into the darkness as the massive shadow of a ship emerged with several large spotlights that pierced the darkness. For a moment they all feared that the ship would ram right into them, but then a long blast of the horn signaled they had been spotted. Suddenly the darkness was illuminated by a brilliant flash of lightning. Kaitlyn glanced up to see an enormous wave off in the distance rising out of the depths of the ocean. It looked like a solid, impenetrable wall.

"They'll never get us aboard in time," Kaitlyn screamed as she pointed at the approaching swell. Matthew turned to look as another flash of lightning lit the sky. The wall of water was about twenty feet high and building momentum as it thundered toward them.

"Yes they will," Dillon shouted as he jumped to his feet.

Several men aboard the ship were already lowering large cables down to them.

"Someone help me," Dillon shouted. "We need to hook the cables to the bow and the stern so they can lift us up."

Kaitlyn watched as the men raced to beat the wave. Jackson caught the first cable and quickly fastened it to the bow, but the second cable slipped from Dillon's grasp. On the second attempt, he caught it and quickly fastened it to the stern. Dillon immediately began flailing his arms up toward the ship.

"Take us up *now!*" he begged.

Within seconds, the lifeboat began to be lifted out of the water. Kaitlyn's eyes flashed from the ship that towered next to them to the wave that seemed to be gaining velocity.

*"Hurry,"* she screamed. "It's coming!"

At least fifteen members of the Search and Rescue team were waiting to grab them once they reached the top. With the lifeboat swaying beneath them, they all climbed onto the deck and ran toward the cabin of the ship. The wave was only seconds from them.

"This is it," Flip called out as the door was slammed behind them.

Sam, Morgan, and Eleanor huddled together around Benton in a corner of the cabin, while Donald, Rhonda, Flip, and Gracie sat close together, all of them gripping a desk that was bolted to the floor. Pete and several of the rescue crew also braced themselves with anything they could find that was bolted down. Kaitlyn and Matthew wrapped their arms around a pole near the center of the cabin.

For an excruciating moment, there was almost complete silence. Even the movement of the water seemed to change. It was as if the wave were pulling all the surrounding water into its building mountain. Then they heard it. At first it sounded like thunder, then it grew until it seemed like the moaning of the ocean itself. The front of the ship rose sharply as it began to climb the wall of water. The silence in the cabin was instantly gone. Everyone began to scream. Several people lost their grip and went flying into the back wall. They were just too weak to hold on. Kaitlyn clung to the pole until her knuckles were white and her arms were weak and trembling. Then, in a shock of sound and force, the wave plunged over the top of them, engulfing the ship. She could hear the shatter of glass, followed immediately by a tremendous spray of water. Instantly the lights began to flicker, inspiring another surge of ear-piercing screams. Then, just when the ship was tilted so sharply that Kaitlyn feared it would capsize, it crested and began its descent. Kaitlyn's eyes shot around the ship anxiously. She could feel her whole body shaking as she waited to see if there would be a second wall of water. Everyone else seemed to be doing the same thing. Though the ocean continued to beat upon them and the waves continued to swell, a second wave didn't come. After what seemed an eternity, the rocking of the rescue ship slowly leveled out and Kaitlyn watched as the water began to drain from the cabin. The giant waves and pounding rain of the storm eventually passed, leaving only the rolling of a stormy sea. Kaitlyn let go of the pole and let her arms fall limply to her sides. Then she turned to Matthew. He had one arm wrapped around her and the other around the pole. His hair was wet and plastered to his face and every muscle in his body was pulled taut, but as he turned to look at her, a smile twitched at the corners of his lips.

"We did it," he whispered.

Kaitlyn's body began to tingle as the realization slowly hit her. They *had* made it. They were alive. The silence that had filled the cabin just seconds ago now turned to sobs of joy and relief. Kaitlyn threw her arms around Matthew.

"It's all over," she cried.

Matthew smiled. "We're going home."

# CHAPTER 27

As soon as they emerged from the rescue ship, a swarm of reporters enveloped them, flashing cameras and thrusting microphones in their faces. Kaitlyn was shocked to find that they even knew their names. The press must have gotten notice of their identities. The Coast Guard tried to get them to the waiting ambulances as quickly as possible, but a few of the ambulances had not yet arrived, including Kaitlyn's.

Kaitlyn stammered as a reporter in a dress suit and heels pummeled her with questions. Before she could form a complete sentence, the reporter spotted someone behind Kaitlyn. She immediately turned, directed the cameraman to follow her, and raced across the deck. Kaitlyn looked over her shoulder to see Rhonda wheeled out to a cluster of reporters armed with microphones. Rhonda immediately transformed back to her former self, playing it to the hilt. Kaitlyn expected the reporters to stay with Rhonda and, from the look on her face, so did she. Instead, as soon as Sam, Morgan, Eleanor, Benton, and little Madison were wheeled out, the reporters rushed right for them. Apparently they viewed a family stranded at sea as a lead story over a spoiled little rich girl.

From the corner of her eye, Kaitlyn saw Donald slip across the dock to a waiting ambulance. Kaitlyn shook her head with a smile. She didn't waste time looking for her parents, whom she knew would still be on a plane heading to Miami. Karen, Gracie, Madison, and Gary had already been taken to a nearby hospital. Kaitlyn and the others on the rescue ship had gotten word that once they'd gotten to the hospital, Gary had escaped. Due to the seriousness of Karen's and Amber's condition, and since the Coast Guard didn't have the full story, he had slipped away relatively unnoticed. As of an hour ago, he was still at large.

Kaitlyn allowed her eyes to sweep across the chaos to rest on Pete. He spotted her at the same time. He quickly turned and said something to the rescue worker behind him, who then immediately wheeled him over to her.

"I talked to my dad on the ship's phone," Pete began eagerly. "He's already waiting for me at the hospital."

Kaitlyn smiled and reached out to grab his hand. "I'm going to miss you," she said.

Pete's eyes widened. "Do you think we'll ever see each other again?"

Kaitlyn tilted her head and arched her brows in mock offense. "You don't think you're going to get rid of me that easy, do you? Minnesota and Miami are just a plane ride away with no ocean in between," she added with a quick smile.

Kaitlyn turned as another ambulance arrived at the curb.

"This one's yours, miss," said the man who was pushing Kaitlyn's wheelchair.

Kaitlyn nodded and then turned back to Pete.

"I've got to go," she said, then leaned over and kissed Pete on the cheek. "When I come to Miami, you can take me to the docks and we'll watch the fishermen unload their catch."

Pete lowered his head, his long lashes unable to hide the tender emotion in his eyes.

"Good-bye, Pete," Kaitlyn said softly.

Kaitlyn was amazed at the bond they had formed in only a few days. Throughout this entire ordeal she had wanted nothing more than to be rescued and get off those lifeboats, but now there was a pulling at her heart. In all the commotion of the rescue there had been very little time for good-byes. Kaitlyn craned her neck around to scan the dock behind her. The whole area was crawling with the news media and emergency personnel. Kaitlyn's eyes raced from face to face, but the person she most wanted to find was nowhere to be seen.

\* \* \*

Kaitlyn's eyelashes fluttered and then flew open to stare up into the face that stood above her.

"Hello," a young woman dressed in green scrubs said with a smile. "I didn't mean to wake you. I just need to take your blood pressure. Standard procedure," she added with a shrug. "Then I'll leave and let you sleep."

Kaitlyn squinted her eyes to read the clock on the wall.

"It's almost six o'clock," the nurse offered.

Kaitlyn rubbed her eyes. "It feels like I just went to bed and it's almost time to get up."

The woman continued pumping the black rubber ball connected to the blood-pressure cup.

"Your body has gone through quite a shock."

Kaitlyn turned her head toward the chair next to her bed. Her mother had her head propped up with a couple of pillows and was sleeping soundly. Marjorie had flatly refused to join her husband and Kenny at the hotel last night, insisting that she needed to stay up at the hospital with her daughter. And Brent hadn't even attempted to talk her out of it. He had simply kissed his wife tenderly and whispered that he loved her.

"Everything looks good," the nurse offered with a reassuring smile. "I'm going to go and let you get some rest, but if you need anything, just ring the nurses' station."

Kaitlyn thanked the nurse as she left and then looked up at the blank television screen that was on the wall across from her bed. Kaitlyn's father had told her that their ordeal had been plastered all over the television for days. Last night she had been so tired that nothing short of an atomic blast could have interrupted her sleep, but now she was wide awake and curious to hear about the evacuation. All she knew for sure was that there had been only a handful of deaths, most of which occurred in the boiler room, and that the *Lady of the Islands* had sunk completely, making investigation into the explosion tedious if not impossible.

Kaitlyn took one more look over at her mom, then quietly slid out of bed. She grabbed her robe, slowly opened the door, and slipped out into the hall.

The hall was empty and quiet except for a few nurses talking and laughing softly down at the nurses' station. Kaitlyn tiptoed past them unnoticed and then headed toward the lounge. Maybe she would go in and see if the television was on. Her father had said that their rescue had made the national news. Kaitlyn rounded the corner and then entered the small room that served as a waiting room for the families of patients. The TV was on, but it was the person sitting in front of it that caught Kaitlyn's attention.

*"Matthew?"*

It was said softly, but Matthew spun his head around as if she had shouted.

"Kaitlyn!"

Kaitlyn could not help but smile at his reaction.

"What are you doing?" Matthew asked as he looked down at his watch. "It's not even six o'clock yet."

"I guess I could ask you the same thing."

"I couldn't sleep," Matthew admitted. "I finally get a nice soft bed and all I can do is toss and turn. How are you feeling?"

"Weak. How about you?"

Matthew looked down at his wrapped leg. "The doctor said he doesn't think there's any permanent nerve damage from the tourniquet."

"Really?"

Matthew nodded. "He seemed very surprised, but I told him I had a good doctor."

Kaitlyn could feel the blood rush to her face. "I looked for you back at the dock. I was afraid I wasn't going to get a chance to say good-bye."

Matthew reached out and took her hand in his as Kaitlyn slipped into the chair next to him. Then they both glanced up at a bulletin on the TV screen. Several officers were escorting a man in handcuffs into a hospital. They both recognized the man immediately.

"I guess Gary didn't make it very far," Kaitlyn said with a shake of her head.

"I have a feeling that was his last taste of freedom for a while."

Then they both sat there for several minutes, watching the still blackness out the window coming to life with streaks of bright orange, yellow, and gentle hints of pink.

"It's beautiful," Kaitlyn whispered.

They both sat there, neither wanting to take the next inevitable step. Kaitlyn could feel her chin begin to tremble. *What are you doing? Tell him how you feel. Don't let him go never knowing.*

"Matthew, I need to tell you something." She let her breath out hard. "Matthew, I—"

"I know," he began. "And that makes it even more difficult to say good-bye. Kaitlyn, believe me, I wish that things were different, but—"

This time it was Kaitlyn's turn to cut him off. "I know," she said sadly.

Matthew ran his finger across her cheek to wipe at the tear that was sliding down her face. Then his eyes ran across all the features of her face as if he were committing them to memory.

"Kaitlyn!" A voice from the doorway brought her head around sharply.

Both Kaitlyn and Matthew turned to look at the figure in the doorway.

"Greg!" Kaitlyn exclaimed as she quickly stood.

Greg was to her in four quick strides. He scooped her up into his arms and kissed her.

"I was so afraid I had lost you," he said as he pulled back. "Are you all right?"

"Yes . . . I'm fine," she stammered.

Kaitlyn glanced from Greg back to Matthew. When she saw the look in Matthew's eyes she wanted to turn away.

"Greg, this is Matthew. We were on the lifeboat together. Actually, he was the one who got me off the ship when it was burning."

Greg immediately stuck his hand out to Matthew, who struggled to his feet to shake his hand.

"Thank you, Matthew." Greg's tone was smooth, but his eyes were rock-hard and challenging. Greg turned back toward Kaitlyn. "I don't know what I would have done if I'd lost you."

"I'd better get back to my room," Matthew began awkwardly. Then he turned to Kaitlyn, his eyes saying everything that he could not. "Good-bye, Kaitlyn."

# CHAPTER 28

Matthew stared over at the phone on the counter, then looked back down at the ledger before him. He picked up the pencil next to it and began to make notes, but again his head lifted to glance over at the phone. He had been doing this for at least a half hour now. Finally he rubbed his eyes, pushed his hair back off his forehead, and leaned back to look blankly up at the ceiling.

"I know the books aren't in the best condition, but is it really all that bad?" Jonathan Wright asked with a gentle smile as he stood watching his son from the doorway.

Jonathan knew that Matthew's frustration had nothing to do with the company books and everything to do with a young woman who lived across the country. He had watched anxiously as his son dealt with his feelings over the past couple of days. Several times he had wanted to pull him aside and remind him that the choices he made now would affect the rest of his life, but he had remained silent. Matthew had been taught since he was a little boy about the importance of a temple marriage. He was a man now. He would have to decide for himself.

"I'm sorry, Dad. I guess I'm not very good company."

"It'll be all right, son."

*"How?"* Matthew shook his head and then turned back to look at the phone. "I'm just supposed to pretend that I don't have feelings for her?"

Jonathan crossed the room and placed his hand on Matthew's shoulder. He could feel the turmoil brooding within him.

"When you were a little boy you stole a pack of baseball trading cards from Mike's Grocery. Do you remember?"

Matthew lifted his eyes to his dad. The frustration was still evident on his face but now it was mixed with confusion.

"Your mom found them in your pants pocket that night. The next day she put the pack of cards on the table next to your breakfast."

Matthew nodded his head in recollection. "I remember."

"She didn't say a word about it during breakfast," Jonathan continued.

"I know. It just about killed me. I kept staring at the cards and waiting for the lecture, but it never came. After breakfast she looked at the cards and then at me. My heart was beating a mile a minute, but all she said was, 'Matthew, you've got to decide what you want most.' An hour later I walked to the grocery store with the cards in my hand and told them what I'd done."

"But you really wanted those cards."

"I guess I wanted to be honest more. If I had kept the cards I might have been happy for a couple of days but—" Matthew stopped, the realization of his own words written all over his face. "Eventually I would have known I had made a mistake."

Matthew's shoulders slumped as he let out a long sigh.

Jonathan nodded grimly. "This is too big a decision to make a mistake, Matthew." Jonathan gripped his shoulder and then crossed to the door. Before he opened it, he looked back at his son, who was staring listlessly at the phone.

* * *

Kaitlyn jerked around as the phone on the kitchen counter began to ring. She watched anxiously as her mother picked up the receiver.

"Hello? Just a minute." Marjorie turned to her daughter with a smile. "Kaitlyn, it's for you."

Kaitlyn hurried over and took the phone. "Hello?"

"Hi, Kaitlyn," Amber said cheerily into the phone.

Kaitlyn smiled, even though a part of her had hoped it would be Matthew. Since the rescue three weeks before, Amber, Gracie, and she were inseparable. Other than Amber's weeklong stay in the hospital in Miami, the three of them had seen each other almost every day. The last few days, though, Kaitlyn had stayed at home to do a few things with her family and with Greg.

"Hey, Amber. How are you feeling?"

Though she would still have a long recovery ahead of her—including countless hours of physical therapy—Amber's doctors were confident she would eventually be able to walk with only a slight limp.

"Homebound. I eat, drink, sleep, and then eat again. Last night Gracie came over with some videos—two or three gory, shark-chomping, ship-sinking horror flicks. After the first shark movie and Gracie's rundown of our own encounter, my parents kicked her out."

Kaitlyn laughed. "I know. Where do you think she ended up after she left your house? I guess it's safe to say that Gracie is recovering just fine."

"Actually, there's something I need to talk to you about."

"What?" Kaitlyn asked curiously. Then her voice suddenly grew anxious. "Is something wrong? Are you having complications with your legs?"

"Oh, no," Amber rushed on. "It's nothing like that."

"Well?" Kaitlyn pressed. "What is it?"

Amber took a deep breath. "I looked up the Mormon missionaries."

Kaitlyn could feel her blood instantly chill.

When there was no response, Amber rushed on. "They've been coming over to my house every day this week to teach me." Again she paused. "Kaitlyn, I'm getting baptized as soon as the casts come off my legs."

Kaitlyn let her breath out hard.

"Kaitlyn, did you hear me?"

"I heard you."

"I know how you feel about this church, and I'm not even going to try and change your mind," Amber rushed on, "but it would mean a lot to me if you'd come."

Kaitlyn sat for several seconds without saying a word. "Are you *sure* this is what you want to do?" she finally asked.

"Yes!"

Kaitlyn shook her head. How could Amber get caught up in something like this?

"Will you come?" Amber asked nervously.

"I don't agree with your decision," Kaitlyn admitted bluntly, "but I'll come."

Kaitlyn could hear a huge sigh of relief on the other end of the phone.

"You don't know what this means to me."

Kaitlyn swallowed hard. "What choice do I have? We're friends."

There was a short pause. "Have you heard from anyone since the rescue?" Amber asked hesitantly.

Kaitlyn knew who Amber was referring to, but she was not in the mood to talk about him, especially after Amber's announcement.

"I talked to Eleanor a couple of days ago," Kaitlyn offered. "She said they're all recovering. She also said that she's sending us all a big batch of homemade chocolate-chip cookies."

Amber hesitated for just a second before she eased into the next subject. "How are things going with Greg?"

"Okay."

"What about your feelings for Matthew?"

Kaitlyn could feel the tears instantly brimming in her eyes. "Amber, I'm sorry. I just can't talk about him."

"Does Greg know?"

"He knows something, but he's not pushing me."

"You know Greg wants to marry you?"

Kaitlyn let out a long sigh. Amber wasn't telling her anything that she didn't already know. She could see it on his face every time they were together. "I know."

"What are you going to do?"

Kaitlyn sat silent for several seconds. "I don't know."

\* \* \*

Kaitlyn pulled up in front of the church and turned off her car, then sat for a minute just looking at the building. It didn't look like anything special. Though the grass was freshly mowed and the shrubs trimmed, it didn't appear any different from some of the other churches in town. Kaitlyn looked down at her watch and then let out a long sigh. Amber had told her that the baptism started at four o'clock and it was now four twenty. Kaitlyn had been late getting off work, and the traffic getting home was heavy. Except that was not entirely true and she knew it—she had purposely lagged around at work and then knowingly selected the most congested route home. If she had not already committed to attend

Amber's baptism, she would have skipped the whole thing and taken Kenny to a movie.

Kaitlyn climbed out of the car and made her way to the front door. A man in a suit was heading to the door at the same time and smiled warmly at her.

"Are you here for the baptism?"

Kaitlyn nodded her head. "Yes, but I think I'm running a little late."

"Mormon standard time, huh?" the man said with a shrug. Then he extended his hand to Kaitlyn. "Brother Henson," he said.

"Kaitlyn Winters."

"Nice to meet you, Kaitlyn," he said as he stood back and opened the door for her.

Kaitlyn followed him down the hall toward a lobby, mainly because she didn't have any idea where she was going. As she glanced around the hall, she noticed a bulletin board with a large map of the world and several photos of young men and women in suits and dresses next to it. Addresses in places like Houston, Texas, and Guatemala City were posted below the pictures.

Kaitlyn then glanced at a large picture on the wall as they reached the lobby. Though she had not seen this particular painting before, she guessed it was of Jesus Christ. He was standing amid the clouds with His hands stretched out. Kaitlyn found herself staring at the picture.

"Have you ever been here before?"

"No," Kaitlyn quickly offered.

Brother Henson's smile broadened. "Well, we're glad to have you." Then he motioned her toward a set of double doors and opened one of them for her.

Kaitlyn looked at the room before her. It was pretty, but nothing like some of the cathedrals and churches she had been in before. Several rows of benches faced an elevated stage, which held a few rows of seats facing the congregation. A piano and an organ stood on either side of the stage, and a man in a dark suit was speaking behind a dark wooden pulpit that rose from the middle. A vase of bright yellow lilies was placed next to the pulpit.

"It was nice meeting you, Kaitlyn," Brother Henson whispered as she passed.

Kaitlyn smiled politely and then scanned the rows of benches, looking for a place to sit. Her attention was briefly distracted by a little boy, no more than two years old, who was turned around in his seat and waving at the people behind him who couldn't resist smiling and waving back. He squealed with delight—which immediately caught his mother's attention. She put a finger to her lips and then turned and whispered her apology to the people behind her. They just dismissed it with genuine smiles. A movement attracted Kaitlyn's attention. Gracie was motioning to her from the end of the pew in front of the family. Kaitlyn quickly made her way to Gracie and took a seat.

"Hey, girl, you're late," Gracie said as she scooted over.

"Mormon standard time," Kaitlyn shot right back.

"What?"

"I have no idea," Kaitlyn said with a shrug of her shoulders. "Where's Amber?"

Gracie pointed toward the first row of benches facing the pulpit. It only took a moment to find her. She was dressed all in white, and her auburn hair was pulled back in a neat ponytail. Her mom and dad were sitting just to her right. Kaitlyn glanced at the man to Amber's left, who was also dressed in white. On his left were two young men in dark suits. Kaitlyn's eyes went instinctively back to the man in white beside Amber. Though his back was to her, there was something familiar about him. Kaitlyn stared at the back of his head, then, just as the realization began to dawn, he turned and whispered something to Amber. Kaitlyn could feel her breath catch.

"Matthew," she whispered.

Her heart began to race, and her whole body instantly flooded with emotion. Kaitlyn turned to Gracie, but from the look on her face, she wasn't surprised to see him.

"What is he doing here?" Kaitlyn whispered.

"It makes sense, doesn't it?" Gracie whispered back. "Matthew's the one who first told her about this church."

"How come no one told me he was coming?" Kaitlyn asked, keeping her voice low so as not to disrupt the speaker.

"I just found out myself when I got here. I guess Amber wanted to surprise us."

Kaitlyn could feel her stomach tighten into a knot.

"I think she's having the elders confirm her, though," Gracie added.

Kaitlyn turned back to Gracie. "Confirm her?"

"Hey, I'm learning a few things," Gracie said proudly. "How could I not? Amber hasn't stopped talking about all of it for weeks now. I have to admit," Gracie added, almost as an afterthought. "It *is* kind of interesting."

Kaitlyn's jaw dropped.

"Hey, I didn't say I was ready to jump in the water myself," Gracie quickly added. "But there is something different about Amber. I'm not sure what it is, but I like it."

Before Kaitlyn could comment, the man at the pulpit dismissed the congregation to the baptismal font. Kaitlyn watched as Amber stood and reached for her walker. She had only been out of her casts for a couple of weeks now and was still having difficulty walking. Matthew stood and steadied her with his hand, then the two of them slowly started down the aisle opposite Kaitlyn and Gracie, followed immediately by those in the front few rows. Kaitlyn could feel butterflies in the pit of her stomach as she watched Matthew tenderly guiding Amber. She had spent the last couple of months trying to forget those feelings, and now here they were, just as strong as when she was on the lifeboat.

The small room that housed the baptismal font was filled to capacity. Several people stood in the back to allow Amber's parents and those closest to her to have the seats up front. Kaitlyn followed Gracie to the edge of the font, where the two of them sat down next to Amber's parents. Two little boys darted away from their parents and sat down on the floor right in front of the baptismal font to get a better look. They looked like miniature versions of the two elders that took the seats next to Kaitlyn—only one little boy's tie was cockeyed, and the other boy had a wayward lock of hair at the back of his head that stuck straight up.

Kaitlyn and Gracie bent over and said hello to Amber's parents. From talking with Amber, Kaitlyn knew her friend's parents had recently agreed to start meeting with the missionaries. Kaitlyn turned her attention to the font. Matthew was just descending the stairs from the left side of the room. He immediately crossed through the font and climbed the stairs on the other side. When he descended them again, he had Amber in his arms. Though she was able to walk, stairs were still out of the question. When they reached the bottom of the stairs, Matthew set Amber down, and the two of them positioned themselves in the center of the font. Kaitlyn stared at the two of them standing in the water, both of them clothed in white. Then she watched as Matthew put Amber's left hand on his left forearm and held her right wrist in his left hand. He then raised his right arm to form an angle and closed his eyes. Reluctantly Kaitlyn followed the example of the others around her and lowered her head. As Matthew began to speak, Kaitlyn lifted her head again. A warmth was spreading through her body just as it had when Matthew had placed his hands on Amber's head and prayed for her on the boat. The feeling seemed to surround her, filling her with peace. Kaitlyn watched as Matthew finished the prayer and leaned Amber back, submerging her in the water. When he brought her back up, Amber's face lit into a smile. She almost seemed to radiate. Kaitlyn thought back to what Gracie had said about this church making a difference in Amber. There was the difference right there. She was happy, and not an I-got-a-new-car-and-aced-my-midterms happy. This was more. Kaitlyn watched in silence as Matthew bent down and carefully lifted her back into his arms and carried her up the stairs. A lady from Amber's new church welcomed her with a dry towel and a hug and then put an arm around her to help her into the dressing room.

Though everyone else had gone back into the chapel, Kaitlyn stopped to sit in the lobby. She felt guilty, knowing she should be in there with Amber, but she just couldn't. She needed time to be alone, to think. Her eyes went to the picture on the wall of the Savior. Almost without thinking, Kaitlyn stood and walked over to it.

"Hello, Kaitlyn."

Kaitlyn almost jumped. She whirled around to face the voice behind her. His blue eyes seemed to show every bit of the emotion that she was feeling.

"Matthew!"

Matthew smiled. "How have you been?"

"Good," Kaitlyn said. "And you?"

Matthew glanced down at his leg and then twisted it around for Kaitlyn to see. "Much better, thanks."

They both turned as several people started filing out of the chapel. Gracie was near the front of the group. As soon as she saw Matthew, she walked over and gave him a big hug.

"You look great."

"Thanks," Matthew said with a broad grin. "So do you."

Gracie twirled around. "Why, thank you very much."

Kaitlyn stared at the two of them. Why was it so easy for them?

"Matthew," Gracie began, "Amber wants a few pictures with you outside. Do you mind?"

"No. Where is she?"

"I think she's still trying to make it out of the chapel," Gracie said.

Matthew turned back to Kaitlyn. "I guess I better go," he said.

Kaitlyn nodded, trying not to let her feelings show.

"I'll keep her company," Gracie said as she linked her arm with Kaitlyn's.

They both watched as Matthew disappeared back into the chapel.

"Are you okay?" Gracie asked sympathetically.

"Gracie, am I ever going to get over him? I thought I was doing better, but then I see him and it starts all over again." Kaitlyn could feel her eyes burning.

"Come on," Gracie said as she started toward the door. "Let's go for a walk."

The two of them walked outside and sat down in the shade of a tree. Kaitlyn closed her eyes and listened to the chatter of a bird lost somewhere in its limbs.

"So what's really going on with you?" Gracie finally blurted out.

Kaitlyn opened her eyes. "I thought that was obvious."

"I'm not talking about Matthew. I'm talking about you."

Kaitlyn shook her head and then lifted her brow. "I don't know what you're talking about."

"Do you want to know what I think?" Gracie asked boldly.

"I have a feeling you're going to tell me regardless."

"I don't think it's God you're angry at. I think you're using Him as a defense so you don't have to face what's really bothering you. The truth is, you can't forgive yourself. Somewhere along the way, you've twisted Leslie's accident around until it's somehow your fault."

Kaitlyn started to stand. "Gracie, I don't need this right now."

Gracie reached out and took her by the arm. "This is exactly what you need. Kaitlyn, you can run from the truth, but unless you face it, the pain is *not* going to go away."

Kaitlyn pulled her arm away and headed to her car. She could feel hot tears burning her cheeks. Then, from the corner of her eye, she saw Matthew and Amber open the door and walk out toward the parking lot. Kaitlyn wiped at her cheeks and then jumped into her car and started the engine. Though her vision was blurred with tears, she could see Matthew in her rearview mirror, standing in the parking lot watching her go.

\* \* \*

Kaitlyn lay in her bed and stared at the ceiling. She could hear the steady pounding of rain on the roof and the rushing of water racing through the rain gutters. It had been raining all day. Kaitlyn had pulled one of her favorite books off the shelf and plopped down on her bed. That had been twenty minutes ago, and she still hadn't opened it. Kaitlyn tossed the book onto her nightstand and crossed to the window. Her neighbor had just pulled into his driveway. Kaitlyn watched as he darted from his car to his front door, using his jacket as an umbrella. He began to shake the water from the jacket once he'd reached the safety of the porch, but stopped short when his front door began to open. His youngest son poked his head around the door and then swung it fully open when he saw his dad. Kaitlyn watched as the boy turned his head back toward the house and called out excitedly. In a moment, another little head bobbed into view at the front door, followed quickly by their mother. She scooted the boys back into the house and then leaned out to kiss her husband. He must not have been satisfied with her half-hearted peck, because he quickly grabbed her and kissed her again, more boldly this time. His wife swatted playfully at him as she pulled back, glancing around to make sure none of the neighbors had seen.

Kaitlyn stepped back from the window. A scene that usually would have brought a smile to her lips left her feeling suddenly empty. She pulled the shade down and turned back to face her room, where her eyes fell on the wilted roses on her dresser. Kaitlyn walked over to reread the note that was attached. Of course, she didn't need to read it to know what it said; she had memorized its contents over the last week and a half. As she reached for the note, one of the drier petals fell from a rose. "Dear Kaitlyn," the note read. "I will never forget you. I wish you the very best in life. Love, Matthew."

The roses had arrived the week after Amber's baptism. Kaitlyn had placed them on her dresser and slowly watched as they'd wilted and died along with her hopes of ever having a relationship with Matthew.

Kaitlyn looked up as someone knocked on her bedroom door.

"Hi, honey, do you have a minute?" she heard her dad ask.

"Sure. Come in," Kaitlyn said as she walked over and sat back down on her bed.

Brent entered and sat down on the bed next to her.

"Gracie called again." Kaitlyn's father took a thoughtful breath. "She told me about what happened."

Kaitlyn started to stand.

"Just sit back down," her father said as he gently took her hand.

Brent took a deep breath. "We should have had this talk eight months ago, but I was so consumed with what I was feeling that I guess I didn't see what you were going through."

Kaitlyn started to say something, but Brent held up his hand. "When your sister died, I blamed myself."

"*Why?*"

"I never should have allowed either one of you to go out on those roads alone that day. But I did. And for five months the guilt gnawed at me until there was almost nothing left."

Brent looked at Kaitlyn, his eyes more intense than she had ever seen them. "It almost destroyed me. It almost destroyed my marriage."

"But it was *my* fault," Kaitlyn cried. "*I* was the one who suggested going to see Greg. Leslie would never have gone if it wasn't for me."

"Sweetheart, you didn't kill Leslie that day any more than I did. She died in an accident. I don't know why it happened—maybe I never will. But after watching you and hearing all that you went through on the lifeboat, I realized something. Difficult things in our life aren't just what happen to us. If allowed, they can form us into who we are."

Kaitlyn's eyes were wide.

"Look at you. You're not the same little girl that left on that cruise. You're a strong woman. On the lifeboat you comforted others when you were afraid yourself, you dove into shark-infested waters to save a little boy, you put others' needs in front of your own."

Then his eyes grew tender. "But until you let go of the guilt and the anger that you've built up, you can't start the healing. Trust me, I know."

As Kaitlyn looked into her father's eyes she could feel the invisible walls that she had built to protect herself tumbling around her. A flood of emotions enveloped her, replacing the anger and guilt that had been there before. Kaitlyn fell into her father's arms and sobbed, allowing the myriad of emotions that had consumed her for months to overflow and spill out.

# CHAPTER 29

"Miss, would you like some coffee?"

Kaitlyn looked up at the woman before her. She was tall, with strawberry-blond hair and big green eyes, and she was wearing a simple, pink, knee-length dress and a white apron.

"No thank you. Just a glass of water and a turkey sandwich, please," Kaitlyn said as she closed her menu and handed it to the waitress, who smiled and disappeared into the kitchen.

Kaitlyn glanced around the little diner. Another waitress in her forties with big hair and a big smile was at the cash register talking across the diner to a couple of men sitting in a booth. From the sound of the conversation, Kaitlyn assumed the men were regulars.

Kaitlyn reached into her purse and pulled out the invitation she had placed there two days ago. She looked down at the name that was written neatly across the front and ran her finger over the name. It was hard to believe it had been seven months since the rescue; so much had happened in that time. One of the most important things that had happened was the change in her parents. The night that her father had told her to stop blaming herself, he had also opened up and shared with her mom that he had been shouldering the guilt for Leslie's death. Kaitlyn's mom had thought that he was just losing interest in her, and fear had kept her from saying anything. Kaitlyn smiled. Now her parents were happier than she had seen them in a long time.

Kaitlyn smiled as the waitress returned with her water, then she quickly tucked the invitation back into her purse.

"Thank you," she said gratefully as she picked up the glass and took a sip. The water was sweet and cool. It was funny, but since the rescue, Kaitlyn found herself appreciating things that she had never before noticed.

The short, middle-aged man that stood in front of a waist-high wall separating the dining area from the kitchen hit a bell and slid a plate onto the counter before returning to the grill. Kaitlyn's waitress immediately headed toward the plate.

"How's married life treating you?" one of the regulars asked Kaitlyn's waitress as she passed.

A huge smile quickly spread across her face. "Just wonderful. You need to try it, Neal."

"That's right," the big-haired waitress at the register agreed as she snapped her gum.

"How can I?" Neal asked. "The best gal in Vail just got hitched."

The big-haired waitress quickly scribbled something on her ticket pad. "Just for that, you can forget your free coffee."

"Aw, now. Don't be like that. You're the second best," Neal teased.

The waitress put one hand on her hip and pointed to the door with the other. "You just go on and get," she ordered.

The man plopped some money down on the table and then headed to the door. Just before he opened it, he turned back to the big-haired waitress.

"Are we still on for Saturday?"

"Seven o'clock sharp," she said without missing a beat. "And don't be late this time."

Kaitlyn looked up as her waitress returned with a big smile on her face.

"Don't mind them," she said. "They've been carrying on like this for years." Then she placed the sandwich down in front of Kaitlyn. "You let me know if you need anything else."

Kaitlyn glanced down at the waitress's ring as she slid the ticket on the table. The diamond wasn't exceptionally large, but the setting was unusual and quite pretty.

"Thank you," Kaitlyn said. "By the way, could you give me directions to Wright Bait and Tackle?"

"Two streets up on your left. You can't miss it," the waitress offered as she looked at Kaitlyn curiously.

"You wouldn't happen to know Matthew Wright, would you?" Kaitlyn questioned hesitantly.

"I sure do. I sit across the table from him every morning for breakfast—or at least I did before I got married. Matthew's my brother."

\* \* \*

Kaitlyn walked along the flower-lined stone path that led to the front door of the shop. It only took a glance to see why Matthew would want to work there; it was beautiful. Large, fragrant pine trees dotted the landscape. Although she couldn't see it, Kaitlyn could hear the soft gurgling of a nearby stream. The air was sweet with the scent of honeysuckle and rang with the chattering of birds and squirrels. It was everything that Matthew had said it was. The building itself was constructed of dark brown wood with gray rocks cemented about three feet up the base of the structure. Kaitlyn paused when she reached the front of the store. There, nailed to the door, was the sign that Matthew had made. Kaitlyn smiled and then took a deep breath. When she opened the door, a little bell rang to let the shopkeeper know that someone had entered. Kaitlyn's eyes went directly to the counter, but there was no one there.

"I'll be right there," came a voice from the back room.

Kaitlyn knew the voice instantly. She turned toward the open door that led to the back of the shop. She could hear the thunk of a hammer followed immediately by a yelp of pain. Kaitlyn winced. She had heard that sound many times before when her father had worked on projects in the garage. She started forward just as a figure appeared in the doorway, his head bent to appraise his thumb.

"Maybe you should put some ice on that," Kaitlyn offered.

Matthew's head shot up to look at the woman before him. For a second Kaitlyn thought he might drop the hammer he was holding, but instead he just stared.

*"Kaitlyn?"* Matthew said in disbelief. "How . . . ?"

Kaitlyn had caught him completely off guard and, for a second, she felt a little guilty.

"You told me that your shop was in Vail, so when I got up here I stopped in at the diner just up the road to ask for directions."

"What are you . . . ? I mean, why . . . ?" Matthew began to shake his head. "I can't believe it's you. That you're here," he finally offered.

"I told you that one day I might drop in," she said simply.

They both stood there, neither knowing what to say next. Matthew glanced down at his thumb, which was already a nice shade of purple.

"Here, let me take a look," Kaitlyn said as she stepped forward and took his hand in hers. Matthew looked up and for a second neither one of them moved.

"It's fine," Matthew began as he pulled it away and walked over to a sink behind the front counter. He turned on the faucet and ran it under the water. "So, how have you been? You look great," he offered, though he avoided eye contact.

"Just about anything is an improvement from dark circles and sunken eyes," Kaitlyn teased.

"You didn't look like that at the baptism."

Kaitlyn felt a twinge of guilt. "I'm sorry I left that day without saying good-bye."

"Don't worry about it," Matthew said with a shake of his head. Then he came back around and leaned against the counter. "You cut your hair."

Kaitlyn reached up and touched her hair. It was shoulder length with several layers in the back that flipped up. "I guess I was ready for a change."

"It looks really good on you."

Kaitlyn smiled appreciatively. "Thanks. How have you been?"

"I'm fine. My parents just left on a mission, so I've been running the place. I've also been taking independent study courses toward a management degree."

"I'm glad you're finally doing what you really want to do."

"I wanted to call you but . . ." he hesitated. "I decided it was probably best to leave the past in the past."

Kaitlyn didn't say anything; she just watched Matthew, who was obviously uncomfortable.

"How's Amber?" he finally asked to break the silence.

"She's doing fine. She's working really hard with her physical therapist because she's determined that as soon as she turns twenty-one she's leaving on a mission."

"Trust her to do it too," Matthew mused, his face relaxing a little. "Have you kept in touch with the others?"

"Eleanor has a publisher and is writing a book about our experience."

"Good for her. What about little Benton and Madison?" Matthew quickly added.

"Madison had some pretty severe nightmares for a while, but Sam and Morgan got her a good counselor and she's doing fine. Both she and Benton have some kidney damage from going so long without water. They'll be on medication for the rest of their lives, but otherwise they've recovered well. Sam is still working as a used car salesman, but he said if he wins a cruise this year he's giving it away."

Matthew burst out laughing. "I can't say I blame him on that one."

"I guess you heard about Karen? She managed to hold on until they got her to the hospital, but she died two days later."

Matthew nodded. "I know."

"I met her son Trevor, though," Kaitlyn said softly. "I had to make good on a promise I made to his mom."

They were both quiet for a moment, their minds caught up in the loss.

"I saw Rhonda interviewed on a couple of morning news shows right after the accident," Matthew said.

"I know. Her five minutes of fame led to a job as a newscaster doing the weather in Buffalo."

Matthew shook his head. "What about Donald?"

"Rhonda followed him around for a couple of months," Kaitlyn began, "but he ended up falling for a brilliant computer whiz who didn't have two nickels to rub together. From what I hear, she's absolutely adorable and they're getting pretty serious."

"Do you remember me telling you about Tia?" Matthew began. "The little girl from Mexico?"

"I remember."

"About a month after we got home, Donald called me and asked for her address. Tia's father called me a couple of days later. Apparently, Donald sent her a top-of-the-line wheelchair and an airplane ticket for her and all her family to come to the States to visit with a specialist."

Kaitlyn smiled. "That's wonderful!"

"What about Pete? Did he go to court yet?"

"Because of Pete's testimony," Kaitlyn began, "Gary was convicted on all counts and sentenced to ten years in prison."

Again there was an awkward stretch of silence.

"Gracie and Flip are dating."

"Flip and Gracie?" Matthew asked with a broad grin.

Kaitlyn broke into a huge smile, too. "The two of them started calling and e-mailing each other after the rescue. Flip flew up to see her a couple of times, bringing a few brochures from science colleges around Miami with him. At semester break Gracie packed up and transferred to Florida International. I don't think she's ready for marriage yet, but I think it's heading in that direction."

"How about you and Greg? When are you getting married?"

Kaitlyn reached into her purse, pulled out an invitation, and handed it to Matthew. The smile on Matthew's face instantly vanished. Kaitlyn stepped back and watched him open it. Matthew stared down at the invitation and then back at Kaitlyn, his expression a combination of astonishment and elation.

"You're getting baptized?"

Kaitlyn smiled.

"What—what happened?" Matthew stuttered. "I mean—how?"

Kaitlyn was delighted by his reaction. "Amber came over to my house one weekend after she was baptized and *accidentally* left her Book of Mormon. I glared at the book for almost two hours before I finally picked it up. Then I couldn't put it down." Kaitlyn paused, the wonder of it all rushing back to her. "After I was finished, I did what you said."

Matthew's eyes widened.

"I prayed about it."

Matthew smiled so wide his cheeks looked like they were about to burst.

"I felt that same warm feeling I had when you gave Amber and Karen a blessing. Though Karen's still bothered me."

"Because she died." It was a statement, not a question.

Kaitlyn nodded.

"Giving a blessing doesn't always mean that the person will live. Sometimes it's a comfort to help them face what will happen."

"I understand that now," Kaitlyn admitted thoughtfully. "Of course, when I told Amber about it all, she dragged me to just about every Church function available. After a month of potlucks, firesides, and Church socials, she brought in the big guns."

"The missionaries," Matthew guessed.

Kaitlyn smiled. "When they taught me about forever families . . . when they told me I could see Leslie again . . ." Kaitlyn's voice caught. "It was like the calm after a storm. After eight months of pain, I finally felt peace."

Matthew's eyes softened.

"There's just one little problem," Kaitlyn quickly added, her expression suddenly serious.

"What?" Matthew asked.

"I need someone to baptize me."

Kaitlyn smiled as she watched her words sink in. Matthew's hesitation was instantly gone. With a look of total exhilaration on his face, he reached out and gathered Kaitlyn into his arms, then almost immediately pulled back.

"What about Greg?" he asked with a look of concern.

"Greg and I aren't dating anymore. A good Mormon boy once told me that he only dates members because he wants a temple marriage. Should I settle for less than eternity?"

Matthew shook his head and smiled. "Never."

"So," Kaitlyn began with a big smile, "after my baptism, what would you say to a dollar movie, a big bowl of green Jell-O, and a handshake at the front door?"

Matthew pulled her into his arms as his face broke into a huge grin. "I think I can do a little better than that."

# ABOUT THE AUTHOR

*The Raging Sea* is Sonia Larsen O'Brien's first novel. She lives in Arkansas with her husband and six children. Though writing is her passion, her greatest joy is her family. Sonia has homeschooled her children for the past five years, which has proven to be both rewarding and extremely challenging. Her other hobbies include jogging, reading, rollerblading, baking her all-time favorite oatmeal chocolate chip cookies, and eating ice cream. She is currently serving as the Relief Society president in her ward.